One moment it was an outsized snakebird—there were many in the marshes here. Then it was not a snakebird but a snake, coiling to strike. Then in succession it became a round ball slowly spinning, a bat with lazy wings, a misty nothing at all.

Until it got there.

Now it assumed human shape again, but the misty figure was no longer pale; it was dark. Dark as the night, almost. So nearly so that Tom Broderick, relaxed on his chair with his cigarette between his fingers, did not become aware of it until it had fully taken shape outside his screen and begun to filter through the mesh. Even then all he saw was a dark shadow, human in form, gliding toward him.

And despite the blazing eyes and hate-warped mouth, it was a human face—one he recognized . . .

SHADES OF EVIL

HUGH B. CAVE

CHARTER
NEW YORK

A Division of Charter Communications Inc.
A GROSSET & DUNLAP COMPANY
51 Madison Avenue
New York, New York 10010

An Ace Charter Original

First Ace Charter Printing August, 1982
Published simultaneously in Canada
Manufactured in the United States of America

2 4 6 8 0 9 7 5 3 1

For Peggie

SHADES OF EVIL

BOOK ONE

The Haunting

1

A Thing from the Lake

The window beside her bed overlooked the lake, and the sound she was hearing was a water sound. A splashing.

Not the single explosive splash of a feeding bass, although the largemouths in the lake did voraciously feed at night sometimes. This must be the sound of wild ducks or wading birds, frightened by a marauder. Or perhaps by the alligator the mystery man in the next apartment, Haydn Clay, claimed to have seen.

Yes, it was a sound of panicky ducks in a frantic race through the reeds and lily pads. They couldn't easily fly out of all that vegetation, so they usually made for open water before taking off. Most of the time they headed toward the strip of white sand the condominium proudly called its beach, then soared with a sharp bank to the left or right to avoid braining themselves against the six-story building itself.

She was hearing the flapping of their wings now. They were airborne. Wondering what they were fleeing from at three A.M., she slipped out of bed and went to a window. The moonlight streamed through her summer-weight nightgown to reveal a remarkably slim and shapely figure for a woman of her age.

Had she awakened her husband? Concerned, because yesterday he had returned from his daily round of golf complaining of chest pains, she turned to peer at his bed. Earlier, on waking and needing a bathroom, she had gone all the way through the apartment to the guest bathroom instead of using the one off their bedroom, to be sure she would not disturb him.

He was asleep on his back, gently snoring. But of course. Had the slight stir of her going to the window aroused him, he would be reaching for her by now, with the moonlight leaving her practically naked like that.

She smiled. "Treasure the good things when you're aging," someone very wise had once said or written. One of the best of all the good things now was Jerry's loving, maybe a little less vigorous than before, but still wonderful. *I'm sixty-four and he's sixty-seven, for heaven's sake, and we still respond to each other's slightest touch.*

But what in the world had caused the ducks to panic at this hour?

She stood there frowning at the beach, which of course wasn't a beach at all, really, but a developer's come-on—a real-estate gimmick common in this part of central Florida where lakes abounded. SWIM AT YOUR OWN RISK the signs said. Where you swam, of course, was in the condo pool, down on the common beyond the shuffleboard courts. This lakeside beach was just white sand trucked in to imitate the oceanfronts of Fort Lauderdale or Boca Raton.

Sure, you could get into a swim suit and loll around soaking up the sun while folks up north shoveled their cars out of snowdrifts. But you couldn't swim here because ten yards out from the trucked-in sand were weeds that felt like a tangle of live snakes and at times did harbor a snake or two. Cottonmouth moccasins, to name just one variety. Not to mention frogs that sometimes gurrumped all night, and—if true—Haydn Clay's alligator.

And, right now, something else. But what *was* it?

She pressed her nose against the screen and tried to identify what she was seeing. A vapor of some sort rising from the water. Swamp smoke? A mist?

If the ducks had been fleeing from it, it must have come in from the area of reeds and pond lilies where they had been, a half acre patch of semi-swamp just off the shore here. Or from beyond, of course, where the water was much deeper. But the thing was rising out of the lake just off the strip of white sand now, and was forming itself into something the way a cloud in the sky sometimes takes on a shape you could put a name to.

Human? As it emerged from the water it seemed to become so. Less amorphous now, it assumed the shape of a person wading up onto the beach, though the water remained still. About the legs of a real person the water would have swirled, no? And the agitation would have been plainly visible in the moonlight.

The thing was leaving footprints in the smooth sand of the beach, though. A whole trail of them. But were they real footprints? There seemed to be no depth to them. They had no shadowed edges, as they ought to have in the moonlight. Yet they were wet—you could tell—and appeared to glow with the strange phosphorescence that sometimes could be seen in the marsh.

What in heaven's name *was* it? And why did she have the distinct feeling it was malevolent, that just by looking at it she might be placing herself in terrible peril?

"Jerry," she said in a whisper. Then, louder: "Jerry, wake up!"

"Uh?" Opening his eyes, he saw her at the window and sat up in bed, frowning at her.

Wrenching her gaze from the thing on the lawn, she turned toward him and cried again, "Jerry!"—annoyed now because he had not recognized her fear and responded to it. A chill of terror raced through her as her gaze twitched back to the unnatural thing below.

"What's up?" Swinging his feet to the floor, Jerry pushed his stiff, stout body erect and stumbled toward her.

"Look down there! What *is* that thing?"

At her side he lifted an arm behind her and let his hand rest on her buttocks. Pure habit; he had even, without thinking, done it at the condo cocktail party last week. Neither sex nor affection was on his mind, though, as he leaned toward the window and gazed incredulously at the misty figure walking, or floating, over the grass.

"I'll be damned."

"Is it real?" Ruby asked him.

He did not reply. Just stared.

"It came out of the lake," she said. "It scared the ducks. They made such a racket getting away from it, they woke me up. Jerry, what *is* it?"

"Somebody's playing tricks," her husband said, remembering a thing he and some other kids in his high school science class had cooked up one memorable Halloween, years ago, to scare the school's principal. You took some gauze or cheesecloth, a mixture of luminous paint, benzine and varnish . . . "A trick," he said again. "Some joker in the building."

"Jerry," she said, "it came out of the *lake*."

"Couldn't have. If you get the stuff wet, it won't work."

"It came out of the lake, I'm telling you!"

"Look," he said, and took his hand away from her to press a pointing finger against the glass. "Now what the hell is it up to?"

The Halloween memory had reached a corner of the building and wavered to a halt. There it stood, a vaguely human shape in a surrealistic painting that included the three-mile long lake with its acres of marsh, the strip of beach gleaming in the moonlight, and the expanse of lawn leading up to the white concrete condominium which in the light of the moon resembled an oversized mausoleum. Here and there a palm tree cast a grotesque shadow on the grass, like a slender woman with a Medusa hairdo. Clusters of flowering shrubs suddenly came to life as small birds awoke and noisily flew out of them.

The thing from the lake just stood there, seeming to peer at the building. As though wondering what the structure was. Or who lived in it.

"I'm wrong," Jerry Ellstrom admitted in a low, uncertain voice. "We kids didn't come up with anything like that."

"Jerry, is it a woman? I mean the ghost, or whatever, of a woman?"

"You've been reading too many of Will Platt's books."

"Look! It's moving again!"

Its study of the building finished, the misty figure was again in motion, walking or floating past the screened veranda of the first-floor apartment on the east corner. Watching it from their third-floor window in 302, the Ellstroms saw it disappear as the building blocked their view. In continued silence for another minute or so they stood there.

"I'll bet I know," Jerry Ellstrom said then with a snort of disgust.

"What?"

"That bastard Helpin, under us. He worked in Hollywood. Some kind of special effects man."

"But why—?"

"Because he hates Ed Lawson, that's why. There isn't anything he wouldn't do to make trouble for Ed."

"Who, with Haydn Clay, saw the alligator," Ruby contributed, frowning.

"Saw something, anyway."

"Jerry, we *both* saw this. It was real!"

"All right, we saw it, but what the hell was it?" There

was a fierceness in his voice that startled and puzzled her. Had he, too, sensed that the lake thing was a creature of evil?

Afraid again, but for him this time, she drew him away from the window. His report yesterday of the pain in his chest had frightened her. Without telling him, she had called their doctor and been advised not to let him exert himself or become excited.

"Come on back to bed, hon," she begged, trying to keep out of her voice the other fear—the unreasonable sense of terror—that she felt now about the nameless thing from the lake. "Come, Jerry. Please. You need your sleep tonight."

He turned for one last look at the now empty condo lawn below and, with a reluctant "Well, all right, if you say so," let her lead him back to the bed. At any other time he almost certainly would have lovingly placed his open hand over her small, soft bottom and pressed his face against hers as they walked toward that bed together. This time, no.

She glanced at the scowl on his face and decided he was worried. Or, like her, was caught up in a cold chill of fear that didn't really make any sense.

2

The Gathering

At 4:20 P.M. the following day, in apartment 604, Willard Platt pulled a page of rough-draft copy from his typewriter and glanced at his watch.

He had begun work at eight after downing a boiled egg and a cup of instant coffee for his breakfast. Had quit at 12:30 to lunch on a tall glass of club soda laced with bourbon, but had become restless and carried the glass back to the small third bedroom he called his study. He still wore the lightweight blue bathrobe he had thrown on over his pajamas when he got out of bed.

He didn't usually work this hard on a book, he thought, scowling, on his way to the bathroom to take a shower. Something about this one was driving him. Was it because he was alone now? No Vicky filling the apartment with sounds as she moved about trying to amuse herself?

In the bathroom he stripped and looked at his image in the mirror-wall over the washbasin. Forty-seven the day after tomorrow, he thought. You don't exactly look it. A bit fat just now, maybe. That's from all those meals of stew peas and such in Jamaica, bless Ima Williams and her idea of a white man's appetite. Most of it is still muscle, though. Nothing to be ashamed of. As for the

..ce—well, hell, it was never anything special, but it'll serve.

He turned on the shower, stepped in, and soaped himself. His soapy hands lingered on his body until he got hard and came, a thing he had learned to do of necessity soon after his marriage twenty-seven years ago. What would the dear ladies of Lakeside Manor think if told that Will Platt's beautiful, sexy-seeming wife was frigid? Or would they believe it?

Probably not. And they most certainly would not believe, even if he himself told them, that in Jamaica she had become a devoted student of obeah and a dangerously evil woman. For that matter, most of the condo ladies would have to go to a dictionary to learn the meaning of the word "obeah"—that it was a particularly powerful and ugly form of West Indian sorcery born long ago in Africa. The idea that their bridge-playing Vicky had studied to become a sorceress . . . well, hell, they just wouldn't buy it.

Anyway, her friends would be at the weekly cocktail party this afternoon and he had better be there to answer questions about her disappearance, or they'd be calling him to find out if he'd heard anything. Condominiums, even small ones like this with its mere twenty-four apartments, were not private places.

Almost every woman here knew, for instance— straight from darling Vicky—what he liked to eat, drink and wear, how many hours a day he usually spent at the typewriter, that he was too impatient to play a decent game of golf, and that he got bored half to death sitting in a boat waiting for a Florida bass to come along and swallow a hapless minnow with a hook through its body.

(He did cast a dry-fly occasionally. But there were precious few fish in this lake smart enough to rise to flies.)

Vicky hadn't told the ladies what happened in the bedroom, of course. Or, rather, what didn't happen. Most of them probably thought she was exactly the right mate for a man who wrote all those torrid love scenes into his novels.

Finished with his shower, he dried himself and walked into his bedroom, where he stood at a window for a moment. In Lakeside Manor all the bedroom windows facing the water were extra wide. He never tired of looking out at this lake, which, thank God, was a wildlife sanctuary and thus had been left pretty much in its natural state. A few of the houses around its edge had wooden piers, but there were no concrete embankments to make the thing resemble a vast swimming pool. More than half the shore, in fact, was marshland, unsuited for development.

I'd better wear something decent. Every dame in the building will be asking me if I've heard anything.

He donned pale green slacks, a dark green shirt, white shoes. Then he went into the kitchen, took a bottle of bourbon and a glass from a closet there, and put them into a brown paper bag.

Okay, Buster, here we go. Brace yourself.

There was the usual cute sign in the elevator, stuck up a few days before by the condo's social director. "April First is now safely behind us, so let's quit fooling around and come out in force for the weekly 'do' at 5 P.M. Wednesday. Bring the usual bottle of something wet and a snack or two to munch on, and we'll be seeing you."

Descending to the ground floor, he stepped out with his paper bag and turned right along the green carpet, at the end of which he emerged into the open where the residents' cars were parked facing one another in neat rows, as if about to kiss. Off to his left, across half an acre of lawn, the pavilion was already crowded.

A woman's deep voice behind him said, "Will, did

ou hear about the dogs?" Like himself, Estelle Quigley had lived in the building since its construction three years before.

He paused, half turned, and waited for her to catch up to him. She was one of the few women in the building he could honestly say he liked: a short, dumpy widow with a mind he constantly envied. Retired now, she had for years owned and run a topflight restaurant in Massachusetts.

"Dogs, Estelle?"

"The two from that house by the golf course, that have been fouling up the common. No one's told you? They were found dead in the road this morning."

"Good God." The animals in question were Great Danes, inseparable. He had always admired them, even while complaining with everyone else at the way their owner encouraged them to use the common for a john. "You mean someone killed them?"

She fell in beside him on his left and they walked together toward the group at the pavilion. "Ed Lawson said there wasn't a mark on them."

"No! Don't tell me someone was ugly enough to poison those beautiful beasts."

"It would seem so, wouldn't it? Unless the vet discovers something else." She shook her head in sadness. "We have some peculiar people around here, Will."

"I didn't think we had any that peculiar. When did this happen? I've been working all day."

"Ed found them just after daylight, on his way over to play golf." Big Ed Lawson loved his golf and played well, but as resident manager had to get in his licks before his working day began.

"Dead in the road, you say?"

"Over there." She pointed to the blacktop that curled in from the main highway to the parking area.

Will was still slowly shaking his head when they reached the pavilion. The Quigley woman left him to join friends, and he stepped to the table where he poured bourbon into his glass and leaned over to fill it at the tap. The pavilion was a roofed circular counter some twenty feet in diameter with a grill in the middle for cookouts.

"You hear about the dogs, Platt?"

Will looked at the speaker and was tempted to be rude and turn away. Carl Helpin, 202. A man who spoke in snarls and said "Platt" when he knew your name as well as anyone else did, and they all called you "Will." A short man with flickery, pale blue eyes. To hell with him. "Yes, I heard."

"Damned queer. The vet says they weren't poisoned."

"Then what killed them?"

"He doesn't know. Like I say, it's damned queer."

"If you ask me," said a woman's voice behind Will, "there is something even worse going on here. Did you see that thing come out of the lake last night, Will?"

He turned and found himself confronted by one of the nicer women in the building. Ruby Ellstrom, 302. Slim, graceful, usually smiling, but now dead solemn as she shook her head at him.

"Something came out of the lake, Ruby?" It was, of course, possible. According to the gossip, Ed Lawson and the new fellow, Haydn Clay, swore they had seen a 'gator. There were some pretty fair-sized turtles, too, and at least one pair of otters.

"Yes, it did. It frightened the ducks, and the noise they made woke me up. You didn't see it?"

Will shook his head. "What was it, exactly?"

"Well, it came up out of the lake after the ducks flew away in a fright. A misty kind of thing, but human. I swear it was human—in shape, at least. I woke Jerry and he saw it too. We think it was a woman, but not a real one. *You* know what I'm trying to say. You've written about that sort of thing."

A woman? Will thought.

"Of course, if you didn't see it, I can't expect you to believe me," Ruby went on. "But maybe someone did, even at that hour. I'm going to ask around."

She went away. Another woman appeared at Will's side, even before he could empty his glass, which at the moment he badly wanted to do. Bee Broderick, 603, his next-door neighbor. Not one he was terribly fond of.

"Will, have you heard anything?"

She meant, of course, had he heard anything from the police or the detective agency people. He shook his head. "No, Bee. Not yet."

"Not a word?"

"They said it would probably be a while."

"Did she take any clothes, Will?"

"I don't know. She has so many clothes and shoes, I can't decide whether any are missing. I've never been one to keep track of such things."

"But she did take a suitcase? You must know that."

"I don't. She has a closet full of luggage. All I know is that she didn't take her car. But she may have been meeting someone, or have arranged for someone to come for her. I just don't know."

Bee stood before him, moving her head slowly from side to side while breathing heavily. To this woman almost everything was an invitation to dramatize. She and her husband had run a motel in Miami before retiring to the Florida heartland, and had known and catered to a number of Miami's entertainment-world people. She even knew a woman in the detective agency he had hired to find Vicky.

"They'll find her, Will. Don't worry," she said, and before turning away, reached out to pat his arm.

Others asked about Vicky in the hour that followed. The disappearance of his wife had really fired their curiosity.

"Do you suppose something happened to her in Jamaica, Will? You do get into some strange situations, you know."

"It's possible. She was a bit edgy and restless before we left there. It's one of the reasons we came back when we did."

"Has she any money, Will?"

"Oh, Vicky always has money. I'm sure that's not a problem."

"She wasn't thinking straight, Will. Could it be change of life?"

"I'm more inclined to blame Jamaica."

"But what did she *do* in Jamaica?"

"Oh, the usual things."

He should have obtained some pictures of Vicky doing some of the things she had done in Jamaica, he decided, even if taking them would have meant resorting to stealth and endangering himself. A shot, for instance, of her sitting in that hellish house on the edge of the island's notorious Cockpit Country, being instructed in the dark arts by the infamous Sister Merle. Confronted with such evidence, the condo ladies might realize that his tall, blond, beautiful Victoria was not the woman they thought they had known so well.

Would pictures convince them? Yes, probably. No one seeing Sister Merle, even in a photograph, could fail to see that the obeah woman was no ordinary creature. Those laser-beam eyes, the love of evil engraved in that threatening face . . . ah, yes, the right kind of photos would surely be convincing. Especially if he had one of Vicky poring over her black opal with the obeah woman, the two of them holding hands across the table while peering down at the stone as though seeking to blend their very souls in its smoky depths.

But, of course, he hadn't any pictures. Only memories that kept him awake nights or gave him nightmares when he slept.

When satisfied they had learned all they were likely to, his questioners drifted away. Will filled his glass again, doubling the bourbon content this time because his mouth felt dry and his temples had begun to throb. It was so hellishly hard to be polite to all these people, yet he knew that not all of them were merely curious; some really liked him.

He sipped the liquor slowly, savoring it, and had almost emptied the glass when his pleasure was interrupted by a return visit from Ruby Ellstrom. The slim redhead had Haydn Clay in tow.

"Will, I've found someone else who saw it!" she declared triumphantly. "Do you two know each other?"

"Not well," Will said, meaning not at all. The silver-haired man was a recent purchaser about whom he had heard little. The board of directors always knew where a newcomer was from, of course—this one was from Los Angeles—but it sometimes took a while to find out how much one was worth, what he did or had done for a living, and such personal matters as the state of his love life. Accepting Clay's hand, Will said with a frown, "You saw it too?"

"I certainly saw something come out of the lake last night."

"Describe it," Ruby Ellstrom urged him. "Mr. Platt writes books about the supernatural."

"Do you, indeed?" Clay said. "Under your own name?"

"And others."

"I must read some. I enjoy that kind of thing."

"His last one," Ruby said, "was about Haiti and zombies and voodoo, and I had nightmares for weeks. But tell him, Mr. Clay. Tell him what you just told me."

Will looked at the man and waited, expecting the usual effort to find words that might impress a man who used them for a living. He was pleasantly surprised when Clay said with a shrug, "Hell, I don't know what I saw.

I'm in 301, walking back to bed after a trip to the john. I heard the ducks. Wondered if the alligator we'd seen was in among 'em. I grabbed a pair of binoculars I keep on my dresser and saw this blob of vapor, mist, fog, whatever it was, sort of gliding up out of the water. It was no illusion. Believe me, I saw it." He paused, scowling. "Another thing. I got the distinct impression it was —well, what's another word for 'vile'? 'Evil'?"

"I had the very same impression," Ruby Ellstrom said in triumph, and turned to wag a finger at Will. "Anyway, he saw it, just as Jerry and I did!"

"I hope you don't think *I* invented it," Will said. That second drink, almost straight, had done what a drink at the typewriter sometimes did: loosened him up and let him shed the shackles a bit. Of course, when he wrote in that condition he almost always had to rewrite.

"No, but I did hope you could explain it," Ruby said.

"I haven't a clue."

A man—over six-feet, craggy-faced and windblown— approached with an unfamiliar woman at his side. To Haydn Clay he said, "Hi, pal," and to Ruby Ellstrom, "Hello, Ruby," and to Will, "You still around? I thought you'd have run for cover by now."

"I'm durable," Will said.

"Want you all to meet the lady who bought 504 from the Lemkes," said big Ed Lawson, the condo's manager, referring to an apartment whose owners had just moved. "She moves in day after tomorrow. Staying over at the motel until her furniture arrives."

He turned to the stranger. "This is the writer I was telling you about, Mrs. Kimball. Willard Pratt. Lives over you on the top floor, but spends a lot of time in the West Indies. You hear a typewriter in the middle of the night, it'll be Will scaring hell out of his readers."

She laughed softly and Will looked at her. Small, almost tiny, but pretty as a picture in every way, from sandaled feet to the top of her saucy dark hair. She was

...aybe forty, a few years younger than he. "Mrs. Kimball," he said.

"Lynne." She had a way of using her voice, too. As if sometimes she used it for singing. "Where in the West Indies? Do you know Jamaica at all?"

"A little."

"I used to live in Mandeville. My husband worked for the bauxite people."

"You must know Christiana, then," Will said.

"We went there on market day sometimes. It was more fun than shopping in Mandeville."

"I've just returned from there."

Peering at them both as they gazed at each other, big Ed Lawson said with a broad grin, "Why don't we all have a drink on this? I'll scout up some ice."

3

Don't Go Down that Lonesome Road

In apartment 602 of Lakeside Manor the Abbotts had finished supper and begun their evening. For LeRoy Abbott this was a routine that almost never varied. Armed with an expensive cigar made 100-odd miles away in Tampa, he would settle into his swivel rocker before the tv, watch anything at all until the cigar was finished, then close his eyes and fall asleep. Seventy-one years old and weighing 260 pounds, he almost never left the apartment after his evening meal.

Before retiring to Florida, Lee Abbott had owned and operated a sand and gravel business in Ohio. His present wife, Constance, twenty-one years younger than he, had been his secretary when his first wife died.

Coming from her bedroom—they slept in separate rooms now—Connie paused beside her husband's chair and said, "How do I look, hon?"

He swiveled his head to squint at her. "Good enough to call on a dame like her, that's for sure. You takin' the car?"

"Why should I? It's beautiful out."

"What about that thing they were talkin' about at the party?" He himself hadn't gone to the cocktail party on the common the day before yesterday. He never went to

17

them. Too much yakety-yak, he said. It was she who had told him about the ghostly what-was-it supposedly seen by the Ellstroms and Haydn Clay.

She frowned. "That's right. And the dogs. Maybe I should take the car, Lee."

But he was already staring at the boob-tube again and surrounding himself with a cloud of smoke that must have made the picture all but invisible to him.

Connie waved good-by and made for the door, stopping briefly at a full-length mirror attached to the wall of the entrance hall. Not bad, she decided. The woman standing there in the glass was a trifle plump, maybe— cooking for a glutton like LeRoy, you were bound to eat too much yourself—but, by God, she still had a good figure, and her hair was as black and shiny as when she had been Connie Pecora. The last few years might have taken the starch out of Lee, but they hadn't had any visible effect on her.

Or any other effect, she thought with a secret smile as she quietly closed the door behind her.

It was about seven o'clock, and warm. The Brodericks in 603 had their door open, and so did Will Platt, the writer, in the apartment next to them. Most people left their doors open now, to let the lake breeze flow through their apartments. As she headed for the elevator she could hear Will Platt's typewriter clicking. Poor fellow. With his wife walking out on him like that, obviously not in her right mind, he must be sick with worry and working at this hour just to keep from thinking about it.

In the elevator she pressed the second-floor button, then when the car stopped went down the hall to 201, the door of which was closed. She rang the bell. The door opened, and the woman who faced her with auburn hair in blue plastic curlers was her best friend Pearl Gautier, a fifty-year-old former nurse.

"Well, hi," Pearl said cheerfully. "Come on in."

Connie wagged her head. "Can't. I'm on my way over

to Mae Henig's." Pearl knew Mae Hennig, played bridge with her sometimes. She didn't know about the rest of it, though. One had to be discreet. "I just stopped by to ask if you're busy tomorrow."

"Uh-uh. In fact, I was thinking of calling to see if you'd like to go shopping."

"Two minds with a single thought. Lakeland?" There were some nice stores in Lakeland and of course LeRoy wouldn't go—"That far to buy a dress?" he'd grumble. "What the hell's wrong with the stores around here?"

"Good," Pearl said. "We can have lunch at the Peony on the way back."

"See you in the morning, then. About nine?"

"Can't we make it earlier?"

"Eight, then." No need to add, "I'll come by for you." Pearl was uncomfortable with LeRoy and never came upstairs.

"Give my best to Mae," Pearl Gautier said.

Connie rode the elevator down to the first floor, turned left along the green carpet, and made for her car: a Continental, because LeRoy had the money and insisted on showing everyone else he had it. As she approached the machine a much more modest car, a compact, pulled into the 504 spot nearby. That one's door swung open and a woman popped out, very nearly as abruptly as a cork from a champagne bottle. Perhaps if she hadn't had a bag of groceries in her arms she would have stepped out even more briskly.

They faced each other. "Well, hello," Connie said. "It's Mrs. Kimball, isn't it?" She'd heard that the new owner had spent the last few years in Jamaica, and that her husband had died down there, of a heart attack or something.

"Yes, I'm Lynne Kimball." Despite the bag of groceries, she managed to extend a hand. Nice hand, Connie thought as she touched it. Smooth, young, like a teenager's, but firm in its grip.

"I'm Connie Abbott. 602. It's nice meeting you, Lynne."

"I'm glad to meet you, Connie. Everyone's so friendly here."

Oh, brother, Connie thought. If you only knew. "Can I help with anything? I mean, do you have more than that to carry? I know you just moved in today."

"Thanks, but this is the last."

She's going to be someone I'll like, Connie decided. No question about it. Bright, cheerful—my God, she looks nineteen years old. "I'm glad we met like this," she said. "I'll be looking forward to seeing you again."

"Thank you. You're kind."

"Night, Lynne."

"Good night, Connie."

Connie watched her for a moment in the glare of the parking area lamps, then slid into the Continental. Out of the parking area she swung left past the common, along the road where the dogs had been found. What *about* those dogs, she wondered uneasily for perhaps the hundredth time.

The talk around the building was that the vet had discovered no poison in their bodies and was completely at a loss for an explanation for their deaths. There were no broken bones. They hadn't been strangled or smothered in any way. "It's almost as if they died of fright," the vet had said.

Of course, he was only a young fellow with little experience. There might be some acceptable explanation later, if the dogs' owner decided to foot the cost of further investigation.

But "died of *fright*"? And on the same night Haydn Clay and the Ellstroms had seen that ghostly thing walk out of the lake and float across the lawn in the direction of the common?

Connie thought about it as she drove along the lake shore, with the moonlit water shining darkly on one side and the golf course a pale green carpet on the other. Less than a quarter mile from the condominium she turned right, drove past three attractive houses backed up to the golf course, and pulled into the driveway of the fourth. A door beside the garage opened as she slid out of the car.

"Hi, Connie," Mae Henig said. "Coming in?" She was taller than Connie and thinner. A few years older.

"Do you mind if I don't, Mae? I'm late."

"Run along. Maybe we can have a drink after."

Connie waved her thanks and, leaving the car there, returned on foot to the road. It was an estate road like the one at the condominium, but a less traveled one, barely wide enough for two cars to pass on it. Actually it served only seven homes. Passing number five, she turned in at number six, and again the door by the driveway swung open as she approached. This one was opened by a man.

He let her step past him in silence, shut the door and, turning, swung her into his arms and placed a big hand on her behind. "How much time do we have, baby?" he asked.

"I'm not sure. If I'm late tonight, he may start to worry."

"Because of what happened to those dogs, you mean?"

"And the thing from the lake." The story had gotten around and she was sure he must have heard it. He played golf daily and almost always had a drink or two at the club afterward.

"Our aquatic ghostie," he said with a grin, brushing her cheek with his lips. "So if Lee gets worried about you, he'll call. No problem."

LeRoy wouldn't call here, of course. He would telephone Mae Henig. In the three months she had been having the affair with Nino he never had phoned, but Mae knew what to do if it should happen. "She's in the bathroom," Mae would say; "I'll have her call you back when she comes out, LeRoy." Then she would call here and Connie would return the call from here. As Nino had said, no problem.

They walked through the living room to the bedroom, Nino's hand still pressing her buttocks. He had to stoop a little to do that; he was six foot four. A very handsome six foot four, too—once a college basketball player of renown, now the Heron Lake Club's most talented golfer. Sometimes she wondered why he had never married. Was it because there had always been women like her?

"You know," he said, starting to undress, "this story about the spook in the lake has got the whole place talking. What's your opinion?"

"They saw something. At least, the Ellstroms did—they're good, sober people and wouldn't have invented a thing like that just to make waves. I don't know about Clay. He's new."

"The Ellstroms saw something, then. But what?"

"Well, it was some kind of mist, maybe, rising from the lake. The stuff you see in swamps sometimes under certain conditions. Parts of our lake are pretty marshy, you know. There's often a mist over the water in the morning."

He shook his head, and she sensed he was going to be argumentative this evening. "They're supposed to have seen this weirdie in the middle of the night, lady. And it wasn't just hanging over the water. It came *out* of the lake and floated up over the condo lawn. It had the shape of a *woman*."

"Oh, come on. Ruby was the one who told that story, and you know her, how she tends to exaggerate."

"You just said—"

"I mean, even if she was *trying* to tell it straight. So they saw something at three in the morning, or whatever. They must have at least been sleepy. It wasn't a ghost—or do you believe in such things? *Do* you?"

He was Italian, and she knew what a free-wheeling imagination he had. Especially in bed. "Of course I believe in ghosts," he said indignantly. "Or in spirits, certainly."

"Spirits of what?"

"The dead, for God's sake. How do we know some woman who drowned in the lake, or *was* drowned in the lake, isn't trying to come back? Answer me that!"

It wasn't going to be one of their finest evenings together, she thought dourly as she removed her dress, bra and panties in that order and watched him take off the last of his clothes. Damn. She wished the Ellstroms and Haydn Clay had kept their stupid mouths shut, or at least admitted they'd simply been taken in by some trick of the moonlight.

But there was something else to be considered. If the thing from the lake hadn't killed those two big, beautiful Great Danes, what had?

Nino sat on the bed and looked at her. "Let's try to work this out, baby. This apparition—"

"Listen, you big lug, I didn't come here to discuss the condo's ghost with you. I have to get back!"

He gazed solemnly at her face for a moment, then lay back and lifted his arms to her—his familiar invitation for her to lie on top of him. One of those big hands cupped her bottom again as their mouths and tongues blended; then the warmth of him crept into her and she began to rub herself against him.

"Getting warmed up for the game," they both called it now. With LeRoy, even in the best of times, it had never been like this but always cut and dried—on, off, and out. With him she had felt absolutely nothing and was fairly certain he could not have felt much more.

After a while the big man under her whispered against her lips, "Come on, baby," and she rose to her knees to make love with him. He had such long arms he could take hold of her feet in that position.

How many other women had ridden St. George with the bottoms of their feet in their lover's hands, she wondered. Not many, for sure. The trouble was, it made her come like a house afire, always before he did, and then he had to shift his grip to her waist and move her up and down until he came too. That was great, though. Like being afloat on a warm, heaving sea.

Spent, they lay beside each other with her head on his shoulder, and let half an hour drift by in silence. It was like that with them now. The questions had all been asked and answered. She knew what Nino desired from her; he knew what she needed from him. Everyone's life should be so simple, she thought. So fulfilling. But when he fell asleep with one of those big, gentle hands on her breast, she nudged him.

"Hey, I have to go."

"So soon?"

"We'll both fall asleep if I stay here. I wish we could."

"Me too, baby."

"But I can't." She rose on one elbow and touched her lips lightly to his mouth, then slid off the bed. While she was dressing, he leaned from the bed, pulled her to him, and pressed his lips against the front of her panties.

"Uh-uh, we haven't time," Connie said. "Bye, darling."

"So long, baby. Sunday, maybe?"

"I'll try. I'll call you."

She didn't want a drink at Mae Henig's. After what had just happened it would be boring to sit and talk about bridge. Anyway, LeRoy just might be really worried because of the talk about the dogs, and if allowed to fret too long could be reluctant to let her out again.

She had to ring Mae's bell and say thanks, of course; couldn't just step into the Continental and drive home. When she did so, and explained why she felt she shouldn't stop, Mae was obviously disappointed.

"Don't tell me LeRoy believes that crazy tale about the lake thing."

"Well, I don't know, Mae. Maybe not. But something did kill those dogs."

"They were poisoned. You know that as well as I do."

"The vet said—"

"Who cares what the vet said? Someone got tired of having them mess up the common and put poison out for them. Something that would *fool* a vet."

"All right, Mae. But I'll still run along. Lee's been in a rotten mood all day and I don't want him mad at me. And Mae—"

"Yes?"

"Thanks. I don't know what I'd do without you."

They touched hands and Connie departed. The time was ten-forty, she noticed as she backed the car out of the driveway. No traffic at this hour. Off to her right now, as she made the turn onto Lakeshore Drive, the water lay dark and quiet. The moon, so bright the past few nights, was dim behind a veil of clouds. A sweet smell of night-blooming flowers rode the air flowing through the car's open windows.

In the near distance, again to her right as she approached the turn to the condominium, she could see lights in some of the apartments. Not many at this hour, of course. Most of the residents had gone to sleep and, anyway, not all the units were occupied. Some owners went north when winter ended.

But wait. What in the name of God was rising from the weedy shallows ahead of her?

She slowed the car and leaned over the wheel to peer through the windshield. The glass was smeared and hard to see through because those pesky little insects, the love bugs, had arrived ahead of schedule this year, and of course LeRoy hadn't bothered to wipe the dead ones off the car after driving to town this morning. Was it the distortion from the bug-spattered glass that made her think she was seeing a blob of mist floating toward the road?

Or *was* it mist? The kind you sometimes saw in the mornings was atmospheric; she knew that. It usually covered all or most of the lake. This was almost human in size and shape and becoming more so every moment.

Yes, it possessed a head and a body, legs and arms . . . legs that appeared to be walking now, not drifting or floating, and arms that reached out for something.

For what?

They could be reaching for her, she suddenly realized. Though still on the strip of grass between the lake and the road, the thing had changed direction and was heading for the car. When the edge of the headlight glare touched it, it seemed to absorb the light and glow from within. For some reason—perhaps because of the ring she wore—she thought of the inner fire of an opal.

Now it was in the road!

The shuddering moan of terror she heard then was from her own wide-open mouth as she sucked in a breath. Her hands tightened so fiercely on the wheel that her knuckles cracked. Everything she had heard about the lake thing at the cocktail party came rushing back to her, filling her with panic. She screamed, but no sound came out.

The thing was striding straight toward her.

Connie's right foot fumbled for the brake pedal and brought the car to a lurching halt. She groped for the control that would run the automatic windows up, then panicked further at the thought of sealing herself in the car while under attack. Should she floor the gas pedal and try to get past the thing or would it somehow stop her if she tried?

All at once she had a mental picture of the two Great Danes lying dead in the road only a few hundred yards from here. Maybe they, too, had panicked at the sight of this unnatural thing and tried to get past it in a foolish race for home.

What, dear God, should she *do?*

The thing slowly approached, swaying slightly from side to side now as though actually made of mist and affected by the slight breeze from the lake. But if made of mist, why did it seem so human? So *malevolently* human.

Connie flung the door open and hurled herself out of the car. A heel caught. Hitting the road on hands and knees, she skidded to its edge, leaving skin from palms and kneecaps on the blacktop. Sobbing now, scarcely knowing what she was doing, she rose staggering to her feet and began running in the direction she had come from.

Running, she screamed for help until the sound broke into fragments and her voice became only a whimper. And she kept turning her head to see what was happening behind her.

What was happening was that the thing from the lake was shapeless again. At least, it was less human in outline and floating again rather than walking. It floated so swiftly now, just above the blacktop, that she knew she could not outdistance it no matter how desperately she tried.

And now she felt a thing that reduced all the rest of what was happening to insignificance. From the depths of the misty blob pursuing her, some irresistible force was reaching out for her, touching her like an icy hand, clawing its way into her and turning *her* to ice. Some force she sensed was evil, wholly evil, and bent on destroying her in some hideous way.

"Oh God," she sobbed. "Oh God, help me!"

Fleeing from such a pursuer was senseless. Faced with that terrible truth at last, she whirled and thrust out her hands in a hopeless effort to keep the apparition at bay. But it would not be denied. In a final swift convulsion the mist leaped forward to engulf her.

Anyone passing—though no one did pass at that time —would surely have thought her last awful shrieks, fading away to silence, were emanating from the heart of the misty blob itself.

4

The Pool

It was the talk of the weekly cocktail party, of course.

"The way I reconstruct it," said Bee Broderick, "a man who lives over there was returning home about eleven o'clock and saw the car standing empty in the road, with its lights on and the motor running. He got out to investigate but couldn't find anything to explain why it had been abandoned, so he drove on and discovered Connie lying at the road's edge a hundred yards or so farther on. He thought she must have got out of the car for some reason and been hit by another vehicle."

"You don't suppose he hit her himself and is just saying that?" Estelle Quigley offered.

"Nobody hit her, Estelle," said Bee. "This man—his name is Emmons—drove on home and phoned the police. They took her to the hospital, but she was dead on arrival. An autopsy revealed absolutely nothing."

"The way it was with the dogs," Nicola Helpin said.

"All I can say," injected Carl Helpin in his customary growl, "is that something damn queer is going on around here and we'd better get to the bottom of it quick. It only takes a little of this kind of thing to give a place a bad name and ruin resale values."

Not many had turned up at the pavilion this Wednesday. Since the tragedy five days ago, the police had been talking to Lakeside Manor's residents and many felt drained. Connie Abbott's husband, LeRoy, was under sedation in his apartment with a nurse in attendance—mostly because he had lost his wife, no doubt, but also because the investigation had disclosed that while Connie had pretended to be visiting Mae Henig that evening, she had actually gone from Mae's house to Nino Viotti's. To add to LeRoy's agony, this had come out in some of the newspaper accounts.

"And now," Bee Broderick said, "the police want to know if her having an affair with Nino had any bearing on what happened to her."

"But nobody knew she was seeing him," someone said.

"Mae Henig did."

The police had been thorough. Hearing about the dogs, they questioned the animals' owner for most of an afternoon, but he was unable to name anyone who might have been sufficiently annoyed to kill them. Hearing about the "lake thing" supposedly seen by the Ellstroms and Haydn Clay, they questioned those three for most of another afternoon, after which they came with a boat on a trailer and spent a full day slowly cruising the shore and searching the marshy areas of the lake itself. When that turned up nothing of interest, they dragged the part of the lake from which the thing was said to have materialized. With intense curiosity the residents of the condominium watched them, but the dragging produced nothing.

"What I want to know," said Pearl Gautier at the pavilion party, "is how someone can die and they can't tell what caused it. For heaven's sake, I talked to Connie before she went out that night, and she was absolutely all right. We were going to Lakeland in the morning."

No one responded. Tom Broderick turned to Will

Platt, who had come to the gathering just to listen. "Will, is this one of your kind of mysteries? Something unexplainable?"

"I have no idea."

Will's tone must have implied annoyance, for the older man put a hand out to touch him on the arm. "I'm sorry. I was forgetting you have a mystery of your own."

"It's all right, Tom. No offense." At this point, deciding he was not going to learn anything because no one knew anything, Will Platt quietly left the group and walked back to the building, where to relieve his tenseness he ignored the elevator, climbed the stairs to his top-floor apartment, and poured himself half a glass of bourbon.

In Lakeside Manor for the next few days some people were more active than others. Jerome and Ruby Ellstrom spent much of their time on their veranda, discussing what they thought they had seen earlier and watching with keen interest the behavior of their next-door neighbor, Haydn Clay.

The condominium owned a number of rowboats and a canoe. In one of the boats Clay seemed to be repeating, day after day, what the police had done. Not the dragging, but the patient exploration of the weeds and shallows from one end of the lake to the other. On a body of water the size of Heron Lake this was no small job.

"He's going to have sunstroke," Ruby Ellstrom predicted. "He ought to have sense enough to wear a hat. Doesn't he know our Florida sun at all?"

Her husband shrugged. "Who knows what he knows? About all anyone can tell you is that he came here from Los Angeles, same as Carl Helpin."

Haydn Clay was about sixty, of average height and build, silver haired and articulate. Reservedly friendly with all in the building, he seemed to find genuine companionship only with manager Ed Lawson, who was a widower. Big Ed sometimes shared the boat with him now as he explored the lake. At times Ed rowed, at times he peered through binoculars as the craft prowled the edges of marshy areas it could not penetrate.

"Do you suppose they're looking for that 'gator they said they saw?" Jerone Ellstrom asked his wife.

"I think they're trying to find the thing *we* saw," she said. "The thing I think killed Connie Abbott and those two dogs. And you know something? I believe if we keep our eyes open we just might see it again . . . though I'm not at all sure I want to." She frowned at him. "Do *you* want to?"

"No, I don't."

She hesitated. "We felt something when we saw it, didn't we, Jerry? I mean really."

"I know I did. I'm still feeling it."

"Then you don't think we ought to . . ."

"No, I don't."

But they did for a while. For five nights they attempted a vigil, sometimes sitting quietly on their veranda until as late as two in the morning. They were not young, however, and when the hours began to tell on them they returned to their usual routine of going to bed early. Then, if their fears would let them, they made their usual quiet love before dropping off to sleep. But now it was a different kind of sleep, full of dreams and anxious awakenings.

Will Platt, meanwhile, had met the new owner, Lynn Kimball, a second time.

It had been Will's custom, one abandoned only briefly when his wife disappeared, to go to the pool every afternoon and swim thirty or forty laps to keep himself in shape. A swimmer in college, he was still good at it and enjoyed it, especially after a morning at the typewriter. Did teachers of "creative writing"—whatever that was —ever tell their students that inspiration consisted mainly of gluing one's butt to a chair and assaulting a typewriter until one's shoulders felt like wire coat-hangers?

This afternoon, when he arrived at the pool, she was there before him. Alone.

And lovely.

How old was she, really? Not his age, surely, with a figure like hers. Yet most people who bought into Lakeside Manor were either retired or contemplating retirement. This was central Florida, a rural region of vast orange groves, lakes to water them, and small towns. No work for outsiders, or at least very little.

"Hi," he said as she surfaced close to where he stood at the pool's edge. "Mind if I join you?"

"Not at all." Lovely voice, like a girl's. "I was just going to quit, it's so lonely here."

He dived in, swam the length of the pool under water and returned to her with an easy crawl. "I'm Willard Platt. Will."

"I know. We were introduced at the pavilion before I moved in."

"I didn't think you'd remember."

"I'm Lynne Kimball."

"*I* know."

She laughed, and he felt instantly at ease with her. "You swim well," she said.

"Used to, maybe. Not any more."

"Shall we do a few laps?"

If he swam well, she swam better, or at least more gracefully. It pleased him to watch her as they did four lengths of the pool together. Lovely, he thought again. A perfect little body, beautiful legs, dainty feet. The feet created half the commotion his did, and her arms moved seemingly without effort, yet she easily kept up with him.

They stopped at the deep end and clung side by side to the tiled gutter. "What did Ed Lawson mean when he said if I heard a typewriter in the night, it would be you scaring your readers?" she asked.

"I live over you."

"I know that. I mean—"

"Oh, that. Well, most of my work is fantasy. What's known now as dark fantasy."

"I like that kind of thing. You wrote a novel about Haiti and voodoo called *Darkling,* didn't you?"

He nodded.

"I've read it," she said. "Bought it in Jamaica, at a bookshop in Mandeville. I remember thinking whoever wrote it must have spent a lot of time in the islands."

"I have."

"What's your latest?"

"A sequel to that, more or less, but it won't be out until July. The latest to come out was a collection of shorter fantasy things I did some years ago for various magazines."

"Called what?"

"Not After Midnight."

"I'd like to read it."

"I'm not sure you ought to, after what's been happening around here. A woman alone."

She laughed, but was quickly solemn again. "What has been happening here, in your opinion? I mean, what killed those dogs, Mr. Platt?"

"Will, please. I can't imagine what killed them. Had there been only one dog, I might have thought someone who knew him walked up and pulled a plastic bag over his head to smother him. But unless two people did the dogs in . . ." He shrugged. "How about another lap or two?"

They did four more lengths of the pool—on their backs this time, lazily—and talked while swimming. "What about the woman who was found dead?" Lynne Kimball asked.

"I'm guessing it was a heart attack."

"But why did she leave her car with the lights on and the engine running? What made her do that?"

"People who have heart attacks sometimes panic."

"Are you convinced the Ellstroms and—what's the man's name? Clay?—really saw something come out of the lake? They were talking about it at the cocktail party, remember."

"Mrs. Kimball, I—"

"Lynne, please."

"I don't know Haydn Clay. He's new here. But the Ellstroms are good people. If they say they saw something come out of the lake, they saw it. *What* they saw is something else again."

"May I borrow your last book?" she asked. "I'll be careful of it, I promise."

"Of course. I'll leave it in your package mail box."

"Thank you. I ought to go now. I'm still sorting things out and trying to put them away."

He watched her grasp the handrails of the ladder near the pool's deep end and swing herself up as though she were made of air. He marveled at the perfection of her tiny feet again, at the way her small, round bottom seemed to wink at him just before she stepped from the ladder. She was wearing a one-piece yellow swimsuit, he realized for the first time. Why hadn't he been aware of that before, when he had been so very much aware of what was inside it?

Lynne Kimball, he thought. A widow who knew the islands, or at least knew Jamaica. They should have things to talk about. He had never been able to talk with Vicky about anything that mattered.

She plucked a yellow robe from one of the poolside chairs, slipped into it and tucked her feet into rubber thongs. "So long," she said. "See you later." And suddenly the pool was no longer interesting.

He swam a few more laps and walked back to the condominium, where he climbed the stairs because it now seemed important to make an effort to stay in shape. He showered, dressed, found a copy of *Not After Midnight* and went down the hall to the elevator, intending to ride to the first floor and place the book in her package box, as he had promised to.

Funny. When his hand went to the control panel, his finger refused to press the first-floor button. It pressed number five instead.

She opened her door when he knocked.

"I couldn't see much point in taking this all the way downstairs," he said, thrusting the book at her.

"Why—thank you, Mr. Platt."

"Will, damn it."

"I'm sorry. Will you come in for a drink?"

"I was afraid you wouldn't ask me."

She was out of the yellow swimsuit now and wearing a dress of sea island cotton hand-embroidered with small, streamer-tailed doctor birds. Jamaican, of course. She wore no makeup. Perhaps she never did. Closing the door behind him, he followed her into the apartment. She liked simple furnishings, he observed. And, by God, she had a bookcase full of books, something very few apartments in this building could boast of. Hallelujah!

"What do you drink, Will?"

"Bourbon if you have it. Otherwise anything."

"I have some Jim Beam."

"Perfect. With tap water, please. In case no one has told you yet, our tap water comes from an artesian well and is high class stuff. May I help you?"

She took bourbon herself, explaining that what she really liked was a certain very light Jamaican rum, but she was out of it now. "I returned from Jamaica over a year ago, when my husband died there," she said. "We had an apartment in Pompano Beach, and I thought I'd go into selling real estate there. I used to in North Carolina before my marriage. But after a while I realized Pompano had changed in the two years I'd been away.

It was noisier, more crowded, really awful after the almost English countryside atmosphere of Mandeville. So I sold out and bought this place."

"And now?" he asked as they moved into the living room with their drinks and sat facing each other on comfortable easy chairs.

"Well, Kevin left me well off, so there's no hurry. But I thought I might go into real estate here. It's an up-and-coming part of Florida, and I'm sure I could keep myself busy."

"I'm sure you could."

"Now tell me what you were doing in Jamaica," she said, gazing at him with interest as she sipped her drink. "And in Christiana, of all places. No one lives in Christiana without a reason."

5

Memories of Margal

In apartment 603, Tom Broderick sat alone in the living room with a section of the Sunday paper he had been saving to read slowly, without interruption, after Beatrice went to bed. It was an account of the recent happenings, headlined STILL NO CLUES TO THE BAFFLING HERON LAKE MYSTERY.

What, it asked, was the "ghostly creature with its aura of evil" that the Ellstroms and Haydn Clay claimed to have seen rise from the lake and cross the lawn in the moonlight toward the road? What had destroyed the two Great Danes found there, when two of the most respected veterinarians in the area had failed to find any physical injury or trace of poison? Finally, what had killed Constance Abbott on her way home from her tryst with her lover?

The article went on to point out that there had been a mystery at Lakeside Manor even before these strange events. Why, it asked, should the wife of a noted author of occult books have suddenly disappeared and left no trace?

The reporter had been to Miami and interviewed—though not very successfully, he admitted—people at the private detective agency employed by Willard Platt to find his wife. Yes, many women left their husbands and many men their wives, but there were peculiar circumstances here to be taken into account. Mrs. Platt had disappeared soon after her return from the West Indian island of Jamaica, the home of voodoo-related obeah. Her husband had written extensively about voodoo and might well have gone to Jamaica on this occasion to investigate obeah. Could there be a connection between his stay in Jamaica and the thing that seemed now to be living in Heron Lake and preying on the Platts' neighbors in Lakeside Manor?

There followed a summary of the contents of Will Platt's most recent books, in an apparent attempt to show that he, of all the Manor's residents, might be expected to explain what was going on—if, the article subtly hinted, he was not actually the force behind it. Slouched down in his easy chair with the paper resting on his overlarge belly, Tom Broderick was reading this part again when he heard the bedroom door open.

Tom's stout, horsey-looking wife stood there in a flowered dressing gown and looked at him with an expression of anxiety. "Are you all right, hon?"

She worried about him, always had, even when they were running their motel together in Miami. Actually, Bee had been the one who ran the motel; all he had done was amuse the guests by cracking jokes he had picked up from his theatrical pals. Long, long ago he had tried to be an entertainer himself, but failed to make the grade.

"I'm fine, baby."

She came to him, pressed her plump body against his protruding belly, and touched her lips to his. "Don't stay up too late drinking, now."

"I'm not drinking. I'm reading that story about this place. The fellow seems to think Will Platt might know more than he's admitting. Might even be responsible, somehow."

"He's crazy," Bee said indignantly. "Will Platt is just

a nice, hardworking man who happens to write creepy books. Why, I'll bet if we could look through the bedroom wall here, we'd see him at his typewriter right this minute, even if we can't hear him any more."

One of the reasons she so liked Will Platt was for his consideration for other people. When told they could hear his typewriter in their bedroom, sometimes late enough at night to be annoyed by it, he had soundproofed the wall of his study and put a thick mat of carpet under his desk.

But at the moment, at quarter to ten this Sunday evening, Will Platt was not writing a book.

"What brought me here," Will was saying to Lynne Kimball, "was the same thing that brought you, I suppose. Vicky and I had a home outside Boston. That's where I grew up. When the West Indies became my bread and butter, so to speak, we moved to Fort Lauderdale to be closer to my work. Then Lauderdale got too crowded and we found this place."

"Does your wife like it here, Will? I mean, is it possible she left because she doesn't? This part of Florida hasn't much to offer except golf and fishing, after all. And the summers are hot."

Will allowed a brief silence to pass while gazing at her. They were seated in his living room, he in an easy chair, she on the sofa. Twice he had been to her apartment. This time he had phoned and asked her to come to his for a drink.

They were on their second drinks now, and he said quietly, "There's something I haven't told you, Lynne."

"Oh?"

"Before my wife and I left Jamaica we agreed to a divorce. She was planning to leave here anyway and go out to California where she has a twin sister she's fond of. The only thing that surprised me about her disappearance was the timing of it."

"I see."

No, you don't, he thought. To understand the whole of it you would have to know what took place in that obeah house in the Cockpit. You would have to have seen Vicky sitting there with its owner, being instructed in the evils of sorcery, or holding Sister Merle's hands while they both peered into the flaming depths of that damned opal from Pachuca. You . . .

"If you expected her to go, why did you employ a detective agency to find her?" Lynne asked with a frown.

"Because I lived in a condominium."

The lifting of her eyebrows said, "What is that supposed to mean?"

"Let me tell you how it happened," he said. "I woke up earlier than usual that morning—five-thirty, to be exact—and noticed her bedroom door was open and the room empty. I went through the apartment looking for her, then got dressed and checked the parking lot for her car because she sometimes got up that early and went for a ride around the lake."

He paused. "The car was there. But I drove around the lake myself, anyway, then returned and looked to see whether any of her clothes were missing."

"And?"

"I couldn't tell. She had so many."

Lynne slowly nodded.

"Well, I didn't know what to do, so I just sat and tried to think things out. And I decided she must have planned it, must have arranged for someone to pick her up and drive her to an airport. The agency people haven't found her name on any passenger list for that day, but she could have used another name."

Again he paused. "Anyway, I blame Jamaica. We came back from there when we did because of her strange behavior, really. I mean I would have stayed longer. But she'll turn up in L.A., I know she will.

Meanwhile, to answer your question, if I'd been living in a house when this happened, I wouldn't have gone to a detective agency. No one would have questioned what I did. Here, damn it, she was missed the day she walked out."

Will had been gazing at the carpet while he talked. Now he looked at Lynne. "She had a bridge date with one group, a golf date with another—the whole social routine. And she hadn't told a soul about our pending divorce, so there was nothing to explain her disappearance. I had to call the police and hire a private eye to protect myself. Don't you see?"

"Yes, of course." Until now, Lynne had seemed to be on the defensive—a little, at least—sitting there rather stiffly, even primly, as though afraid she might invite an attempt at intimacy if she seemed too casual about being in his apartment. Now she visibly relaxed. Nudging her shoes off, she lifted her tiny feet onto the sofa and looped her arms around her knees. Tonight she wore white slacks and a pale green blouse that made her look more than ever like a teenager.

"So what you think, then, is that she won't come back here even if she's found," Lynne said.

He nodded.

"What will you do in that event? Stay here alone?"

"I've been alone for years."

"Oh?"

"You've never met my wife, so this won't shock you as it might some others around here. They know her as a physically attractive woman who was always friendly and easy to talk to. So she was. But the honeymoon wasn't even over before I realized I'd married a lesbian."

"A lesbian?"

"Not a practicing one, perhaps. It wasn't as acceptable a life-style then as it is now. But she was completely frigid. 'Don't make love to me. If you insist on sex, I suppose I can't refuse, but don't expect me to enjoy it.

Just get it over with in a hurry.' "

"Why did you go on with such a marriage?" Lynne asked quietly.

"I suppose I was the eternal optimist, hoping she'd change."

"She never did? Not even a little?"

After gazing at her in silence for a few seconds, Will decided he liked this woman well enough to be honest with her. "A couple of years ago she changed very much. But not in the way you mean."

Lynne waited.

"She went with me to Haiti when I was doing some background work for my last novel, and she got into voodoo there. When I say she 'got into voodoo,' you would have to know Vicky to understand what I'm telling you. She never does anything casually. We were based in Jacmel, on the south coast, and she sought out a notorious sorcerer named Margal. She became his pupil. What she learned from him made her a wholly evil woman."

"Evil in what way, Will?"

"Margal had devilish powers. He could reach you with his mind and force you to obey him. He could make *your* mind do tricks. You might be riding a mule through a rain forest, and the forest would suddenly burst into flames—or you would think it had, and perhaps kill yourself trying to escape. You could be crossing a mere trickle of water and it might suddenly, in your mind, become a raging flood that could drown you."

Shaking his head, Will paused. "There was no door you could lock to keep that man at bay, no barrier he couldn't breach in his quest for more and more power. If you believe in demons, he was one. And Vicky wanted to be like him. She wanted to possess the same unholy talents."

"Did she succeed?"

"We weren't in Haiti long enough, thank God. But in Jamaica she tried again, with an obeah woman named Sister Merle who was a kind of female Margal." He took in a deep breath. "I didn't want to take Vicky to Jamaica, and I didn't go there to work on a book, as the people here think. I went because an old friend in deep trouble there sent for me."

He paused again for a moment to marshal his thoughts. "It's a long story. I knew I'd be getting into obeah; Sam Norman made that clear when he asked me to go down there. I had a dread that Vicky might become a catalyst for the evil forces Sam was up against, and be a real danger to him. So I refused to take her, and we quarreled about it—just one more quarrel in a long string of them, all based on the fact that our marriage was a failure. But she turned up in Jamaica anyway." He stopped again. "I'm talking too much."

"No," Lynne said. "I want to know about you. My husband is dead and I'm free, but you're not. If you were just a man whose wife walked out and left him feeling sorry for himself, just a man looking for someone to drink with until she returned . . . But you're not, are you?"

"I feel as free as you, for the first time since my marriage."

"When was that, by the way?"

"When I was just out of college."

"Good God," she breathed. "Let's have another drink."

In the kitchen, while they were refilling their glasses, Will Platt put his hands on her shoulders and kissed her on the mouth. And she responded.

6

A Grim and Tender Evening

It was quiet now in the Broderick apartment. Bee had gone back to bed while Tom, his usual nightcap of Scotch and water in hand, sat in the dark on the veranda and gazed out at the lake. He was thinking of LeRoy Abbott in the apartment to his left.

It was a shame, really. The poor guy should have guessed Connie was playing around with somebody, the way she always went out alone at night. It was tough, though, having the whole thing come out in the papers after she was found dead. And how had the police learned about Nino Viotti?

LeRoy had aged ten years in the nine days since his wife's death. If he left his apartment, it was only to shuffle up and down the hall for exercise. He'd lost weight, which for him was something. His face was the color and texture of dough. If Bee hadn't been taking food to him a couple of times a day, he'd probably be starving.

And now this new piece in today's paper. It was bound to start the talk up again and add to the poor guy's misery. A shame.

Tom drank an inch of his nightcap and let his gaze roam over the lake. The night was moonless, but there was almost always some light in the sky here. Enough to reveal the movement of the water, at any rate. It was moving tonight under a gentle but steady breeze from the east. A nice cool breeze for this time of year.

Maybe he ought to tell Bee, if she was still awake. The veranda, just a big open-air room with screens for three of its walls, was always cooler than the bedroom. Unless, of course, the air conditioning was on. Neither of them liked air conditioning much.

He leaned sideways to pull open the drawer of a table. He took out a pack of cigarettes, tapped one loose and lit it. Bee didn't like him to smoke, and he never did when she was around. Lately he didn't even smoke when she was not around, but he felt the need tonight. Returning the pack to the drawer, he leaned back on his chair.

He could still see most of the lake. The balcony was on the building's top floor, six stories above the ground. But seated near the back of it and relaxed as he was, he could not look down at the beach. And just as he had been leaning back, the thing came out of shallow water less than ten feet from the sand.

An amorphous thing, white and slow, as though some creature in the lake had breathed out a mouthful of mist in imitation of cigarette smoke drifting from the Broderick veranda. A nothing, really, except that it was white on a dark night, pale against dark water, and so surely would have caught Tom's eye had he been in a position to look down on it.

When all of it was clear of the water, floating on the surface, it drifted across the beach and onto the lawn. There it stopped and swirled into something resembling a human figure, and with its head atilt seemed to study the building in front of it. Beginning at the ground floor, its gaze—if it possessed anything like eyes to gaze with —traveled slowly up the face of the structure as though reading the contents of the verandas.

At this hour on a Sunday night the verandas of Lakeside Manor were usually deserted. Not everyone went to bed early, of course, but those still up would not be out looking at the lake; they would be watching the news or a movie on television. One or two might even be reading a book. Tonight only the Broderick porch showed any sign of life, and the thing on the lawn could not have seen into that from where it stood so far below.

It just might, however, have seen the curl of smoke from Tom's cigarette, or from his mouth as he exhaled. Against the dark sky the smoke, to one with keen enough vision, might have been visible as it drifted out through the screen.

The thing began to change shape again. No longer human, it rose from the grass and floated upward. It was the size of a man but kept changing shape as it rose, the way a small cloud might change if caught in wavering currents of air.

One moment it was an outsized snakebird—there were many in the marshes here—with serpentine neck characteristically darting forward and back. Then it was not a snakebird but a snake, coiling to strike. Then in succession it became a round ball slowly spinning, a bat with lazy wings, a misty nothing at all.

Until it got there.

Now it assumed human shape again, but the misty figure was no longer pale; it was dark. Dark as the night, almost. So nearly so that Tom Broderick, relaxed on his chair with his cigarette between his fingers, did not become aware of it until it had fully taken shape outside his screen and begun to filter through the mesh. Even then all he saw was a dark shadow, human in form, gliding toward him.

Rising in haste, Tom uttered a grunt of alarm and dropped his cigarette onto the veranda carpet. "What the hell," he said, and then his eyes bulged with fear as the advancing thing, though still dark as oilfire smoke, became more human in shape . . . and developed a face.

At least, it had human features. But Tom had never

seen such a countenance before, even in his wildest liquor-inspired nightmares!

The eyes in this advancing death mask were aglow with some hellish fire that seemed capable of reducing him to a cinder. The mouth was a wide-open leer of hate in which the teeth were white fangs framing a bottomless hole. And the whole hideous thing kept *moving*. Its outlines writhed as though subject to shifting internal pressures. "There's an evil force inside it fighting in fury to get out" was the thought that flashed into Tom's mind.

But it was a face. And despite the blazing eyes and hate-warped mouth, it was a human face—one he recognized. "My God!" Tom croaked, stumbling backward with his hands upflung to fend the creature off.

The awful mouth seemed to snarl in reply, though he was sure it made no sound. Wildly retreating, Tom knocked over the chair he had been sitting on.

Behind the chair, the sliding glass door to the living room was open. He tripped over the low sill and went sprawling through to land on his back on the living-room carpet.

As the smoky figure flowed over him, he threw up his hands and clawed at it, frantically striving to keep it at bay. A yell of total terror erupted from him now, with all the air in his heaving chest behind it.

When the outcry ended he was still on his back, feebly struggling under an amorphous cloud of writhing darkness. The face was there in the cloud, but fading now and seemingly about to disappear.

No matter. It had accomplished its purpose. Above the cloud Tom's hands twitched helplessly, like the upthrust white wings of a wading bird that was caught in a pool of black pitch.

The bedroom door flew open then in response to his scream. Rushing out in her nightgown, his wife shrilled in panic. "Tom! Tom! What's the matter?"

* * *

"Will, what was that?"

Lynne Kimball sat up in bed, gazing wide-eyed at the wall between Will Platt's bedroom and the apartment next door. She was naked.

Will sat up, too, and put an arm across her shoulders. "A man yelling, it sounded like."

They were silent then, both of them, listening.

It had begun in the kitchen, when he kissed her. Their drinks replenished, they returned to the living room and sat together on the sofa. In a moment, the drinks forgotten, they were lying side by side, each seeking to find out whether the casual kiss in the kitchen was something to build on.

It was.

"Shall we go into the bedroom?" Lynne asked after a while.

"Let's."

He began to unbutton his sport shirt as he followed her across the living room, was out of it by the time they stood beside the bed. Gazing at him, she said quietly, "Everything, Will?" and he was startled. In the twenty-seven years he had been married to Victoria, nothing like this had happened even once.

Was it happening? Was this beautiful girl-woman really standing before him with her hands raised to unzip her dress? Or was he dreaming it?

He nodded in reply to her question. When she did step out of the dress and nervously shucked her bra and panties he made up his mind to find out at once just how real she was. Because if he were going to commit to a new relationship, it had to be one he was sure of.

She stood before him naked, a lovely thing with a solemn little smile on her lips. With the breasts and tummy of a teenager. The arms and legs of a girl athlete. In silence she watched him finish undressing, then stepped forthrightly into his arms and lifted her mouth to his and held it there.

When the kiss ended and he raised his head, he saw that her eyes were closed. She was breathing hard. From waist to knees there was a slippery film of moisture between their bodies.

He eased her onto the big double bed and sat beside her, looking at her. "Have you read all of that book of mine yet?"

She nodded.

"The story called *Alauda?*"

"Yes, Will."

"You didn't dislike that story?"

"I liked it very much."

"Even the love scene?"

"Especially the love scene."

Was she being truthful? He had to know. Had to know *now,* before this promising adventure reached a point of no return. "I want to be the man in that story," he said. "I never have been such a man—never had the chance to be—but I want to be now, with you, unless you say no."

She lifted her hands to his face, drew his head down and kissed him. "I can't imagine not liking anything you might do to me," she said.

But he lay beside her first, wanting to be sure. Wanting her to feel as right with him as he suddenly felt with her. Though it had happened very quickly between them, it was no light thing. He was in some ways a deeply religious man. Something more than chance, he already felt, had sent him to the pool that day when she was swimming there alone.

He held her in his arms, lightly caressing her body with his fingertips, her face with his lips. And then they heard the sound from the next apartment and were startled into sitting up.

They listened for a repetition. It didn't come. What came was the sound, muffled by the wall, of a woman screaming.

"That's Bee Broderick, next door," Will said. "She's not the screaming kind. I'd better check."

He slid quickly from the bed and into his clothes. Lynne was dressed and right behind him as he strode from the room. Down the hall they went to the door of 603, and Will banged it with his fist. No sound came from the apartment now. But no one opened the door, either.

He grasped the knob and found the door unlocked. Taking the brief entrance hall in three strides, he froze to a halt and stared at Bee Broderick, kneeling beside something on the floor at the far end of the living room, just inside the open door to the veranda. She wore a nightgown and was quietly sobbing.

He halted beside her and looked down. The thing on the floor was her husband, Tom—on his back, mouth and eyes wide open, face convulsed into something barely human. Will knelt, gently easing the woman aside. He reached for the man's wrist. After a few seconds he dropped the wrist and put an ear to Tom's chest. He could detect no pulse, no heartbeat, no sound of breathing.

Still on his knees he looked about the room, then at the veranda. Nothing seemed out of order except an overturned veranda chair and an unbroken length of cigarette ash on the green carpet. He looked at the dead man's wife and reached for her hand.

"Bee, what happened?"

"I heard him call out." Her voice was barely loud enough. "I was in bed. I ran out here. He was like this with . . . with something dark on top of him. Dark like smoke."

"Smoke?"

"Like smoke but *alive*. I don't know what it was. When it saw me, it flowed out onto the veranda and just . . . just disappeared through the screen. He was still alive then, trying to tell me something."

"Tell you what?"

She shook her head. "One word. Just one word. He said it over and over. It sounded like 'bat' but he was dying; he hardly had any voice left."

"Bat?"

"I think so. I'm not sure. I think that's what he was saying. Over and over again, just that one word. Bat."

7

Jurzak

Lakeside Manor was all but deserted. The snowbirds had gone back north and now, following the death of Tom Broderick the week before, most residents left had moved to a nearby motel.

Not for them the terror of continuing to dwell in a haunted condominium where two dogs, a woman and a man had mysteriously perished within the past three weeks. They would spend their nights, at least, at the motel until the killer was found.

The Ellstroms were among those who had departed. They might be high on the creature's list, they decided, because they, along with Haydn Clay, had been the first to see it. Pearl Gautier, the former nurse who had been Connie Abbott's best friend, had also decided it was unsafe to linger, especially for a woman living alone.

Estelle Quigley, the no-nonsense former restaurant owner from Massachusetts, had surprised Will Platt by leaving. He had thought her a tough old girl who would stick it out. LeRoy Abbott had caused no lifted eyebrows at all by departing. Why should he remain after the murder of his wife and the humiliating disclosure that she had been another man's mistress?

Remaining were Carl Helpin and his wife, Haydn

Clay, and manager Ed Lawson. Clay and Lawson spent much of their time together in a rowboat on the lake. Bee Broderick lingered too, determined to find the cause of her husband's death. And, of course, the two whose sudden friendship had set in motion a wave of gossip throughout the condo—Will Platt and Lynne Kimball.

"You know something, Will Platt?" said the girl-woman in Will's arms. "We've been sleeping together just a week now, and I feel more married to you than I ever felt with my husband."

"I've been telling you. It wasn't an accident that we met at the pool that day. I have deep convictions about such things."

"Have you, really?"

Will drew her closer and kissed her. It was two in the morning and they were in bed in his apartment. Sometimes they used hers, sometimes his; it didn't seem to matter. Actually they were not in bed, either, but on it, naked, with nothing over them. Both were accustomed to warm climates. They could, of course, have closed the windows and turned on the air conditioning, but they preferred the windows open.

"What I think, lady," Will said, "is that the good Lord is trying to prove something with us."

"Prove what?"

"I think he's fed up with the way things are going in this world of his. The increasing violence. The way such violence is being accepted as a normal way of life—if you don't like something, organize a gang and trash it or kill it. He didn't expect this kind of behavior, I'm sure. When he made man and woman, he planned on their loving each other, the way we're doing right this minute."

"I'll buy that," Lynne said. Snuggling closer, she let a hand wander over his body, just barely touching him with the tips of her fingers. It was a thing she had never done with her husband. Very early in her life with him she had discovered that his idea of making love to a woman was to get himself between her legs as rapidly as possible, even if it made her feel like a punching bag. Will Platt, on the other hand, liked to touch and be touched, and both of them, in the short time they had been doing it, had discovered a surprising variety of ways to please each other.

"The minute I saw you at the pool," he said presently, "I felt something I'd never felt in my life before. Not even with Vicky, when she was young and lovely and I thought I'd go crazy if I couldn't marry her. With you I felt—"

"What?"

"A certainty. We were being brought together for a reason. We were exactly right for each other."

She put her lips against the side of his neck and said in a low voice, "Thank you. I felt something like that too. I love you, Will Platt."

"I love you. How could I help it?"

But he had problems elsewhere.

The story in the Sunday newspaper the day of Tom Broderick's death had done him no good at all. The police and the county sheriff's people, reading it, had soaked up the insinuations concerning his possible connection with the mystery. In the week since the latest attack of the lake thing, he had been interviewed three times by different investigators.

A homicide investigator named Jurzak from the sheriff's department had been the most difficult. Short, fat, with a face resembling a small gray watermelon, he had at first seemed to be the one most easily disposed of, but behind his watery gray eyes and dull manner lay a brilliant imagination.

"Tell me about your wife, Mr. Platt."

"What?"

"Your wife, who ran away some weeks ago. When did she disappear, actually?"

"March twenty-ninth."

"That long ago, was it?" Jurzak took time to adjust his bulk more comfortably on the sofa and stare at his knees for a moment. "Anyway, tell me about her."

Will felt a twinge of apprehension. "What is there to say?"

"Well now, it seems you've told others she wasn't acting just right when you returned with her from—where was it?"

"Jamaica."

"Right. Jamaica. Where you were into some kind of voodoo business for your next book, no?"

Will hesitated. No one here knew his real reason for going to Jamaica. "No. That was pure speculation on the part of the man who wrote the newspaper story. I *was* worried about her when we returned, however."

"Why?"

"She wasn't herself."

"Could you be a little more specific, Mr. Platt?"

"She seemed troubled. Something was making her edgy and nervous."

"Then she left you."

"Then she left me."

Jurzak's hands were on his knees. His gaze slowly ascended from the hairy backs of them to Will's face. "Before she began acting edgy, Mr. Platt, how did the two of you get along? Any problems?"

"We had our disagreements at times. Nothing serious."

"I hear you're pretty friendly with someone else now. A woman here in the building."

Will felt sure his shrug was convincing. "She lived in Jamaica for a time. We find things to talk about. If you know this building, you know most of the talk is about bridge and golf."

"Nothing between you, eh?"

"Nothing between us. I'm still a married man hoping to find my wife."

"You hear anything at all from that agency in Miami?"

"They phone me every few days."

"But nothing to report, eh? No word about her from Los Angeles, where you thought she might go?"

Will shook his head.

The homicide investigator looked thoughtful for a moment, then said, "Do you have any idea, Mr. Platt, what might have caused the deaths of Mr. Broderick and Mrs. Abbott? And those two dogs?"

"No, I don't."

"There wasn't a mark on any of them to show what they died from. Seems to me it might be sort of up your alley, with you writing so much about West Indian voodoo and such."

"I'm a novelist, that's all. I don't practice what I write about. I mean, it almost sounds as if you're accusing me of . . ."

"No, no. Just wondering if you've run into anything like this before—in your research or folk stories, whatever."

"I haven't. I'm as puzzled as you are."

Jurzak departed then. Even shook hands in a friendly way and ventured his opinion that the mystery of Heron Lake would soon be unraveled, with so many investigations now in progress. His presence remained after his departure, however, and for the rest of that day Will kept trying to recall exactly what each of them had said.

I should have used a hidden tape recorder, he thought. Or would he have smelled it out somehow?

Three days after his conversation with Will Platt, Jurzak talked with Carl Helpin. The best way to learn the worst about the Manor's residents was to win the confidence of a man most of them disliked, he felt.

"I understand you've been in the building about as long as anyone, Mr. Helpin. Maybe you can help me with the backgrounds of some of these people."

They made an odd pair sitting there face to face in the Helpin living room—both short, Helpin heavy-shouldered but otherwise scrawny, Jurzak fat all over. On a chair some distance from them, Helpin's wife Nicola worked at needlepoint.

"Let's start with that writer fellow on the top floor," Jurzak suggested. "What's your opinion of him, Mr. Helpin?"

"Platt's nobody to waste your time on. Turns out a bunch of tripe about voodoo, ESP, sorcery, and stuff like that. My guess is he makes most of it up."

"You've read it?"

"You must be kidding."

"You would discount him as a suspect, then?"

"I sure wouldn't put him near the top of the list."

The fat man placed his pudgy hands on his knees and gazed at them. "Who would you put at the top, Mr. Helpin?"

"Our manager, Lawson, and Haydn Clay in 301."

"Why those two?"

"Lawson is about to lose his job here. He sure will if *I* have anything to say about it. And Clay is a bad one."

"What could they gain by killing people, Mr. Helpin?"

"They can ruin the condo; that's what they can do. Maybe you've heard how some of our people want to sell but can't find a realtor to handle their apartments."

"Yes, I've heard." Jurzak's face took on a frown. "You say Clay is bad? In what way? I've been told no one knows much about him."

"I know about him. I looked him up."

"Do you always investigate people who buy in here, Mr. Helpin?"

"We don't have to. Most people move in, they tell you

about themselves. I didn't hide the fact I came from Hollywood and worked in the film industry."

Jurzak's eyebrows went up a little. "Oh? You were an actor?"

The answer came not from Helpin but from his wife, who had stopped working on her needlepoint and was attentively listening. "My husband was a special effects man," she said calmly. "I was the actress."

"You, Mrs. Helpin?" Jurzak was obviously surprised.

"Not one you've ever heard of, I'm sure. Perhaps I might have been, had I kept at it, but I didn't; when I married Carl, he insisted I drop it." Jurzak had the distinct impression she was not happy, now, that she had let her husband persuade her. "Carl worked mostly on science fiction and horror pictures," she said with a shrug, returning to her needlework.

Jurzak looked at Helpin again. "Horror pictures?"

"Yeah. What's happening here would make a good one, don't you think? Maybe I'll try a script and send it to one of my old buddies. That is, if Platt isn't already doing a book about it."

"Tell me about Haydn Clay. You were about to when—"

"I was interrupted. Yeah." Helpin shot his wife a look that promised he would return to her later. "What I was going to tell you is that when I saw Lawson and Clay out there on the lake in a rowboat night after night, I got mighty curious. Oh, sure, they were supposed to have seen a 'gator a while back, and we were supposed to think they were trying to find out where it was holed up. But I didn't buy that. What they were up to had something to do with the killings, I figured."

"So?"

"So I made a point of finding out about Clay's background."

"How did you do that?"

Helpin grinned. "It was easy. He's from L.A. . . . . we

knew that. All I had to do was call up a buddy of mine there and put him to work. And you know what he came up with? Are you ready for this? Haydn Clay was in real estate out there, and his reputation was none too good. He was even into blockbusting for a while and got himself blacklisted. You know what blockbusting is?"

Jurzak nodded.

"Enough said, then. So now you tell me what Ed Lawson and Haydn Clay are up to when they take a rowboat out on the lake here at five in the morning or after dark. Are you prepared to say they're not up to something shady connected with these killings, so they can give this condo a bad name and Clay can buy it for pennies?"

"I'll look into it," Jurzak said.

Helpin's grin was a twisted thing of triumph. "You do that, buddy. You be sure you do it."

8

Footprints in the Night

At eleven o'clock that night Will Platt finished a three-hour sting at his typewriter and went to the telephone. He dialed Lynne Kimball's number.

"Hello."

"Hello, love. What are you doing?"

"Waiting for you," she said without hesitation. "How's the work going?"

"Finished for now. I'm dripping, though. Need a shower. Then I'll be down."

"I was just about to take a shower myself," she said. "In fact, I'm standing here with nothing on. Why don't you—" Her last three words bumped into his interruption of "Why don't I," and they both laughed. "Two minds with a single sexy thought," she said.

"Correction. A single loving thought. After three hours at the word-machine, sex is the last thing on my mind."

"Hurry down anyway," she urged.

He would be staying in 504 all night, he knew, so before leaving he went through his apartment to be sure the right windows were open to catch the cooling night breeze. And, of course, the sliding glass door to the porch; unless that were left open, most of the lake wind

61

would be walled out. Locking the hallway door behind
him, he descended the stairs to the floor below and
found Lynne's door ajar.

"Close it, will you?" she called from the larger bathroom, the one with the shower stall. "I'm in here."

He closed it and pushed the button to lock it, then
walked to the bathroom intending to kiss her. He had
not seen her since sharing a light supper with her at six
that evening.

She was adjusting the water, with the upper half of her
body inside the curtain. She turned as he entered the
bathroom, her shoulders damp from the shower's spray.
"I missed you," she said, reaching up to kiss him.

He felt the heat of her body against him and her wet
hands pressing against his back under the loose shirt he
was wearing. "Just wait, Lynne," he said as he began to
shed his clothes, tossing them out of the bathroom onto
the hall carpet. When he stepped under the cool water,
she followed him. Though they had never done this before, it seemed they both knew instinctively what to do.

He soaped her body and she soaped his, turning the
motions into a prolonged caress. It aroused them both.
When he went into her she was warm and wet and waiting, and both were oblivious to the water cascading over
them. It ended with a quiet meeting of mouths, a stepping back to gaze at each other with new understanding,
and her saying at last, in a whisper, "Why didn't we find
each other years ago, Will?"

"It wasn't time."

"You really believe that, don't you?"

He nodded, then drew her close again and held her
soapy, slippery body against his own and fitted his lips
to hers. This time the kiss went on and on, and they
began swaying from side to side together as though hearing a seductive music in the sound of the water.

When he let her go, he said, "All my life, Lynne darling. All my *life* I've been waiting for someone like you.

Do you know I'd even given up thinking about it? Or believing there might be such a woman?"

"We've got something special," she said. "I don't think many people find it."

"Very few."

They stepped out of the shower and dried themselves, pausing every now and then to dry parts of each other. Then they turned out the lights and went to bed. Through the open windows they heard the murmur of the lake lapping the sandy beach, and now and then the breeze rustled the fronds of the palm trees on the lawn.

Will lay on his back and she moved closer to him, resting her cheek on his chest. Her free hand slid down to cover his sex, not teasingly but as though wanting to sleep there. He looped his arm around her and let his fingers lie on her breast.

He began chuckling.

"What's funny?"

"I just thought of a little ditty I heard once in England. Don't know who wrote it or where it came from, but for us it was made to order."

"Tell me," she murmured sleepily.

> "Here's to us and here's to Blighty
> I in pajamas, you in a nighty
> But since we're both a trifle flighty
> Why the pajamas, wherefor the nighty?
> Twas never intended by God Almighty."

Her laughter tickled his shoulder. "Very nice. I'll bet you wrote it, though."

"I didn't. Honest."

"Well, you should have. Go to sleep now, darling. Night."

"Night, my love. For now."

Will awoke first. Lynne was still in his arms, asleep with her cheek on his chest. Amused, he raised his head enough to look down at her hand, still resting in the same place on his body. The movement waked her and she opened her eyes.

"Hi," she said. "What time is it?"

He raised himself a little more to see the illuminated clock on the chest of drawers beyond the end of the bed. "Three-twenty."

"If it's that late, I need a bathroom."

"You have a built-in alarm?"

"Something like that. You should know by now."

As a matter of fact he needed a bathroom himself, so while she went to the one off the bedroom they were using, he walked through the living room to the other. When he returned through the living room, he saw her standing on the carpeted veranda, looking out at the lake. Still naked, of course.

For some reason he suddenly remembered he had not seen his wife naked more than half a dozen times in all the years of his marriage.

Joining Lynne, he stood at her side and put an arm around her waist. "What are you looking at?"

"Nothing. It's just so pretty in the moonlight."

The moon was in its first quarter and she was right: the lake in that faint light, barely touched by a breath of breeze, appealed to whatever instinct it was in him that made him enjoy writing tales of mystery and imagination. In the marshy sector just beyond the artificial white sand beach, hundreds of white water lilies seemed to glow in the half light.

In the marsh a frog began grunting. Arms around each other now, they stood by the veranda screen, listening and trying to locate the grunter. A cloud swam under the moon fragment, and the lake became dark for a few minutes. When the light washed over it again, Will said, "Look out there beyond the marsh. The far edge. Do you see something?"

"Like smoke rising."

"Yes, dark smoke. That's what Bee Broderick called it, remember?"

They watched a dark gray shape rise from the water among spikes of pond grass that in daylight were topped with showy blue blossoms. Free of the surface, it floated like a small dark cloud toward the beach. Lynne reached for Will's hand, and her fingers trembled as she clung to it. "Should we stay out here, Will? After what happened to Tom Broderick?"

"Wait."

"But—"

"If it comes this way, we'll go inside and shut the door. Even leave the apartment, if you like." He pressed his face against the screen. "You don't have binoculars, do you?"

She shook her head.

In silence they watched the thing drift toward them, saw it float out onto the sand, which in the faint moon-light was weirdly pale, as though sprayed with offwhite paint.

"My God, look," Will breathed.

The amorphous blur was now assuming shape. On the sand now it gathered itself into something nearly human and female, the smoke still swirling and writhing but more real every instant. Then it walked up over the beach and onto the lawn, where it stopped and looked up.

"Can it see us, do you suppose?" Lynne whispered.

Will shook his head. "Not without a light on up here."

"But if it can—"

"All right, let's move. God knows what it is or what it *can* see. Or what it wants." Stepping back from the screen, he drew her with him into the living room and closed and locked the sliding glass door, being careful to make no sound that might reach the senses of the thing below. Then he walked her the length of the living room to the hall door and, without opening the door, said, "Let's wait here a minute."

They stood side by side, naked, watching the veranda. A cloud was passing in front of the quarter moon again, a larger one this time, and the veranda was dark. So was the apartment. Moments passed in silence except for the sound of their breathing, his slow and deep, hers a little faster. He was holding her hand and it felt sticky in his own. Not hot but sticky. He released it.

Just then he thought he saw something, and reached behind him to grasp the doorknob in case they had to flee. What he thought he saw was dark, like the veranda and the night sky beyond the screen, but visible in the way certain moving things—bats, for instance?—could be visible in not quite total darkness. This was no bat, though, unless it was one as large as a human being and able to rise through the night without moving its wings.

He doubted his senses as it seemed to float up past the veranda. Most of all he doubted the legitimacy of his feeling that the thing was ugly, evil, and bent on committing some hellish act. Yet the feeling was so strong within him, it chilled his body and made him tremble.

"Lynne," he whispered, "did you see something out there?"

"I think so."

"What in God's name was it?"

"A woman, I think. But not a real one. A shadow of one." She groped for his hand. "Will, yours is the only apartment above this!"

"Wait," he said in a voice only she could hear. "Let's see if it comes back down."

They waited, staring through the glass door at the porch with its outer wall of screening. The moon-sliver reappeared in the sky. The veranda, the screen, the lake became more visible. Ten minutes went by. An ache settled in the calf of his left leg. He leaned over and rubbed it, but still kept his gaze fixed on the veranda.

Suddenly he felt the nearness of something evil again and knew the thing was returning. As it drifted back down into view, he froze in the act of massaging his leg, and Lynne stiffened at his side.

But this time there was no way that it could be considered human—and womanly—in appearance. Swirling, twisting, constantly changing form like a column of dark smoke above an invisible fire, it spiraled swiftly past the porch and was gone.

Will straightened and stepped forward.

"No," Lynne whispered. "No, Will, don't!"

"I just want to see where it goes." Crossing the room, he slid open the veranda door, stepped across to the screen, and peered down. Despite her fear, Lynne came to his side.

The thing had descended rapidly; it was over the water, half way out to the area of reeds and lily pads. And now it was only a shapeless blob.

Could it change shape at will? Assume any form that served its purpose?

Side by side, bodies touching, they watched it hover for a moment over a spot near the center of the marsh and then spiral down out of sight. *Like the genie into the bottle,* Will thought, staring in fear and amazement at the point of disappearance.

There was a sudden violent swirling of the dark water then, as though on becoming submerged the thing had changed shape again, this time convulsively. The movement was not repeated, and in a moment the lake was as calm as before, shining softly in the moonglow. Will turned away.

"Lynne, I'm going upstairs."

"What for?"

"I left my veranda door wide open."

Will headed for the bathroom hall where his clothes still lay on the carpet. But by the time he was into them, Lynne was dressed too.

"I'm going with you."

"Now wait. All I want is to find out—"

"You're not leaving me alone here, Will Platt. That thing may decide to come back!"

"All right." He steered her to the hall door, glancing at his watch as he did so. They still had not switched on any lights, but the watch had a luminous dial. "Five to four," he said, frowning. "We've been at this for thirty-five minutes."

They climbed the stairs in silence to the floor above. Unlocking the door of his apartment, Will entered first. Sensing no alien presence, he thumbed a light switch.

Then he stood motionless, gazing at the living room carpet.

The carpet here was a good one, pale gold and smooth as a golf-course green. Vicky had picked it out, and she had expensive tastes. On it now were lines of dark wet spots resembling human footprints, blurred at the edges. They ran in all directions from the veranda, where they seemed to have originated.

Their maker had obviously searched both bedrooms, both bathrooms, the kitchen, the study, crossing and recrossing the living room a number of times.

"Will," Lynne whispered behind him, "what—"

"Get out of here!"

"But—"

He turned and made her step back into the hall, where she might have a chance to run from danger. "Wait out here!" he ordered sharply, and shut the door on her. Then, facing the wet footprints again, he walked slowly the length of the living room and out onto the veranda.

The intruder had come through the screen at a point near the middle of the porch, the footprints beginning between a pair of red clay pots filled with sweet basil that even now scented the air with its minty fragrance. But he was aware of another, less agreeable odor, too. A swamp smell. A reek of decaying vegetation.

Squatting on his heels, he pressed his right palm onto one of the soggy spots on the veranda carpet, then lifted the hand and sniffed it.

Was it a swamp smell? All he could be sure of was that it was nothing he had ever encountered before or was anxious to again. It filled him with the same fear, the same sense of the presence of evil, that had seized him when Lynne and he watched the thing on its way up here.

In spite of his fear he made himself explore the apartment, confirming his first belief that the intruder had thoroughly searched it. It was empty now, however, except for those sodden marks of the thing's feet.

Opening the hall door, he drew Lynne in from the corridor and showed her what he had found. "What do you think of the smell?"

She made a face. "It's awful. Will, I think you should call the police."

"No."

"Why not?"

"My God, lady, how can I? Don't you see? I'd have to tell them where I was when this happened, and I'm supposed to be desperately searching for my wife."

After gazing at his troubled face in silence for a few seconds, Lynne reached for his hand. "Let's go back down to my place and talk about it," she said quietly. "Because we have to do something, darling. This horrible thing that killed Connie Abbott and Tom Broderick is after you now. And believe me, I don't want to lose you."

BOOK TWO

The Sorceress

9

"I'll Turn You into Dirt!"

He had not told Lynne Kimball the whole truth about Jamaica. Perhaps he never would. Certainly he had not told the people of Lakeside Manor. They took it for granted he had gone to the island to do a book. However, with a long novel just completed and in the hands of his agent, he was under no pressure to work his head off. What he wanted to do was work on a solution to the ever more acute Vicky problem. Then came the phone call from Sam Norman.

Sam. They had met when he went to Haiti, with Vicky, to search out background material for the voodoo book. The town of Jacmel on Haiti's south coast, well off the beaten track, had seemed a likely place to dig into voodoo at that time. It had an intriguing reputation for strange happenings.

Renting a car in Port-au-Prince, he had driven to Jacmel, taken a room at something called the Pension Forban, and discovered he was not the only white man on the premises. Young Sam Norman, doing an A.I.D. job in agriculture, had been living at the same little hotel for months.

Great. An old hand in Haiti, Sam spoke fluent Creole and knew the country as well as any outsider could. He was also having troubles with some local fellow on the dark fringe of voodoo, a bocor named Margal who was giving him fits, and that made it even easier for Will Platt and Sam Norman to become friends in a hurry. When you were prey to such troubles, it was nice to have someone to sit with at the pension's little self-service bar and talk things out.

The trouble with the sorcerer had turned into a strange adventure, but in the end Sam Norman had met a Schweitzer Hospital nurse who was right for him, had married her and gone back to the States. Fine. Every month or so they swapped letters, grateful that in the normal dullness of traveling from birth to death they had run into each other and were able to stay in touch, even without the promise of future meetings.

Then, in March, the phone call came.

"Will? Sam Norman, in Jamaica."

"Jamaica, Sam?"

"The U.N. asked me to look into some obeah trouble a man of theirs was having here. I'm out in the sticks, in Christiana, not in Kingston."

"For God's sake. What do you mean, obeah trouble?"

"Just that. You remember Margal, the bocor who damned near destroyed me?"

"Of course. He and—" Will caught himself. He had been about to say, "He and Vicky were thick as thieves," but suddenly became aware that Vicky was standing only a few feet away, listening to him. "Yes, of course," he finished lamely.

"This is pretty much the same cup of tea, except it's a woman. And there really is trouble, Will. *I'm* in trouble up to my neck. Can you possibly come down for a few days to lend a hand? I know it's a hell of a thing to ask, but I need you. I really do."

Will had stared at the phone in silence. Actually in something of a daze. He was in the heartland of Florida.

To get to Jamaica he first had to reach an airport from which planes flew there. And what would he tell Vicky?

He said at last, "Okay, Sam. When?"

"The sooner the better. Make your arrangements, hey? I'll call you back in a couple of hours to find out when I'm to meet you."

"Meet me where? Montego Bay?"

"Right. It's a shade closer than Kingston. Easier, too."

"Give me your number. I'll call you."

"Will, you can't. I'm at a pay phone."

It was like that sometimes in the islands. You learned to live with it. Rent an expensive house from which the phone had been removed, and you might discover you couldn't get one for months because there were ninety-nine applications ahead of yours. But you might rent a falling-down shack and find it had a phone in it and the damned thing still worked. Crazy.

He turned to Vicky, who was still standing there. "That was Sam Norman, Vicky. I have to go to Jamaica."

"Good. I need a change from this stuffy place."

"I have to go alone."

Her smile vanished. Her eyes glittered. "Alone? Why?"

Because, he thought, *this is like the Margal business, and if you go with me and get yourself involved in sorcery again, God knows what might happen. Sam is in trouble with obeah and doesn't need you to make it more dangerous.*

But what he said was, "It's a hurry-up thing, no time for planning. I'll be back in a couple of days, no doubt."

"How do you know?"

"Well, I don't *know,* naturally. A friend is in trouble, you stay as long as he needs you. But it can't be a big deal."

"Oh, of course."

He used the phone to arrange transportation from Miami to Montego Bay, then looked at Vicky again. It was six-thirty on a Saturday evening, and she was dressing for dinner at the club. Wearing only panties and a bra, she stood there as though waiting for him to come and put his arms around her. But he knew that if he did, she would become marble.

He shrugged. It was an old, old story. "Look," he said. "Sam says he needs me. He's a friend. The best friend I have. I'm going down there to see what I can do, and when I've done it or decided I can't do it, I'll come back. What do you care? *You* haven't needed me since you married me."

"Do you mind telling me where in Jamaica you're going?" she said with the mock politeness that infuriated him.

"Christiana. It's a town in the center of the island, near Mandeville."

"Another Jacmel?" Her eyes were really bright with interest now.

"No," he said, "it's not another Jacmel. Jamaica isn't Haiti."

"What kind of trouble is Sam in?"

"Something about a U.N. man teaching agriculture."

"What do you know about agriculture?"

He had said the wrong thing, he realized. It was a common failing of his when they were engaged in their little battles of wit. He tried to shrug it off. "I'm sorry. Sam didn't go into details."

After gazing at him in silence for a few seconds, she shrugged and walked away.

He had taken her to the club that night, and had thought of trying to make love to her when they returned—one last try, because he was leaving for a while —but decided against it. He slept for a few hours, got up, packed a bag with the things he expected to need for a short stay in Jamaica, and departed without even looking into her room to say goodbye.

An hour and twenty minutes after takeoff he was waiting for his bag at the conveyor belt in MoBay, as he had done more than a few times in the past, and feeling the sweat trickle down his ribs under his sport shirt because, of course, the air conditioning was out of order.

Sam Norman was waiting, looking young, rugged, and grateful.

The vehicle in the airport parking area was a Land Rover that belonged, Sam explained, to the United Nations. "I'm living in their fellow's cottage, and he's disappeared. You can stay there too. Lots of room, and he's got the best cook in all Jamaica, I swear. Will, by God, it's good to see you. Shades of Jacmel."

"This *is* a shade of Jacmel, isn't it?" Will said. "I mean—the same kind of thing you ran into with Margal."

"I think. But this is obeah, not voodoo."

"There's a difference?"

"There is a difference. Anyway, Margal wasn't really voodoo either, was he? We understand that. He was a bocor."

"A sorcerer."

"Right. And so, if I'm not mistaken, is the lady I'm up against this time."

They were away from the airport now, Sam driving, the north coast road stretching wide and empty ahead. Will knew this road. It was the one you traveled from MoBay to Ocho Rios, to Port Antonio, past many of the tourist hotels, even on to the capital city of Kingston if you were stupid enough to want to go there. New to him, though, was the road onto which Sam turned just after they had passed through the handsome old seacoast town of Falmouth.

This was a narrow strip of blacktop that snaked

through fields of sugarcane at first, and then began to climb. In seemingly endless loops it ascended through a wilderness of deep sinks and formations of limestone that resembled everything from giant animals to whitewashed reproductions of the Hudson River Palisades. "The Cockpit Country," Sam said, interrupting talk of their adventures in Haiti. "Know it, do you?"

Will wagged his head. "Heard of it, that's all."

"It's a geological freak, the only one of its kind in the world."

From the air the terrain probably resembled a huge World War I no man's land, Will decided, its giant shellholes overgrown with forest and scrub. The road skirted the tops of deep depressions, often with uncomfortably steep drops just a few feet beyond the vehicle's tires. Put a collection of chamber pots together, he thought whimsically, and we're a bug running along their rims trying to find a way out of the maze without tumbling to destruction.

"She lives here in the Cockpit," Sam said, breaking a silence.

"Who does?"

"Sister Merle, the obeah woman I've been telling you about. The dame who told our U.N. fellow, Juan Cerrado, she was going to turn him into dirt to make his fields grow better."

"That's what she said?" Will turned on the seat to frown at his companion.

Sam nodded and shrugged at the same time. "The U.N. sent him here to teach the peasant farmers a few new things about farming, just as A.I.D. sent me to Haiti. You remember what happened to me in Jacmel. Margal was grabbing most of what my farmers earned, and I fought him. Cerrado found this obeah woman doing the same thing, and fought her."

They were nearing the village of Wait-a-Bit and Will found himself gazing at steep hillsides bristling with yam sticks. For miles he had been full of admiration for the peasants who farmed this land; they seemed to have planted every inch of earth they could find among the fantastic formations of limestone. Here the soil seemed to be better and more plentiful, though it still would have broken the heart of any farmer in Florida.

"And?" he said.

"As I told you, he's disappeared."

"What do you mean by that, exactly?"

"He's simply vanished, Will. I know it sounds crazy, but it's true. Friday before last he went to market with Ima Williams, the cook. Friday and Saturday are market days in Christiana. He wanted to look at the vegetables being offered—it was a thing he did every now and then to help him decide how his program was going. That day he didn't come back."

"Nine days ago."

"Nine days ago, and nobody's seen him. Not a soul."

"What have you done?"

"I went to the police and they're trying to find him—so far without turning up a clue. I've talked to everyone in town who will talk to me. I've driven over every road in the district, stopping at shops and talking to those people. Nobody's seen him."

"And this obeah woman who threatened him—you've spoken to her?"

"Her, too. It was after I'd walked in to her place and questioned her that I decided to phone you."

They were making the turn onto the Christiana road, and there had been long silences between fragments of talk because both men were accustomed to thinking before speaking. "Walked to her place?" Will Platt said. "She's that hard to get to?"

"You have to leave your car and follow a footpath. Cockpit Country was a hideout for escaped slaves in the old days, and some of the soldiers who went after them were never heard from again. I had a feeling I might not be heard from again either. Will, how long can you stay with me on this?"

"I didn't bring a time clock."

"Good. Because I like this Juan Cerrado. He's young and pig-headed but really wants to help these people. Has a degree in tropical agriculture and knows what he's doing."

The Land Rover was climbing toward a scarred gray concrete structure with a sign in front that said CHRISTIANA POST OFFICE. "One minute you talk about him in the past tense," Will said. "Then he's alive again."

"That's because he's gone, but I can't believe she's had him killed. All he was doing was threatening part of her income. Probably a small part, at that."

"Just as you threatened Margal's and nearly got yourself killed for it. Is she as powerful as Margal, do you think?"

"She's certainly just as evil."

"For instance."

"Well, there are many stories. I'd better tell you just one at this time. Obeah, of course, is outlawed here. Every now and then someone gets picked up by the police for practicing it and is fined or jailed. About a year ago, I've been told, two cops from Sister Merle's district paid her a visit one evening in response to some complaints they'd been receiving. It was a hot night and her door was open. Without making their presence known, they looked in and saw her seated at a table with a lighted black candle in front of her. In one hand she held a Bible, in the other a rum bottle. Sound familiar to you, does it?"

"The usual," Will agreed, but sensed something less usual coming.

"After a while she left the house, taking the Bible and bottle with her, and the two cops followed. She went down a Cockpit path to a little graveyard. There she got down on her knees in front of a stone, tapped the stone with the Bible, poured the contents of the bottle over it —and the cops testified in court that it didn't smell like rum —and barked out a command. 'Mordecai, Mordecai, arise!' she shouted. 'Our master calleth! Turn to the north, south, east and west! Come to my house tonight to perform with me the powers of demons!' "

Knowing what he did about bocorism, to which this was certainly related through a common African origin, Will was not even tempted to smile.

"At this point the cops decided they'd heard and seen enough, and showed themselves," Sam Norman went on. "They grabbed the Bible and bottle for evidence and she demanded them back, calling the two men a string of names that should have curled their hair. All this came out at her trial. Another thing that came out was that when she wouldn't shut up and go with them peaceably, one of the cops, a man named Dorney, slapped her across the face pretty hard with his left hand. Keep that in mind, Will; it was his left hand. When he did it, she quit cursing them, stopped resisting, and just stood there staring at his hand. Then suddenly she stepped forward and spat on it."

Sam paused. "Do I need to tell you the rest of this?"

"Tell me anyway."

"The Magistrate found her not guilty, for some reason. She was released and went home. A couple of days later Dorney turned up at a hospital in Mandeville, complaining that his left hand wouldn't stop itching and was driving him crazy. There was nothing wrong with the hand that the medics could see, except that the man had scratched it almost down to the bone."

"And it got worse," Will said, nodding. He had heard a similar tale in Haiti and taken the time to check it out, and had found it to be true.

"It got worse. They kept the fellow in the hospital, and still it got worse. They bandaged the hand so he couldn't continue to scratch it, and *still* the flesh fell away. Then one day Sister Merle appeared in the doorway of his hospital room, walked over to his bed, looked down at him with what he later described as the most horrible smile he had ever seen, and said to him, 'Does your hand hurt a little, corporal? You're going to lose it, you know. Foolish man, you never should have slapped Sister Merle.' And she walked out.''

"Did he lose the hand?"

Without shifting his gaze from the road, Sam nodded. "They had to amputate. For a time they thought he might lose his arm as well."

"Your obeah woman sounds formidable, Sam."

Again Sam nodded. "At least we know what we're up against. Shall I take you back to the airport?"

"No way. Keep going."

It was Sunday. The town of Christiana was all but deserted. The four-wheel-drive vehicle droned downhill and up between rows of closed shops. It purred past a silent market gate and a theater displaying gaudy posters advertising Chinese karate flicks.

Another turn on the roller coaster, and it climbed again past a drab shed in front of which mountains of Red Stripe beer boxes were stacked, and a ramshackle garage that looked as though all cars were repaired at the road's edge and had been dripping oil there since Columbus discovered the island.

At last it put commercial things behind and sped between gracefully antique wooden homes with verandas and gardens and fences and gates, until Sam Norman brought it to a halt in front of a gate from which dangled a massive padlock.

"Home."

Unlocking the gate and swinging it open, Sam drove the Land Rover into a curving dirt driveway between hedges of hibiscus and stopped it before a long wooden veranda. A flight of wide steps led to weathered double doors that opened before the vehicle came to a stop. In the doorway a tall black woman, maybe thirty-five years old, held a long-fingered hand above her eyes to shield them from the early afternoon sun so she could see who was arriving.

"Ima, lend a hand here, will you, please?"

She came down the steps like a peasant woman descending a mountain trail with something heavy on her head—straight as a eucalyptus tree and just as supple. Handsome, Will thought. So many of the country women were handsome.

"Ima, this is Mr. Platt, come to help me find Mr. Juan." This was typical, too: Mr. Juan, not Mr. Cerrado. Soon he would be Mr. Will, not Mr. Platt. "I haven't asked him, but he must be hungry. Could you whip up something?"

"Of course." She looked at Will in an appraising way. They were good at that, especially with white men. "Do you like our food, Mr. Platt?"

"What did you have for your lunch?"

"Stew-peas, sir."

A dish made with red beans or gungo peas, pigtail, maybe some chicken. "Is there any left?" They always cooked a lot of stew-peas; it took so long with spices and extras to achieve the proper flavor.

"Oh yes, sir, plenty."

"Then I'd like some. Indeed I would."

Her smile was wary but revealed beautifully white teeth—a rarity among peasants, who usually lost everything to yank-out country dentists before they reached her age. Lifting his suitcase from the Land Rover, she swept inside with it while he looked at Sam and approvingly nodded.

"She's the best," Sam said.

"Lucky you."

"Not me. Juan. To be candid, I think he was sleeping with her before I got here, and I don't blame him."

After Will had eaten his fill, the two men went into the parlor where Sam filled glasses with a light, smooth Venezuelan rum. As they sat and relaxed with their drinks, Will looked at his friend's troubled face, and knew this would probably be their last quiet moment. "All right, Sam, what do we do?"

"As I told you, he disappeared a week ago Friday when he went with Ima to market. You don't know Christiana, but it's like—well, even Jacmel—on market day. People come in from miles around, not on foot like in Haiti, but by bus and community taxi. You know the sort of taxi I mean: so much for the ride, and pack 'em in till they're sitting on one another's shoulders."

Sam paused to sip his drink. "Anyway, the market is a mob scene. You walk down from the street through five or six different levels until you come out at the bottom." He paused again, and shrugged. "Juan went with her to see what the higglers were selling, and when she looked for him to drive her back, she couldn't find him. She walked home and told me. I went up and searched the whole damned town for him, couldn't find him either, and brought the Rover back."

"And haven't seen him since."

"Right."

"What did Sister Merle say when you questioned her?"

"Denied she knew him, at first. When I pointed out I had proof she not only knew him but had threatened to turn him into dirt, she ended up threatening *me.*"

"You haven't told me what she looks like, Sam."

"She's a small, ugly woman, almost a dwarf. About sixty, I'd say."

"Black, of course."

"Not so very. I think the people here would call her medium brown. She's had some kind of disease. Her face looks as though someone ran a harrow over it."

"What's your plan? We call on her together?"

Sam looked thoughtful for a few seconds, then slowly moved his head up and down. "I think we have to. I've done everything else I can think of, and I'm still on square one after nine days. Sister Merle is the only enemy Juan had."

"We go tomorrow?"

"If you're game to face a sorcerer maybe as awesomely powerful as Margal."

Will shrugged. "I'm here, good buddy. And I didn't come for a vacation."

10

To the Lair of the Sorceress

"You must not go there!" Ima Williams pleaded with them. "That woman has already threatened Mr. Sam. If you dare to confront her again, she may do something terrible!"

Will looked at the tall black woman with respect and said quietly, "What can she do, Ima?" Sam and he were eating the breakfast and she served them: scrambled eggs, some kind of cornmeal fritters done in deep oil, and cups of hot, sweetened chocolate, the source of which was one of the cacao trees in the yard.

"That woman is able to make people obey her will."

"You mean she'll have someone harm us?"

"She may make *you* do things!"

Recalling Sam Norman's tale of the policeman's hand, Will asked, "What things, Ima?"

"A man she once put a spell on refused to touch food and wasted away from hunger," she said. "A young higgler who was foolish enough to taunt her one day in the market died on the way home that evening by walking off a cliff in the dark. She didn't walk off by accident, you can be sure. She was obeying a *command*."

"You seem to know a good deal about obeah, Ima."

"Ima is a hounsi kanzo," Sam Norman said.

Will looked at the woman in astonishment. "A hounsi kanzo? In Jamaica? I didn't know there was voodoo here."

"I was born in Haiti," she told him. "In Léogane. Ima Williams is not my real name. People in this country had trouble pronouncing my name, so I borrowed one from a woman I was fond of in Cedar Valley, up in the Blue Mountains, when she died. And, yes, I am kanzo."

In the voodoo heirarchy, Will knew, being kanzo placed her just beneath a mambo, or priestess. It meant she had undergone years of study and self-discipline, then endured tests with fire and boiling oil, which rejected all but the most devoted.

He looked at Sam. "Why didn't you tell me?"

"I knew she would tell you herself, in her own good time."

"And I do not want you to go to Sister Merle," Ima said emphatically. "I beg you not to go there. She is one of the most evil women who ever lived. Even I, a hounsi, am afraid of her. When I tried to help Mr. Juan against her, I failed."

Keenly interested, Will said, "How did you try to help Juan, Ima?"

She hesitated. "I—tried to reach into her mind. But she sent me a message instead."

"She got into *your* mind, you mean?"

"To tell me . . . she told me she would destroy me when it pleased her to do so." This time Ima addressed her plea to Sam. "Please, Mr. Sam, do not confront her again! Sister Merle is feared all over this part of the island—in Christiana, Devon, Mile Gully, Coleyville, all through the Cockpit, even in Mandeville. Don't go!"

"I'm afraid we have to, Ima," Sam replied gently. "I've done everything else I can think of, and Juan is still missing. But we'll be careful." Finishing his chocolate, he stood up. "You ready, Will?"

As they went out to the Land Rover in the yard, the Haitian woman stood in the doorway staring after them, wringing her long-fingered hands as though afraid she might never see them again.

It was Monday and the road to town, so deserted on the weekend, was filled with school kids in uniform. Almost all the schools in this poor country required uniforms, Will recalled, even though many families couldn't afford them and their children had to stay at home.

The town itself was busy for so early an hour. But only the town. Once Sam had maneuvered the Land Rover through the clutter of cars and trucks that filled the shopping district, the school kids coming in from the other side presented the only problem.

"Sam, what are we going to say to this woman?"

"I thought I'd leave that to you."

"Me?"

"Obviously I didn't say the right things when I called on her before. You know more about this stuff than I do."

"The hell I do."

"Well, you know more words. And more about the West Indies in general. You're older and wiser."

"Thanks. Remind me to mention you in my will."

It was the same road they had traveled yesterday, on the fringe of the virtually uninhabited Cockpit Country. Studying a grimy map he found on the Rover's seat, Will saw that for miles to right and left what he thought he was seeing was what he was seeing: a wilderness so inhospitable to man that few men, even among the tough Jamaicans, had cared to challenge it. Winding little dirt roads ran off the blacktop now and then, but were soon swallowed up by the wild terrain. On reaching the village with the odd name Wait-a-Bit, he felt he had been riding for hours.

"How far are we from Christiana, Sam?"

"About ten miles."

"I thought we'd come fifty."

Sam Norman laughed.

Beyond Wait-a-Bit Sam slowed to fifteen miles an hour, found what he was looking for, and turned left onto a red dirt road that quickly began to think of itself as a corkscrew. *We meet something on this,* Will thought, *and we're in trouble.* Why, he wondered, had the magnificent little World War II Jeep, so slim and tidy, been blown up into vehicles like this that required nearly as much road as a bus?

Both sides of the way were lined at first with yam fields, bristling sticks jabbing their fingers at the sky, and with occasional clumps of bananas and plantains. Then even those disappeared, and the track snaked down into a forest of rock formations in which nothing so ambitious could be grown. Here, among the stones, tiny patches of the same red earth supported handfuls of cabbages or callaloo.

And, of course, ganja. If you knew the spiky leaf of Jamaica's marijuana, you could spot it quickly enough, even with the naked eye. Here in the Cockpit, strangers were likely to be looked upon as government agents snooping for the stuff, and some who may have seen too much were not heard from again.

"Where does this road go, Sam?"

"I don't really know. Haven't been the whole way."

"How did you find it?"

"Juan Cerrado showed me the turnoff back there one day, and told me how to get to the woman's house. When I actually came here, though, after he disappeared, I couldn't find the footpath and had to pay a fellow to guide me."

Sam pointed down to his right, at a peasant hut precariously perched on the slope. "That's where I got him. He was working in his yard and I called down to him.

Decent sort, about thirty, named Mowatt. We won't need him today, though. I know the way now."

The road looped on down for another half mile or so and leveled out to traverse a ridge. On both sides of the razorback the land fell away into deep sinks the sides of which were partly green with scrub, partly gleaming white with fangs of limestone that resembled the bleached teeth of huge dead animals. "That's where the lady lives," Sam said. "Down there on the left. See the path?"

Will did, but only just. "Aren't we stopping?"

"Not here. Can't block the road, even if it isn't used much. Anyway, we have to go past the next bend to find a turning place."

On reaching the point where the road widened, Sam pulled the vehicle off and parked it. They walked back and the sun blazed down on them in a fury of brilliance. Even under a cloudless sky the land seemed empty and hostile.

"I wonder why the old girl lives in a place like this."

"For privacy, probably."

"But she has to deal with people, doesn't she? To make a living as a sorceress?"

"They find her; don't worry. But obeah is outlawed, remember. In a place as remote as this the police aren't likely to bother her so much."

"Were you scared, coming in here alone?"

"Let's say I was uneasy, after hearing about those two cops who did bother her."

There was no marker to indicate where the obeah woman's path went, or that anyone lived on it. It angled down from the road, not too steeply at first, to disappear among limestone formations that looked like huge white sponges. Beyond the sponges it twisted on down into dusty scrub and candelabra cactus.

No ordinary person would want to live in such an unfriendly setting, Will decided. The few farmers who challenged the Cockpit were obviously the toughest of a tough breed, grimly scratching a living from pockets of soil despite the heat, the desolation, the lack of water, roads, and human company. But the pockets of soil here along Sister Merle's path were too few and too small even for them. The obeah woman had no neighbors.

The sun's fierce heat bored through his hat—thank God he had worn one!—and soaked his hair with sweat as he doggedly trudged down the slope at Sam's heels. The sweat burned his face and made it itch.

"Just a little more," his companion called back without halting. And he saw the house.

It was not what he had expected. Here in this forsaken wilderness a house should be a small, crooked thing of wattle and daub, with a roof of rusty zinc. One room, maybe, or two at the most. From the looks of its exterior this one had at least four. Its walls were carpenter-built of the local Caribbean pine. Its roof was of aluminum that shone like a mirror.

Sam had stopped. Reaching him, Will said in a hushed voice, "Brother!"

"Something, isn't it? Must have cost plenty in a place like this, too. Wait'll you see the inside. If she invites us in, that is." Sam moved forward again, halting for a second time just outside the open door. "Sister Merle? Are you home?"

Silence.

"She must be, or the door wouldn't be wide open," Sam said. Then again, "Sister Merle! Sam Norman here. Are you at home?"

Will heard a chair scrape the floor inside, then footsteps. Staring at the door, recalling Sam's description of the woman as being almost a dwarf with a face that seemed to have been run over by a harrow, he nevertheless gasped when she suddenly appeared in the opening. Small and ugly and all of sixty years old, too, as Sam had said. But he had not mentioned the eyes.

She focused them on Sam for a moment the way a cat
might scrutinize a mouse it contemplated devouring.
Then her gaze shifted to Will and looked him over.

"Who this man is?"

"Friend of mine, Sister. His name is Will Platt."

"From where? I never see him before."

"He's visiting from the States."

"Why you bring him here? You know we don' like
strangers!"

"Sister, I'll be explaining that. May we come in and
talk to you?"

While speaking to Sam she had been studying Will, as
though suspicious and needing time to make up her
mind about him. With a shrug of her misshapen shoulders she said, "Very well, you come," and turned her
back on them.

Will was astonished again as he entered the house.
The large front room in which he found himself was
lavishly furnished. Sister Merle shuffled across the
polished pine floor to an overstuffed sofa and motioned
her callers to be seated on matching chairs.

On a table of blue mahoe against one wall stood a
large battery-operated radio which must have cost a
small fortune. A second table supported a lineup of
kerosene pressure lamps, much more expensive than the
ordinary household lamps used by most peasants.

Through an open door Will could see into a kitchen
that contained a kerosene fridge and a gas stove. Who,
for God's sake, lugged gas cylinders in here? Even the
small ones would give a strong man fits on that trail.

"Well, Mr. Norman?"

"Sister Merle, I still haven't found my colleague, Juan
Cerrado. I'm hoping you can help me."

She may have expected it. Her shrug seemed automatic. "I don' know where him is. I told you when you
came here before. *Nobody* knows where him is."

"Sister Merle, people say you have certain powers.

Could you help us find Juan if I paid you for your services?"

"What powers I supposed to have?"

Will studied her, trying to read her face and body movements while those eyes drilled Sam again. It was not a simple thing to do. Except for the eyes and the physical ugliness for which, of course, she could not be held accountable, she was as seemingly neutral as the plain gray dress she wore. "What powers?" she said again, sharply.

"Well, you're said to be an obeah woman."

"Obeah! You think a woman like me goin' bother herself with that foolishness?"

"Sister, don't call it foolishness. My friend here is an expert on Haitian voodoo. Is that a joke?"

Seemingly startled, the woman transferred her gaze to Will.

"He has written books about voodoo," Sam said. "He knows its secrets."

"Is so?" she demanded, gazing at Will.

He nodded, knowing Sam wanted her to think so. "Perhaps with your help," he said, "I can find Mr. Norman's colleague."

She seemed to consider the suggestion for a moment, then slowly wagged her head. "Me don' know nuttin'," she said, the patois noticeably thickening as she altered her image to that of a simple peasant.

"We've heard," Sam said, "that when Juan disappeared from the market, he came here to see you." It was a hook baited with pure conjecture, Will guessed, but she might rise to it.

"Uh-uh. Him never did."

"Then why would people say he did?"

She moved her bony shoulders. "To make some kind of trouble for me, must be. Not everyone calls me friend."

"Sister Merle," Sam persisted, "do you suppose you

and Mr. Platt here can work together on this and find some answers? I've got to locate that man."

She studied Will again, but he had a feeling she was merely letting a polite amount of time pass before answering. "If you a big voodoo man, Marse Platt," she said, "you don' need no ignorant country woman like I to help you. No, suh." Suddenly her gaze flicked to the door. "Someone comin'. Now who could that be?"

She was out of her chair and at the door before Will heard the footsteps she must have heard. With a hike of his eyebrows he looked at Sam. Sam briefly made a me-too face. The obeah woman said, "Well, see who here!" and into the house walked a tall black man about thirty, wearing khaki pants, shiny black shoes, no shirt or undershirt.

Seeing Sam, the fellow stopped in his tracks. "Well, good mornin', Mr. Norman," he said.

"Hello, Keith." Sam turned to Will. "This is the man who brought me here before. Keith Mowatt."

"What you come for this mornin'?" Sister Merle asked him, scowling as though displeased.

"Nuttin' much, Sister. Just to bring you the black candles you sen' me for and tell you me couldn't get the tank of gas. Seem like there is a shortage of gas again."

She made a sound of disgust through her nose. "The way this country goin', they is always a shortage of somethin'. Well, all right. Try again tomorrow, you hear?"

"Yes, Sister. Me will do that."

"Go on, now. Me busy."

He dropped a package on the radio table—the black candles to be used in obeah, Will supposed—and went out. Sam Norman stared after him with a peculiar intensity. Sister Merle turned to her callers and said, "Well, Marse Norman, all me can do is wish you luck with what you tryin' to accomplish. Me don't see no way to help you."

She rose and offered her hand. Sam shook it in silence. Will did the same, and they walked out.

Sam set a fast pace on the stiff climb to the road, so fast that Will, running out of breath behind him, at last called out, "Hey, what's the rush?"

"Police station, Will. We've got to get there before that fellow realizes what he did!"

"What are you talking about?"

Without even slowing his pace, Sam called back, "Did you see his shoes?"

"Well, I wondered why he'd shined them like that just to call on an old woman. But shoes are expensive here, aren't they? Maybe he just takes care of them."

"They weren't just shined, Will. They were dyed."

"What?"

"And they're not Jamaican shoes. They're field boots from Maine, ordered by mail from an L.L. Bean catalogue. The last time I saw them they were tan and the feet in them were Juan Cerrado's."

11

The Lockup

Once off the Cockpit road where haste would have been suicidal, Sam pushed the Land Rover to its limit. In front of the Wait-a-Bit police station he brought it to a skidding halt. "Come on!" he said, leaping out.

The station was a small one, with a corporal seated at a scarred desk just inside the door. Sam explained what had happened and what he wanted.

The Red Stripe was young, handsome and slim as a ballet dancer. "Mister, you better go to Christiana about this," he said with a shrug. "We know your Mr. Cerrado is missing, but Christiana's been doing the investigating, not us."

"There isn't time for us to go to Christiana! Mowatt has to be questioned before he realizes what he did and gets rid of those boots!"

"Well, that may be so."

"Corporal, it *is* so! He didn't expect to find us there at Sister Merle's. The Land Rover was parked beyond her path and he didn't see it."

Time passed while the corporal thought it over. At last he stood up and called out to someone unseen, "Lenny, take over here for a bit. I mus' go somewhere." Looking back as they hurried out to the Land Rover,

96

Will saw a man in blue-striped pants emerge from a back room to stand by the desk, frowning after them.

On the way back to Sister Merle's road Sam briefed the corporal on the full story of Juan Cerrado's disappearance. The Red Stripe solemnly shook his head.

"No sensible man would start a fight with that woman, Mr. Norman. He was just beggin' trouble."

"If she's that big in obeah, why haven't you arrested her?"

"Unless somebody in our district complains, what can we do?"

"You mean no one has complained?"

"Not even your Mr. Cerrado, so far as we know in Wait-a-Bit. Maybe he should have."

It was not from this small station, then, Will decided, that the man who had slapped Sister Merle's face had come. Well, there were other stations in the area, no doubt. Of course, if the man who lost his hand *had* come from Wait-a-Bit, the police there would have good reason to leave the obeah woman strictly alone.

They stopped at the top of a footpath winding down the slope to the peasant hut he had pointed out to Will earlier. The corporal led the way. When they reached the hut with its small patch of garden, a young but worn-looking woman came from inside to confront them. Visibly nervous, she gazed at the corporal in silence, waiting for him to address her.

"Good mornin', Celia. Where you man is?"

"Him inside, Corpie."

"Fetch him."

She turned back to the open doorway and spoke to someone in the house. Into the yard slouched the man who had worn the dyed field boots to Sister Merle's home. He was barefoot now. Most of his toenails were split and deformed, Will noticed.

"Is this the man, Mr. Norman?"

"Yes."

"Keith, what happen to you shoes?"

"Shoes, Corpie?"

"The ones you was wearin' when you did call on Sister Merle, little while ago."

"Oh, them." Mowatt turned and went back inside the hut. Reappearing, he held a pair of Jamaican-made dress shoes, old and worn but highly polished.

"Those are not the ones, Corporal," Sam Norman said. "Are they, Will?"

"No. He was wearing field boots, nearly new."

"These the only shoes me own," Mowatt protested. "Don't it so, Celia?"

The woman looked frightened but briskly bobbed her head up and down.

"I'll just have a look," the corporal said, and went into the house.

Sam and Will waited outside with Mowatt and his woman. At first Mowatt ignored them, gazing blankly at the ground, but after a while he raised his head and glowered at them. Reading murder in the man's eyes, Will felt his stomach muscles tighten.

For relief he looked around. If, indeed, Keith Mowatt was an enforcer for Sister Merle, there was nothing about this place to indicate he was well paid for his services. The house was a dirt-floored hovel perched on a skimpy pocket of red earth in the midst of desolation.

The corporal reappeared, holding something in his hand. He held the hand out to Mowatt's woman, palm up. "Is you did use this and lef' the cover off it?"

She hesitated, nodded, then apprehensively glanced at her man.

"Don' you know shoe polish mus' dry out if you don't put back the lid?"

"Yes, sir. But me did use it only a short while ago."

"To shine the shoes him is holdin'. Is that what you sayin'?"

Again she shot a glance at her man, but it was too

late. "Y-yes, sir," she had to admit.

"Now that's interestin'," the policeman said. "Mowatt, is you plannin' to go to town today?"

"Matter of fact, yes."

"Wha' for?"

"Well, me need some t'ings."

"Wha' you need?"

Mowatt was not that fast a thinker, and had to hesitate. When he said, "Well, matches," it was unconvincing. In any case, it was a bad choice.

"You got plenty matches inside," the corporal said. "I just now saw two–three boxes on the table in there."

"Well—"

Suddenly the Red Stripe dropped his patois drawl. "I say you had Celia shine those old shoes of yours so you could say they're the ones you wore to Sister Merle's, if somebody like me came and asked you! Now suppose you go get the ones you really did have on!"

"Is not so, Corpie. These is the ones me had on."

"Celia, go get the others."

The woman looked terrified. With Mowatt glaring at her on one side and the corporal commanding her on the other, she was caught in a crossfire and began to tremble. Suddenly she broke and ran—not into the house but down the footpath that continued past it and disappeared below among scrub growth and limestone crags.

The corporal watched her disappear, then turned to Mowatt again. "The U.N. fellow's boots are not in your house, Mowatt. I looked. Where are they?"

Silence.

"Did you bury them?"

"Me don' know what you talkin' about!"

"All right, you hid them where I'll never find them. But you'll tell me where they are before I get through with you, I promise. Come, we're going to the station." The corporal placed the palm of his right hand against his holster and tapped the leather with his fingertips.

"You first, and walk slow."

They climbed the steep path to the Land Rover, where Red Stripe and Mowatt got in the back. Sam drove on down the road to the turning place he had used before, then back out to the main road, to stop at last in front of the police station again.

The corporal got out and kept a wary eye on his prisoner as Mowatt dropped out after him. "Can I telephone you, Mr. Norman?"

"I'm sorry. I don't have a phone."

"Then if I have anything to report, I'll call the station in Christiana. They'll send a man to your house."

"Thank you."

"Come on, you," the policeman growled at Mowatt.

Before turning away, his prisoner stood motionless for a few seconds, glaring at the two men in the Land Rover. Once more Will Platt felt his stomach muscles tighten as he read the hatred in the man's eyes.

"Did you see that?" Will asked as Sam put the machine in motion.

Sam nodded. "This isn't a game we're playing, is it? All at once it's turned into something that is scaring the hell out of me."

"Will they make that fellow talk, do you think?"

"They might, I suppose. But not if he's more afraid of the obeah woman than of them."

"Sam," Will said after a silence, "what do you think about this boot business? Is your man dead?"

"It looks that way, doesn't it?"

"Unless they've got him in hiding somewhere and took his boots to keep him from escaping. No one barefoot could walk far in that Cockpit Country, for instance." Will raised his right leg and scowled at his foot. "I've just about ruined my shoes this morning."

"Juan once introduced me to a man who had walked across the Cockpit from Quick Step to Windsor Cave," Sam said. "That would be about seven or eight miles as the crow flies, I think—God knows how far on the ground, through those impossible sinks. The fellow said he reduced two pairs of tough hiking boots to shreds and arrived at Windsor with his bleeding feet wrapped in banana trash."

While making the turn onto the Christiana road, Sam was silent. Then with a frown he said, "But what's the profit for them in keeping Juan alive?"

"I've no idea," Will said. "Let's just hope there is one."

12

"Hear Me, Master!"

In a rude little cemetery below her house in the Cockpit, Sister Merle knelt in the shadow of a tall gravestone. The cemetery was the one in which, a long time ago, a policeman had so foolishly slapped her face. It was mid-afternoon and the sun was a fiery golden ball, but she could not be seen from the path because the stone concealed her.

It also concealed what she was doing.

She had scraped a few inches of earth from the grave in question, to reveal a sheet of flattened-out zinc. Now, still on her knees, she removed the zinc and peered into the hole beneath.

The lid of the pine coffin there had long since been knocked in with a shovel—not by her but by one of the men who served her—and sufficient light reached down to disclose a human skeleton. Or, rather, what was left of one after many earlier visits by the sorceress.

Lying prone now at the edge of the hole, Sister Merle reached down with a chunk of limestone and struck the skeleton a sharp blow. Bones broke and, dropping the stone, she reached for one.

It happened to be a clavicle. But the kind of bone did not concern her so long as it was freshly obtained from

102

a grave after the recital of certain ritual words. She had recited the words.

Slithering backward now, she placed the clavicle on the ground behind her and, before rising to her knees, scraped a handful of earth from the grave wall. Her face was a study in concentration. Anyone watching would have noticed a strange, reddish glow in her small, dark eyes, and a movement of her lips. The onlooker would have heard no sound, however, other than the usual humming and buzzing of insects in the afternoon heat, or the occasional croak of a lizard in the dry grass.

Having replaced the sheet of zinc, Sister Merle carefully put back its covering of earth before reaching for the bone again and rising to her feet. The zinc had been a fine idea, she thought, congratulating herself. On her first half-dozen visits to the burying ground, she had been forced to bring along an assistant with a shovel.

Now with everything in the graveyard left the way she had found it, she turned for a last look at the stone. It was of concrete, as most of them were, and the lettering on it had been done by a non-professional with something like a triangular machete file while the concrete was still soft. Little except the name was now legible.

The name was Mordecai Adams.

She trudged on up the winding path to her home, carrying the bone and the handful of earth in a plastic bag. With a key she unlocked her door.

Inside, she relocked the door and drew the bright red curtains at the front-room window. What she was about to do was not for the eyes of any caller who might decide to peer in at her. Not even for the eyes of those who faithfully served her.

Opening a wooden chest on the floor against the far wall, she took out an assortment of items: a tall black candle, a rum bottle, and a number of small, unlabeled jars, the contents of which only she could name. These she carried to a table on which she had spread a carefully ironed black cloth.

She lit the candle, placed an empty bowl on the table and sat down with the bowl between her and the flame. With the curtains drawn, the room would have been nearly dark without the candle flame; with the flame it was full of shadows. Soon a smell of incense filled as well, for while the candles came from a Christiana store, she always melted them down and added certain obligatory herbs before using them.

With her gaze fixed on the flame, the woman began to sway very slowly toward it, then back again, as though at first attracted by it, then repelled. This continued for some time. Then she opened a jar and lifted from it a pinch of its contents, which she placed in the bowl while intoning words in a hoarse singsong.

"Mordecai, arise! I call to you! Through me our master calleth! Turn to the north, south, east, and west. Come and perform with me the powers of demons!"

Now the gaze of her glowing eyes was fixed not on the flickering candle but on an empty chair at the side of the table. She peered at the chair as though waiting with confidence for someone to come and occupy it.

And someone—or something—did. Or was the dim figure that appeared there only a shadow created by a change in the candle's brightness? For the candle did waver as in a sudden draft. It did nearly go out. And when it recovered, it was not as bright again as it had been.

Sister Merle reached for other jars then, murmuring incantations as she added bits and pieces of their contents to the bowl in front of her. "Master, accept this tip of a goat's horn. Master, I give thee the dried blood of a black cat. Master, here is grave dirt, and these are human ashes; this is a cat's foot and this a ground-up toad. Take them and hear my plea, for I serve thee well!"

In the empty chair—if it was empty—the shadowy figure seemed to lean forward to peer into the bowl. But again it could have been an effect produced by the unsteady burning of the candle.

"Master," the sorceress intoned, "I have in my hand now a piece of skin from an unborn kid, with thy name writ in human blood on it. And I have this bone just taken from the grave where Mordecai lies. Thy Mordecai, who taught me and now sits here beside me. Now hear me, Master, while I tell thee what I want from thee in return."

With the bowl half full of her offerings, Sister Merle unscrewed the cap from the rum bottle and poured in an ounce or two of its contents. There was no smell of rum when she did so. Rather, there was one of tar or pitch, though the liquid was free flowing and colorless. Then she took the candle and touched the mixture with its flame.

A small explosion followed. Thick black smoke arose in a cloud above the table, blotting out the misty figure in the other chair. With it came such a stench that even Merle turned her face away and covered her nose with her free hand while returning the candle to its former position.

The stench—was it sulphur?—endured and filled the room. But the candle still burned, and Sister Merle recovered. And the misty figure was still there on the other chair.

Now the obeah woman gazed at the candle and spread both arms wide in a gesture of supplication. "Master, I speak of the man called Keith Mowatt," she called out in a loud voice. "Thou knowest what he did. Thou knowest he must be punished. As I serve thee in all things, so must thou serve me when I am in need. Give my mind the power to punish him!"

Slowly the stench dissipated and the air in the room became clean again. Sister Merle blew out the black candle. Methodically she screwed the tops back on the jars and on the rum bottle, and returned all her paraphernalia to the wooden chest.

But she did not open the curtains. Seating herself again, she placed her elbows on the table and pressed the tips of her fingers to her forehead and closed her eyes.

An hour later she was still in.the same position. Only her lips moved, and no sound came from them.

The figure on the other chair seemed to have departed with the blowing out of the candle.

13

The Cocomacaque

After leaving the Wait-a-Bit police station, Will Platt and Sam Norman spent the rest of the day awaiting word.

None came.

In the morning Ima Williams asked if she might walk to town to do some shopping. "I need some salt fish," she said. "Yesterday I bought some akee from a higgler who came around. If I can find the fish to buy, I can make salt fish and akee for your supper tonight." It was the Jamaican peasant's favorite dish, popular with the elite as well.

"Of course," Sam told her. "Run along."

He and Will continued their wait.

"Do you suppose we might learn something by going to the police here in Christiana?" Will asked.

"I doubt it. They'll come to us when Wait-a-Bit calls them. *If* Wait-a-Bit calls."

Still no one came.

Just after eleven Ima Williams returned with her plastic shopping bag full. Not for her the basket on the head, of course. As housekeeper for a United Nations agricultural expert and now for two other men of means, she was above that. She walked like a peasant, though,

Will noticed. Tall, straight, with that haunting grace and taunting movement of the buttocks.

After carrying her purchases into the kitchen, she came at once to the living room where they sat. Hands on hips, she faced them. "I heard something, Mr. Sam."

"Heard what, Ima?"

"I met an old friend in the grocery across from Len Kirby's hardware. She told me she saw Mr. Juan the morning he disappeared."

Sam smiled his disappointment. "Ima, I'm sure a lot of people saw him that morning. After all, he went to market with you and no doubt wandered all over the place."

"She saw him *leave* the market."

Sam sat up straighter.

"She said he left with two men. One was an obeah man from Silent Hill, a man named Emmanuel Bignall who sometimes works with Sister Merle. She didn't know the other. They got into an old yellow Prefect that was parked down by the bottom market gate, where she was buying charcoal, and went up to the main street and turned left."

Sam's bushy brows were low over his eyes. "The way to Silent Hill, if they turned at Barclay's Bank," he said.

"Yes."

"Emmanuel Bignall, you say?"

She nodded.

"What kind of man is he? What does he look like?"

"He is a big, ugly, black man who hangs around the bar there a lot. The one by the bottom market gate, I mean. I don't know him to talk to, but people say he is afraid of nobody."

Will Platt, speaking for the first time, said, "What's this Silent Hill, Sam?"

"A little village about ten miles from here, on the road from Alston to Dump. A few houses, couple of shops, that's all."

"How could anyone be hiding Juan in a place like that?"

"Well, there are other houses off in the fields and bush, of course. All over this area you find those." Sam took in a breath that swelled his chest. "Will, I'm going there. Right now!"

"We're going, you mean."

"No." Getting to his feet, Sam emphatically wagged his head. "If two of us turn up asking for this Bignall fellow, he may feel threatened. I don't want him running off and hiding. Or even worse, surrounding himself with buddies and trying to put me down. This calls for diplomacy, not a show of strength."

"You should not go there!" Ima Williams said in a voice unusually sharp for her.

"Why not?"

"Silent Hill is too far from anything. If you get into trouble, who can help you?"

"Damn it, Ima, we have to find Juan Cerrado. If he was taken there, that's where I have to look for him."

"Eat some lunch first. Think about it."

"No. The sooner I get there, the better."

She planted her hands on her well curved hips. "Mr. Juan didn't disappear yesterday, you know. He has been gone for days."

"All the more reason for me to get cracking. Handle the gate for me, will you, Will?"

Will followed him out and swung the big iron gate wide while Sam climbed into the Land Rover. As the vehicle passed him, he called out, "Good luck!" and received a wave in return. He stood there for a moment watching the black and white license plate become smaller and finally disappear around a bend in the road. Then, shaking his head, he returned to the house.

In the parlor living room Ima Williams stood with her hands still on her hips and a look of censure on her face.

"There's nothing we can do, Ima," Will said. "Sam's a stubborn man."

"I want to find Mr. Juan just as much as he does! But the police should go there, not him!"

"I'm sure he thought of that. But they don't seem to be getting anywhere with the fellow they arrested yesterday, do they?"

She gazed at him in silence for a few seconds, then turned away. He heard her in the kitchen but did not see her again until she called him for lunch half an hour later. In the dining room he found the table set for one.

"Have you eaten, Ima?"

She shook her head.

"Join me, then."

"You want me to eat with you?"

"You ate with Juan, didn't you?" He was betting she had. And maybe more.

"Well, yes."

"Set another place and bring food for two, then. I'd like to talk to you."

The lunch was an excellent chow mein made with chicken breast and the local pak choy. She had worked for a year, she explained, at the home of a wealthy Chinese family in the capital, where her principal task had been to prepare the food for the man of the family to cook when he came home at night from his place of business. "He taught me much about Chinese cooking." He or someone else had taught her good table manners also, Will decided, and how to speak English with only an occasional lapse into patois. She was quite a woman.

"Tell me about this obeah," he invited while deliberately dawdling over his food.

"What about it?"

"Well, I've written books about voodoo—writing is my job—and I'm wondering what the two may have in common. Are there such things as obeah ceremonies?"

She shook her head. "There are services in pocomania, but not in obeah. Obeah men and women work alone."

Like the witch doctors and sorcerers in Haiti, he thought. "Are most of them unprincipled?"

"Pardon?"

"Are they wicked? Corrupt? Villainous?"

"I think so, yes."

"You go to them when you want something. Is that it?"

"When you want help, or to hurt someone, or to stop someone from hurting you. But mostly when you want to accomplish something wicked yourself."

"And how does the obeah person produce the results you pay him for?"

"Different ones have different methods. They do things with herbs and roots and leaves. With parts of animals. With blood and graveyard dirt, even parts of corpses. Also with special charms that are handed down sometimes from parent to child. They say things no ordinary person can understand. But the most important thing they call upon is the power for evil inside themselves, I am sure."

"By which you mean that to be an obeah person one must be evil to begin with? It can't simply be learned?"

"It can't be learned by ordinary people. The old rites of voodoo can be, of course—voodoo is not evil—but to practice a sorcery such as obeah one must be a follower of the Devil."

Will thought of Vicky and her dark desire to learn from Margal. No question about it, Vicky *had* learned. For a moment he was silent while his companion concentrated on her food. Then he said, "How would you know if an obeah person is trying to harm you, Ima?"

She raised her head to gaze at him, her face almost expressionless. "You might *not* know. You might just get sick, or have something happen to you."

"Such as?"

"Like the market girl who walked off the road's edge and fell down a cliff on her way home. Or if you were a country woman washing your clothes in a stream, you might become dizzy and fall in and drown. Or—and I know this will seem strange to you, but it has happened —you could be eating something perfectly good, like this chow mein, and it would poison you. It might not poison *me* as I eat it with you, but it would poison *you*. A sorceress like Sister Merle speaks to your mind and you are ill, even ill enough to die if she wills you to. Of course, some people are easier to destroy than others."

Ima paused. "I was in a shop once, in a place not far from here called Mile Gully. Three men were talking to a stranger from another district who claimed to be an obeah man, and one jeered at him, telling him obeah was for children and he was stupid to believe in it. They were drinking Dragon Stout. Each had a bottle. Suddenly the man who said obeah was nothing began to choke and dropped his bottle and started to vomit. Then the vomit turned to blood and he fell to the floor, twisting and wriggling like a lizard that had been stepped on."

Again Ima was silent for a few seconds. Then: "Everybody in the shop was terrified and ran out, even the proprietor. *I* ran out, and didn't stop running until I was far from that place and could feel safe. Later I heard say the man died on the floor there before help could be found for him."

"You realize, of course, there could have been something in the bottle that choked him."

"Perhaps. But it was in the *Gleaner* later that the stout left in the bottle was tested and nothing was wrong with it. And they didn't find anything wrong with him when they did an autopsy."

Will let another period of silence go by, then said, "Ima, what do you think has happened to Juan Cerrado?" They had told her about Mowatt.

An expression of infinite sadness settled on her face, especially in her eyes. Her mouth twitched, then drooped. "I think he is dead."

"Sister Merle would do that? Kill a man just because he tried to keep his farmers away from her?"

"Yes. Because if she did not, the people who deal with her would think she was not strong enough to strike back at him."

"What has she done with him?"

She shook her head. "I would not even guess, Mr. Will. But I think you will never find him."

"Thank you for answering my questions, Ima. And for eating lunch with me." He got up, helped himself to a piece of brown-sugar candy from the sideboard, and glanced at his watch. Twelve-forty. It might be hours before Sam returned from Silent Hill. What to do until then?

There was a typewriter on the table in his bedroom, an Italian portable that belonged to Cerrado, he supposed. He searched the table drawer for paper, found some, and sat to type up some notes on what the housekeeper had just told him about obeah.

That done, he went on to put down his impressions of Ima Williams herself, of Sister Merle and her mini-mansion in the desolate Cockpit Country, of Wait-a-Bit and Christiana and all the rest of it.

You never knew. At the moment he had no notion of using any of this in one of his novels, but it had possibilities. Anyway, he had the afternoon to kill.

At six o'clock Sam Norman had not returned. Nor at seven. Nor at eight.

"Ima, what could have happened?"

She was as anxious as he was, he guessed. For two hours she had been pacing about the house or going outside to stand at the gate. Now she sat in the kitchen, by the stove, with her hands tightly clasped in her lap and a look on her face that revealed increasing fear.

"Mr. Will, I don't know. It's dark out now." Her voice was low, a kind of moan.

"Do you know where this Bignall fellow lives? I mean,

is his house in the village or is it off in the bush where getting to it would take time?"

"I don't know. But it shouldn't be taking Mr. Sam this much time, no matter where."

"What can we do? Is there some way I can get there?"

She glanced at a clock on the wall. "Not now, Mr. Will. There are no taxis passing now. We just must have to wait." Rising, she turned to the stove. "Should I get you some supper?"

He shook his head. "When Sam gets here." Returning to the living room, he sat and stared at the door. Should he walk to town, to the police station? What would he say if he did? "Sam Norman drove to Silent Hill to talk to an obeah man and hasn't returned." That might make the difference. But the police hadn't found Juan Cerrado. They hadn't even questioned Sister Merle. They apparently hadn't been able to make Keith Mowatt talk.

Wait.

At nine-thirty Ima Williams insisted he eat something and served him a dish of the salt fish and akee she had promised. He might have enjoyed it had Sam been there. Now he could enjoy nothing. *You know too damned much about the Sister Merles of these islands,* he told himself angrily. *You're scared.*

Ima ate nothing.

It was after eleven when he went into the kitchen for a drink of water and found her again sitting there by the stove. For some reason, perhaps because she was so quiet, he had assumed she was in bed. With a glass of water in his hand he sat and looked at her.

"Ima, is there any place in Silent Hill he could be staying overnight? A guest house? Something like that?"

"No, Mr. Will. Why would he want to stay, anyway, when it's only a few miles from here?"

He drank the water. He poured two inches of rum into the glass and sipped that while standing at the counter. "You should go to bed."

"He may be hungry when he comes."

"He'll have eaten something before now. Anyway, it wouldn't be the first time he and I have thrown a meal together. Go on."

Something in her dark eyes glistened wetly in the light as she stood up. "Well, all right. I won't sleep, though. I'll hear him if he comes."

If he comes, Will thought. Not *when* he comes. She was as scared as he. Finishing his drink, he returned to the living room and threw himself on the sofa.

After a while he dozed.

The sound of a voice awoke him and he looked at the watch on his wrist. Its luminous hands stood at half past four. The voice came from the room Ima Williams occupied, in the servant's quarters behind the kitchen.

He got up off the sofa and walked to Ima's door, which he found closed. Not altogether puzzled, he stood there listening.

The Haitian woman was talking in Creole to one of her voodoo loa, imploring the spirit to help her. To open her eyes and let her see despite the darkness. To lead her along the path she wished to travel. There were many gods in voodoo. Will had not heard of this one—at least, not by the name she used. It could be some minor loa for whom she felt some special affinity. A family deity, perhaps, to whom she turned when in trouble.

With the plea for help he heard a thumping sound, as though the woman on the other side of the door were striking the floor with her foot, or a table with her hand, to make sure the god was paying attention to her. It was a common thing in voodoo services.

Only for a moment did Will hesitate. Then as the voice continued its plea and the thumping sound became more emphatic, he reached for the doorknob and gently turned it.

A slight pressure on the door caused it to inch open. Peering into the room, he was startled.

Ima Williams stood before her dresser, clad only in a thin white nightgown that revealed almost as much of her dark body as if she were naked. On the mahogany dresser was a wooden serving tray on which burned two tall white chandles. There was no other light in the room.

In her right hand the hounsi held a stick about three feet long, an inch or so in diameter, that resembled the trunk of a miniature palm tree. Which, in fact, it was— a dwarf palm that seemed to grow only in the highest, least accessible parts of her native country. Perhaps that explained the reverence with which it was held in voodoo circles.

Will Platt may not have known of the deity to whom she prayed, but he knew the name of the stick. It was a cocomacaque. He himself owned one.

He watched in silence as the woman continued her invocation of the loa. If she were aware of his presence at the door, she gave no sign of it. After perhaps ten minutes she stopped talking and, still clutching the cocomacaque, turned to the bed. Will was startled to realize the bed had not yet been turned down.

Had she been at this ritual ever since retiring to her room?

Throwing herself on the bed, she lay on her back and held the cocomacaque above her at arm's length, gripping an end of it in each hand. Slowly she brought the stick down to her forehead, to hold it there for a moment before lifting it again. After doing this three times, she placed it beside her and folded her arms on her breasts. The only sound in the room then was the almost inaudible whisper of her breathing.

Her breathing became very slow and steady. Her eyes closed. She was asleep, Will decided, or in some kind of trance. Retreating, he silently closed the door and returned to the sofa in the front room, where he sat and pondered what he had just witnessed.

He was still sitting there when he heard Ima's door open and turned to see her coming toward him.

She wore a dark dressing gown over her nightdress now. Halting before him, she frowned and said, "Mr. Will, haven't you been to bed?"

He shook his head. "Nor have you, I think. I heard you talking to your loa."

"Yes." She went to a chair and sat down, facing him. "I have something to tell you."

He gazed at her and waited.

"I asked the loa to let me see what happened," she said, "and my plea was answered. Not wholly answered, but I was allowed to see something. Mr. Sam has been shot."

Will felt as though she had slapped him across the face with a cold, wet towel.

"I saw two men in a room, and one was Mr. Sam," Ima went on in a voice that wept. "The other man had a shotgun and was telling him he would kill him with it. Mr. Sam knocked the gun out of his hands and ran, but the man picked it up and shot him."

"Oh, my God," Will breathed.

"But then I had another vision," Ima went on quickly, though so shaken by her emotions that her voice broke. "I saw Mr. Sam in another house and this time there was an older man with him, and an old woman. He was on a bed and they were doing something to his leg. So I don't think the man with the gun killed him."

Will felt himself come alive again. "Who were these old people, Ima? Did you know them?"

She shook her head.

"Did you know the man with the gun? The one who shot him?"

She frowned. "I could not see his face."

"I don't understand. You recognized Sam, you heard

this man threatening to shoot him, but you couldn't see the fellow's face?"

"No, and that is strange. And it has something to do with Sister Merle, I think." She leaned toward him, her dark eyes flickering. "You remember I told you I tried to help Mr. Juan, but that woman was too powerful for me?"

Will nodded.

"Well, I feel her power all the time now. It is as if—as if she has surrounded me with some kind of wall, to make it impossible for me to see or do certain things. Tonight I called on the loa to help me and they did, yet while I could see Mr. Sam clearly, I could not see the face of the other man. It was just a blur, as if someone had drawn a veil over it."

"But it could have been this obeah man Sam went to see?"

"I suppose it—"

"I'm going there." Will stood up. "Where can I find transportation?"

"What time is it, please?"

He looked at his watch. "Close to six."

"There is nothing we can do until the first taxis start passing. That will be in an hour or so. Why don't you take a shower and change your clothes while I make you some breakfast?"

"Lord, woman, I'm not hungry!"

"You must eat before you go. There is no telling when you may get another chance."

He took her advice, and she had a breakfast of bacon and eggs ready for him when he came from his room. Standing by the table, watching him as he began to eat, she said, "Ken Daniels will be coming by from Devon soon. I'll stop him."

"Who is Ken Daniels?"

"He has a taxi. You must understand, the taxis here are not like those in Kingston. Or in your country, I suppose. Each man here owns his own and drives it home at night to wherever he lives. In the morning he will start work by driving people from his district to Christiana. Will you mind riding as far as town with a lot of black people?"

"No. But how will he be able to take me to Silent Hill?"

"If you can pay, he will take you anywhere."

"I see."

"Ken is a good man. You will like him, I think, and I know you can trust him. Let me go out to the gate and wait for him now."

While watching her from a living-room window, Will checked the Jamaican money in his billfold to be sure he would have enough. It would be expensive, he guessed, to take the taximan from his normal routine and hire him for the best part of the day.

Out at the gate Ima stood tall with her hands folded over her bosom. Then as the rising sun brightened, she lifted one arm to shade her eyes as she peered to her right down the road.

After a while she stepped into the road with a hand uplifted to stop an oncoming car.

14

"Me Never See Him!"

When the taxi stopped and Will got a close look at it, his admiration for the efficiency of Ima Williams faltered a little. It was an old, many-times-dented Austin Cambridge, black with a horizontal stripe of hand-painted lavender under its windows on the side he could see from the veranda.

Ima talked to the driver, a bearded brown man with solid-looking shoulders and chest. Then she hurried back to the house.

"Are you ready, Mr. Will?"

"Well, yes. I guess so."

"As soon as Ken drops these people off in Christiana he will take you to Silent Hill and stay with you as long as you like."

"Ima, thanks." He touched her on the arm and smiled his gratitude as he went past her.

When he got to the car, the man at the wheel thrust out a hand and said gravely, "Sorry I'm so crowded, Mr. Platt. It will be all right after we get to town." Ken Daniels was a big man, easily two hundred pounds, and about forty; he was bearded and had remarkably even, white teeth. For Will, the most striking thing about him was an aura he seemed to have of strength and honesty.

120

Releasing Will's hand after a vigorous clasp, he reached behind him and opened the rear door. The five passengers on the car's rear seat, which was popping its stuffing, squirmed and wriggled to make the necessary room for one more, graciously smiling and exchanging greetings with the white stranger.

In the town, Ken Daniels stopped in front of a grocery store and turned the battered car's nose in to the curb. Having squeezed into the conveyance last, Will was the first to exit. While the others followed, dropping coins into the driver's hand, he waited on the sidewalk. The town's main street was remarkably clean. Across the way an old fellow plied a broom in the gutter.

"Well now, Mr. Platt, you want to go to Silent Hill, correct?" Daniels, his passengers attended to, stood solidly before him, ready to dicker.

"That's right, Mr. Daniels."

"Just call me Ken, if you don't mind. Everybody calls me Ken. Where you want to go in Silent Hill?"

"I don't know. I'm looking for Sam Norman, who went there yesterday morning to find a man named Emmanuel Bignall and hasn't returned."

"All right. What I can do is this. I will drive you there and do whatever we have to, and leave the pay up to you for the time it takes. If I drive somebody to MoBay airport these days, I have to charge eighty dollars because the price of gas and car parts is so high. MoBay and back is a six hour ride, so you can figure today's cost accordingly. Is that okay with you?"

"That's fine with me, Ken."

"Good. We're gone."

While driving through the town, the taximan was silent. After turning down the hill at Barclay's Bank, however, he said with a frown, "Who is this Mr. Norman we are looking for, Mr. Platt?"

"He came here to help the United Nations man, Juan Cerrado."

"I know Mr. Cerrado."

"You must know he is missing, then."

"Yes. He disappeared about ten days ago."

"Sam Norman is trying to find him. I came down from Florida to help Sam. We're old friends."

As the car left Christiana behind, the driver removed his left hand from the wheel to rub his whiskered chin. "And your Mr. Norman went to Silent Hill to seek Emmanual Bignall?" he said without taking his gaze from the steep downgrade.

"That's right."

Silence. The road leveled and spawned some sharp turns. After handling the curves at what would have been reckless speed with a less skillful driver at the wheel, Ken Daniels said quietly, "Emmanuel Bignall is an obeah man. You know that?"

"So I've heard. Are you afraid of obeah?"

"I don't mess with it, but I'm not afraid. Not of people like him, anyhow. He is not big like—well, some others I could name."

"Sister Merle, for instance?"

The driver's gaze flashed to Will's face and away again. "You know about her too, do you?"

"Sam and I called on her the day before yesterday."

"At her place in the Cockpit?"

"Yes."

"You're not a timid man, then. And now you want to call on Bignall."

"I want to find Sam, and it was Bignall he was looking for. Do you know where the fellow lives?"

"I can take you there."

The unpaved road crossed a narrow bridge above a stream, then climbed. There were yam fields on both sides, and now and then a small house. A pickup truck filled with green bananas and ginger root rattled past on its way to Christiana. A dirt road angled off to the left, and Ken Daniels took it.

They passed half a dozen houses and a pair of shops, in one of which men stood around in work clothes drinking beer and listening to a jukebox thunder out reggae. Then more yam fields and some banana walks. Suddenly Will leaned forward to peer through the car's windshield.

"Isn't that a Land Rover parked ahead, Ken?"

Ken eased his foot off the gas. "It is." He brought the taxi to a halt behind the standing vehicle, and they got out. "It's the U.N. Rover, no key in it." Twisting his big frame at the hips, he frowned at a footpath angling down to his right. "That track there goes to Emmanuel Bignall's home."

"How far?"

"Maybe half a mile. You can walk that far?"

Two years ago Will had walked across the Massif du Sud in Haiti, one of the Caribbean's most challenging wildernesses. "I think so. I walked to Sister Merle's."

"So you did. I forgot."

The path was not as difficult as the one to Merle's. Reaching a level some twenty feet below the road, it wound its way leisurely through planted fields where the red earth seemed ablaze in the sun, then through patches of trees where the cool shade was a relief. Bignall's home, too, was unlike the obeah house Will had visited with Sam. Little more than a shack, it stood in the center of a small, weedgrown clearing, with a rusty and dented oil drum at its door to catch rainwater from the roof.

Will tried to recall what Ima Williams had said about Emmanuel Bignall, and the phrase that came to mind was "big, black, and ugly." When Ken Daniels called out, "Manny, you home?" the man who appeared in the doorway in soiled khaki pants and a sweat-stained undershirt, yawning and stretching, well fitted the housekeeper's description.

"Mornin', Manny," the taximan said. "This here is Mr. Platt and we lookin' a friend of his, a man name

Mr. Sam Norman. He did come here yesterday to talk to you."

The whites of the eyes that looked Will over were streaked with red. The eyes themselves were hostile. "You lookin' who, suh?"

"Mr. Sam Norman," Will said. "His Land Rover is out there on the road, where he left it when he came in here."

"Him never come in here," Bignall said, warping his oversized face into an expression of puzzlement. "Nobody never come here yesterday. Not a soul."

Ken Daniels said, "Why his vehicle is out there, then? You tryin' tell us he couldn't find his way in here, when your track don't go nowhere else but here?"

The expression on Bignall's face again changed, this time to anger. "Me tellin' you me never did see him!"

"You was here?"

"The whole entirely day."

"Manny, you not bein' too polite, you know. Why you don't invite us in?"

"Come in if you likes." The big man stepped back from the doorway to let them enter.

The shack was a single room containing a bed and a few other sad bits of furniture. A two-burner oil stove against the far wall looked as though it was used often but cleaned seldom. The obeah man eased his bulk into a rickety chair and waited for his callers to be seated. In silence he scowled at them, obviously resenting their intrusion. Ken Daniels looked questioningly at Will.

"Mr. Bignall, I'll tell you why Mr. Norman came to talk to you," Will said carefully. "He and I are trying to locate Juan Cerrado, the United Nations man who disappeared a week ago last Friday. Yesterday we learned that you and another man drove him away from the Christiana market that day in a Prefect. Mr. Norman wanted to ask you where you took him."

Did the fellow understand ordinary English, or would

Ken have to translate? Ken himself had used the patois, more or less. Perhaps it was common practice when conversing with those whose only tongue it was.

With a ponderous shrug Emmanuel Bignall said, "The two of we never did bring Mr. Cerrado here."

"Where did you take him?"

"*Me* never did take him nowhere. Me was finished in the market and talkin' to Nevil Walters that mornin' when Mr. Cerrado come along. Him say, 'I hear you has a fine farm, Nevil; I would truly like to see it.' Nevil, him say, 'Well, Mr. Cerrado, me goin' home right now and me has a car here, so if you wants to come along, you can come.'

" 'I better follow you in mine,' Mr. Cerrado him say.

" 'No need to do that,' Nevil tell him, 'because me comin' back here with me woman to buy her a dress.' " The obeah man looked innocently at his callers and shrugged his shoulders again. "Does you know where Nevil Walters live, either of you?"

Ken Daniels nodded. To Will he said, "We passed the place on our way here, a couple of miles outside Christiana."

"So what happen," Emmanuel Bignall said, "the two of them did stop at Nevil's and me did walk home from there. Next day me did see Nevil in Case's bar and ask him how things go, and him tell me him did take Mr. Cerrado back to town when him drive the woman in. Them did drop him off at the bank to draw money for him Friday paybill."

"Which bank?" Ken asked casually. "Barclay's or Scotia?"

Bignall hesitated, but only slightly. "Barclay's. How me know, us was drinkin' in Case's when Nevil say this, and him turn and point across the street."

The taximan only nodded.

Will said, "Now tell us why the U.N. Land Rover, which Mr. Norman drove here yesterday, is parked out on the road where your path begins."

"Me have no idea. Me never know it there till you say so."

"Mr. Norman came here to talk to you," Will persisted, speaking slowly and deliberately now. "He didn't know where you live, so he must have asked—probably at one of the shops. He then found the path to this house, took the ignition key out of the vehicle so no one could make off with it, and walked in here. Where is he, Mr. Bignall? What happened to him?"

"It seem a real problem, don't it? For me was here all day yesterday and all last night, and no one did come here to call on me."

To Will's surprise, Ken Daniels interrupted with, "Mr. Platt, maybe we should go talk to Nevil Walters."

Glancing at him, Will saw something that spelled "urgent" in the man's face, and got to his feet. Ken rose with him and turned to the door.

"If me hear anything, me will surely let you know," Emmanuel Bignall said.

Will muttered, "Thanks." Ken said nothing. They walked across the shabby clearing to the footpath by which they had come.

Half way out to the road the taximan said, "Mr. Platt, do you have another key to the Land Rover?"

"There may be one at the house. I don't know."

"It would not be wise to leave the vehicle here. In Jamaica today cars cost a fortune and are being stolen or stripped every day."

"I'll ask Ima if there's another key. Can we stop on the way and talk to this Walters fellow?"

"It would be a waste of time."

"But you said back there—"

"I know. I wanted to get away. Those two have got together and invented a story, Mr. Platt. You noticed what happened when I asked him which bank? They hadn't expected that, and he made a mistake. At least, I think he did. There are only two banks in Christiana, and the one I've seen Juan Cerrado in is the other one, the Bank of Nova Scotia."

"It isn't much to go on," Will protested.

Still speaking over his shoulder while leading the way out to the road, the taximan said, "A man like you could find out if Juan Cerrado withdrew money that day, couldn't he?"

"I don't know."

"I believe you could, if you explain why you need the information. But even if you can't, I am certain Bignall was lying to us."

"Are you? Why?"

"Do you know where Craig Head is?"

"No."

"It is a village beyond Christiana on the road to Troy. The Friday Mr. Cerrado disappeared, I carried some people there because the taxi serving that district broke down and they begged me to take them home from the market."

Ken paused, scowling. "On my way back from Craig Head, Mr. Platt, I saw Nevil Walters's yellow Prefect come streaking out of a side road in front of me, in a real big hurry to get to Christiana, with both Walters and Bignall in it, but no Juan Cerrado. This was well before noon when, if we are to believe Bignall, Mr. Cerrado was at Nevil's farm."

"Where was the Prefect coming from?"

"That road goes to one place. Gourie Forest."

"Where?"

"Gourie Forest. A big pine forest with trails to explore, and Gourie Cave, that is said to be one of the longest and most dangerous caves in all Jamaica."

Taking a hand from the wheel, Ken emphatically gestured with it. "I think we should go there, Mr. Platt, when you have the keys to the Rover and have asked at the banks if Mr. Cerrado took money out that day. Because I don't think he did. And I don't think he was driven to any farm. Bignall told us that pretty story— and, mind you, it's a very likely story right down to the bank business—to throw us off the scent."

Without shifting his gaze from the road, Ken managed somehow to convey the impression that he was peering at Will. "What I think really happened," he said, "is that Juan Cerrado was taken from the Christiana market to Gourie and maybe killed there. And if so, Mr. Platt, your friend Mr. Sam Norman may be there too."

15

The Telegram

Juan Cerrado had no account at Barclay's. He had one at the Bank of Nova Scotia but had not used it on the day of his disappearance or since.

At the house Ima Williams said yes, there was a spare set of keys for the Land Rover. She lifted them from a nail in the kitchen broom closet and put them in Will's hand.

On the way back to Silent Hill in the taxi, Will went over the events of the morning and tried to make sense of them.

It was an exercise in frustration.

"Ken, tell me if I've got this straight. Cerrado made an enemy of your obeah woman, Sister Merle, by telling his farmers to keep away from her. To stop paying her their hard-earned money for services he thought were worthless. Is that right?"

"That is correct, Mr. Platt."

"So you think she may have had him killed."

"Yes."

"But *why,* if she is such a powerful sorceress? Why didn't she just use her obeah on him?"

"The way I understand it, Mr. Platt, some people are easy for an obeah person and some are not. I shouldn't

129

think Mr. Cerrado was one of the easy ones. Then again, I'm told you must believe, though I don't go along with that."

An old notion, Will thought. One that existed in Haiti, too, in connection with bocorism. Unless you believed in the powers of such people, you could not be brought under their influence. His research in Haiti had led him to reject the theory even before Sam Norman's clash with Margal had made a mockery of it.

"What can have happened to Sam, Ken?"

The taximan thoughtfully scratched at his beard. "All I can think of is that he may have walked to Bignall's place and been disposed of."

A chill took Will and he winced. "To stop him from finding out what happened to Cerrado?"

"Yes."

"But if he was disposed of, as you put it, would Bignall have left the Land Rover there?"

"If he could not drive it. I have never seen him drive a car. Few people of his kind know how to."

"Should we go there again and ask him what he was doing with Walters in your Gourie Forest?"

Ken shook his head. "There is a potato storehouse on that road. He is not a potato farmer but could say he went there to see someone. There are houses, too, though not many. He could claim he was calling on a friend." A deep frown changed the shape of the taximan's jaw. "What I think, Mr. Platt—we should ask some of those people in Gourie if they saw a yellow Prefect that day, and who was in it. We can do that today."

The U.N. vehicle was still standing at the roadside by Bignall's path. It started for Will at a turn of the key. Ken, leaning from his taxi, called out, "All right. I will drive to your house and wait for you there."

At the house they parked the lavender-striped taxi in the yard and closed the gate on it for security. After telling an anxious Ima their intentions, they drove in the

Land Rover through Christiana and up the steep grade beyond the town to the road Ken had talked about.

It was unpaved and rough. Circling a large metal storehouse that glistened in the sun, it became even rougher, with fields of corn on both sides. After a sharp left turn the farms yielded to pine trees, tall and straight, taming the harsh sunlight to a cool, dim darkness.

Roads and trails wore Forestry Department signs of rustic design to indicate where they went. Today the whole place seemed empty and eerily silent except for the wind-sigh in the pinetops.

"Your forest is bigger than I expected," Will remarked.

"We would need days to explore it. I just want you to drive the roads now and see the size of the problem."

They finished their tour, during which Will felt he had been magically transported from the tropics to some secret part of the Maine woods. "Now let's talk to people," Ken said.

There were houses on the road by which they had entered. At one after another the taximan asked questions while Will stood by in silence, not knowing how to contribute. Only at the last one, near the potato storehouse, did Ken score.

"The week before last on Friday?" said the woman trying to respond to his questions. "Yes, me did see an old yellow car come by here. It was about eleven o'clock, 'cause me was dressing to go-a-town and fretting 'cause me so late."

"Who you did see in the car, mum?"

"Seem like me remember two men, one o' dem really big an' black."

"Not three?"

"Coulda been three if one was in de back seat. Me never really look, you understand."

Ken gave her a bright new fifty cent coin and thanked her. As they got back into the Land Rover, he said,

"We've done what we can here, don't you think? At least for now. Seems to me what we ought to do next is go to your house and decide on a plan of action."

Will nodded. "Can you stay with me on this for a while, Ken? I can't handle it alone. I don't even speak the language."

A smile touched the taximan's ruggedly handsome face. "Well now, Marse Platt, me sure can and will. Me must have to admit me really curious now."

"You'd better drop the 'Platt' if we're going to be working together. My name's Will."

"Okay, Marse Will."

On reaching the house, Will suddenly realized he should call Florida. "I ought to tell my wife I won't be returning as soon as expected," he said to Ima Williams. "Where's the nearest telephone?"

"When Mr. Sam called you, he used the outdoor pay phone opposite the police station. But some of our neighbors have telephones they would let you use, I am sure."

Not eager to become involved with strangers, Will drove up to the town, then wished he hadn't. The booth looked as though it had been without maintenance for years. The door refused to close properly, and every vehicle snarling up the grade outside added to his hearing problem. But he got through eventually.

When told he might have to stay in Jamaica longer than planned, Vicky seemed indifferent. Too much so, he thought—as if she had rehearsed both her words and her attitude in the event he did make such a call. "Stay as long as you like," she said with a vocal shrug. She was still very angry, he guessed, at not being allowed to accompany him to the island.

"Have I had any mail of importance?"

"Nothing that won't keep. But give me your phone number, in case."

"I don't have a phone. I'm calling from a pay station."

"Your address, then."

He told her she could reach him in care of Juan Cerrado, Christiana.

"No street address?" she asked coldly.

"There's no delivery here. You go to the post office and stand in line. Unless you have a box."

"Well, does Cerrado have a box?"

"He does, but I don't know the number. It doesn't matter. They'll know."

"What about telegrams?"

"Same address. They do deliver those."

"All right," she said. "Enjoy yourself. I'll try not to miss you." And she hung up.

Driving back to the house he had an uneasy feeling he had said too much and had not heard the last of it. Vicky had always been a cold woman, and since her sessions with Margal, she had been a dangerously cunning one as well.

"What now?" he said to Ken Daniels.

"Perhaps we should call on the Christiana police."

They went to the station and the police listened attentively but only shrugged. That the U.N. Land Rover had been found keyless at the entrance to Emmanuel Bignall's track obviously struck the lawmen as being unimportant. Arrest the obeah man and his friend Nevil Walters because of it? On what charge?

"Can't you even question them?"

"You seem to have done that already, Mr. Platt. At least, you've questioned the one most likely to know anything."

"What about Gourie Forest? Will you investigate that lead?"

"We will search the forest, certainly. If your friend Mr. Norman is there, or even the missing Mr. Cerrado, we may be able to find them. Be warned it won't be easy, though. Gourie is no small place."

From the police station Ken and he began on the shops. Covering the ones in town, including small bars on side streets that he never would have found by himself, took more than two hours. Then they used up most of the afternoon touring the shops on surrounding country roads.

The bearded taximan was unhappy. "One of our troubles, I think, is that Mr. Norman did not circulate enough for people to get to know him."

"He did after Cerrado disappeared, Ken. Trying to find him, I mean."

"But it has been such a short time."

"He's white. Wouldn't that—"

"There are some white teachers in schools around here, and among the bauxite people. He wouldn't stand out that much. Anyway, it's evident no one has seen Mr. Norman since he went to talk to Bignall." Ken paused, knuckling his beard. "Look. Why don't we call on Nevil Walters, just in case he knows something?"

"Whatever you say. You're better at this than I am."

Nevil Walters was at his farm. About thirty years old, he showed no hostility—in fact, seemed more than willing to answer questions. As though he was expecting us, Will thought.

The man had a vocabulary, though, that was all too common among certain barely schooled country folk in the island. "We have island-wide spelling bees every year," Ken Daniels explained. "The kids are given lists of words to learn, and they learn them. Then, God help us, they go through life using them to show how educated they are, without a clue to what half of them mean."

In Nevil Walters's case the use of so many meaningless words could have been intentional—a way to avoid honest replies to unwelcome questions. In any event, the interview produced nothing of value.

They returned to Cerrado's house and sat on the veranda to talk about what they could do next. Ima Williams brought them drinks. Before the drinks were finished, a rapping on the gate interrupted their conversation.

"It is Tanny, from the telegraph office," Ken said, leaning forward on his chair to peer at the caller. "Must be for you, Mr. Will."

Will went down the steps, and the fellow handed him a brown envelope and a pencil.

"You must sign the flap and give it back to him," Ken called from the veranda.

Having done so, Will tipped the man and returned to his chair. Intuition told him what the telegram might be, and he scowled in anger as he tore the envelope open.

On the pink sheet inside was the message. ARRIVING MONTEGO BAY NOON TOMORROW IF NOT MET WILL TAKE TAXI TO CHRISTIANA LOVE VICKY

Love? he thought bitterly.

16

The Opal

The plane from Miami was half an hour late. Waiting outside the customs area, Will saw Vicky as she emerged into the afternoon sunlight, following a skycap with a pair of matching suitcases. Beautifully garbed, of course, though her expensive, pearl-gray summer suit looked out of place here.

He made his way forward and touched his wife's hand. Her mechanical smile said, "Look, I'm smiling." In a gesture just as mechanical he brushed her cheek with his lips. "The Land Rover over there," he said to the skycap. Then to Vicky he said, "How was the flight?" It was probably the safest thing to say right now.

"I've had better."

"How have you been, yourself?"

"Bored. That's why I'm here." She turned her head to give him one of her sharp-eyed, warning looks. "I just hope this Christiana of yours is exciting. Is it?"

There was no point, he decided, in reminding her he had not wanted her to come. She was here and he must make the best of a bad—perhaps even a dangerous—situation. "I don't think you'll be bored here."

"Is there voodoo in Jamaica?"

"Obeah."

"Is that the same?"

"Not exactly," he replied wearily, recalling the time she had disappeared in Haiti without telling him where she was going. At four in the morning he had found her at a voodoo ceremony ten miles from the town of Jacmel, where they were living, possessed by a voodoo loa and unable to remember who she was.

At the Land Rover he tipped her skycap and stowed her luggage away himself. "What's this thing?" Vicky demanded, eyeing the vehicle with open displeasure.

"An English jeep. Belongs to the U.N."

"I hope we don't have far to go."

He refrained from commenting as he helped her up onto the seat and they left the airport in silence. Not until they were on the main north-coast road did Vicky say, "Well, are you going to tell me what's been happening since you got here?"

He took his time telling her, so the journey would seem less long to her. She had spent a fair amount of time with him in the islands; this ride through the Cockpit to Christiana would not impress her as it might someone more curious. Between intervals of silence he told of Juan Cerrado's clash with the obeah woman. Of Cerrado's mysterious disappearance. Of Sam Norman's more recent vanishing. Of his own fruitless efforts to find them both.

"You're doing this by yourself?" she asked with a frown at one point.

"I have a fellow named Ken Daniels helping me."

"Can you trust him?"

"You'll be meeting him. You can decide for yourself."

"I'd like to meet this Sister Merle."

He had expected that and already decided how to handle it. "Sister Merle is a dangerous woman, Vicky. She's no one to play your little games with. The one thing I am *not* going to do is take you to see her."

"Well, you can at least tell me about her, can't you?"

That would be a way to keep her from constantly frowning at her watch as the hilly miles rolled out behind them, he decided. In detail he told of his visit with Sam to the obeah woman's house in the Cockpit.

"She sounds like a female Margal," Vicky observed.

"She is. If you want her services, you go to her and pay her. It was because so many of his farmers were giving her so much of their hard-earned money that the U.N. fellow declared war on her."

"And now he's missing."

"Now he's missing. And so is Sam."

"Have *you* been threatened?" Vicky asked, turning her head to study him.

"I'm not sure." He told her about his visit with Ken to the home of Emmanuel Bignall. "Nothing now would surprise me much."

It was mid-afternoon when they reached Christiana. It was Friday, the first of the two market days when people flocked in from miles around. Obviously excited, she kept turning her head from side to side as he drove through. "Why, it's like Jacmel!" she exclaimed.

"Wait until you see it tomorrow morning. Getting past the market gate in a car will take forever. On foot you'll need a suit of armor and a baseball bat."

"But where do they all come from?"

He had been studying maps of the district. "Just about everywhere within reason. Even such wonderfully named places as Balaclava, Auchtembeddie, and the District of Look Behind."

She was pleased, and for the first time since leaving the airport he felt some of his apprehension melt away. With Vicky you never quite knew. You could anticipate a certain mood and encounter one entirely different. She was smiling now. She was thrilled. Maybe her coming to

Jamaica would not be a disaster, after all.

Her mood changed abruptly, though, when she met Ken Daniels at the house. Will saw the change in her face when Ken offered his hand on being introduced. It became even more noticeable when Ima Williams did the same.

She was like that about blacks. If they seemed to feel themselves her equal, she instantly withdrew. To be her equal, a person with skin other than white had to be someone whose services she needed or wanted, as she had wanted those of the bocor in Haiti.

Ima Williams picked up the two suitcases and led Vicky to the bedroom. Ken Daniels said to Will, "While you were gone, I took the liberty of going to Wait-a-Bit."

"To talk to the police, you mean?"

"Yes. And I think we should go there together, first thing in the morning."

"Why, Ken? What's the problem?"

"The fellow hasn't talked. Hasn't said a word. And there is something wrong with him, it seems. They wouldn't let me see him. Said it was none of my business."

"How do you know they'll let me see him?"

"I asked. At first they said no, but when I told them about Mr. Norman's disappearance, they finally agreed. Not with any enthusiasm, mind you, but you'll be permitted to see Mowatt if we go early in the morning. Perhaps even both of us."

"Why early, Ken?"

"They say they are taking him to Spaldings, to the hospital."

"The hospital? But there was nothing wrong with him when Sam and I left him at the station."

"There seems to be now, Will." The bearded man shrugged, then glanced toward the veranda door. "I'd better run along. You'll want to be with your wife."

"No, wait. Stay for supper and tell me more about this."

"In the morning. I'll come by about six."

A good man, Will thought, watching him open the door and depart. A sensitive one, too, well aware of Vicky's instant hostility. What the hell was wrong with Vicky, anyway? And what had happened to the man who wore Juan Cerrado's field boots?

It was unusual for him to be sharing a room with his wife, and when they retired he felt compelled to explain to her why it was necessary. Discounting the housekeeper's room there were but two bedrooms, he told her. The one they were using had been Juan Cerrado's; the other was being used by Sam Norman. True, Sam was missing now and not able to occupy it, but he might turn up at any moment. So, whether she approved of the arrangement or not, they would have to share a room.

"I suppose if we must, we must," she replied with a shrug.

"I didn't ask you to come here, you know," he reminded her.

She merely glared at him.

There were two beds in the room: a mahogany double and a truly handsome single made more recently of guango. He was using the smaller one himself, so it was no sacrifice to offer Vicky the other. After testing it by lying on it fully clothed and squirming a little, she pronounced it adequate.

Not since Haiti had they used a common bedroom, he mused as he sat on the edge of his bed to take off his shoes. Was this to be another Haiti in more ways than one?

Vicky, too, had begun to undress. "May I ask what your plans are for tomorrow?"

"Ken and I have to go to the police station in Wait-a-Bit."

"That sounds interesting. I'll enjoy that."

He shook his head. "I'm afraid not, Vicky. They would never understand. Anyway, we're leaving very early. You'll still be in bed."

"I'm to spend the morning here with Ima, then?" Her beautiful face was a thundercloud.

"Well, the town's within easy walking distance. I'm sure you'll find something to do."

She turned away with a shrug of her shoulders, which were exposed to his gaze now because she had removed everything but bra and panties. Guessing what would happen next, he watched her. As expected, she took her nightgown—an expensive and sexy pink one, with all the frills—and went into the bathroom, closing the door behind her. When she at once turned a tap on in the hand basin, he knew she had done so to smother any sound she might make when seated on the toilet.

Remembering something that had happened on his way to the airport to meet her, he had to smile in spite of himself. On the outskirts of a village called Barbecue Bottom he had passed a woman squatting by the roadside with her dressed hiked up. *She,* caught in the act, had gaily waved to him, showing a mouthful of teeth in a happy grin.

Undressed, he got into bed in the raw, the way he always slept, and linked his hands behind his head while watching the bathroom door, waiting for her to come out. There had been times not so very long ago when he had still wanted her. After all, she was as beautiful today as when he had married her—tall, graceful as a dancer, with a body that seemed made for love.

But he had no such feelings now, knowing the beautiful body housed a heart of pure evil and any man who tried to be intimate with it was flirting with destruction.

The door opened and she came back into the

bedroom, a vision of beauty in the nightgown. Easing herself into the double bed, she said, "Good night, Will," and reached out to switch off the lamp on the table between them.

"Why don't you like Ima?" he asked.

"What?"

"Ima Williams, the housekeeper. Why don't you like her?"

"Her attitude, for one thing. And yours toward her. No one would ever guess she's a servant here, for God's sake."

"She cooked and served your dinner, didn't she?" he challenged, feeling himself bristle.

"As if she were doing me a favor."

"I assure you she's a very fine woman." And wouldn't you be devastated to know, he thought, that she is a servitor of the loa, high up in the voodoo hierarchy!

"Well," she said curtly, "I don't like her and don't intend to pretend I do. By the way, I suppose you know she's Haitian, and in voodoo."

He felt himself stiffen. "She told you that?"

"She didn't need to. When she was getting dinner I went into the kitchen for some ice. She was hard-boiling some eggs for the salad, and I saw her put her hand into the boiling water to take them out. It would be boiling oil at a kanzo service, wouldn't it? So I took a good look at her and guessed she was Haitian, and she admitted it."

"Did she tell you she was kanzo?"

"Yes, when I accused her of it."

"And then?"

"Why, then," Vicky said, her lower lip curling, "I showed her my ring and warned her not to try her simple white magic on me because I could top it in a way she wouldn't like."

She was wearing the ring now, Will observed. She almost always did. It was an opal he had bought for her some years ago in a Mexican town called Pachuca, just a few miles north of Mexico City.

He had since had reason, more than once, to remember that occasion vividly. They had turned in off the main highway because Vicky had heard of an Indian woman in Pachuca who was said to possess certain occult powers. Even then, that long ago, she had been curious about things occult.

The woman turned out to be a crone who lived in a rather decent house, certainly not a hovel, on a dark little street off the zocalo. Vicky spent the evening with her while he walked about the town soaking up its unique atmosphere, thinking he might one day need such an offbeat setting in one of his books. And at the hotel that night, a pleasant place mellow with shadows, kitchen smells and mariachi music, she had shown him the opal.

It was only a stone then, not a ring in an expensive setting. "She says it has unusual powers, Will, and, you know, I think it may have. When I hold it in my hand, I actually feel something."

He was amused. "You feel what?"

"Well, I don't know. A tingling, sort of, but really more than that. Something like . . . as if *I* have acquired a certain kind of power, myself."

"Like the power to persuade me to buy it for you?"

"Will you? You don't have to, you know. All she wants is three hundred dollars, and I have more than that myself."

"It's worth that much, and she trusted you to walk off with it?"

"She said she knew I wouldn't steal it. She could read my thoughts when I held the stone in my hand." Vicky gazed at him with a peculiar intensity. "The opal is said to be a gem of prophecy, you know. Arabs used to believe they came from the sky in flashes of lightning."

"They're also thought to be bad luck," he had reminded her.

"Well, yes, they used to be. But that was mostly because of a novel by Sir Walter Scott—*Anne* of something or other. Its heroine had an opal that reflected all her feelings, like turning fiery red when she was angry. Then after a lot of unhappy adventures she died and—if I remember it right—the stone lost all its colors and turned gray as a gravestone."

"I should read the book," Will said. "Anyway, what will you do with it if you acquire it?"

"Wear it, of course. In a ring." She gazed at the stone as if longing to see it on her finger. "Isn't it just beautiful? Did you know the Empress Josephine owned one that she named 'The Burning of Troy' because its colors were so incredible? And did you know an opal is said to protect its wearer from evil?"

"All right, then. I'll consider it some kind of insurance." Will smiled and shrugged at the same time. The stone was probably not worth anything like what the woman was asking, he told himself. For one thing, it was darker than any opal he had ever seen before, though a kind of spectral fire did seem to burn inside it.

But who cared if the old Indian woman was engaged in a minor con game? His trip with Vicky to Mexico City had been unexpectedly free of friction so far, and if he could keep it that way for a few hundred dollars, he would be a fool to start counting pennies.

After a beautiful, fiery hot breakfast in the morning, Vicky had gone to give the Indian woman the three hundred dollars, and when they left Pachuca an hour later, the opal was in her handbag. A few weeks later, back in the States, she had had it mounted in a gold band for the little finger of her left hand.

She had worn it almost continuously ever since, and had never ceased to claim it was a source of power.

"When you threatened Ima with your ring, what did she say?" Will asked her now.

"Say? Nothing."

"Nothing at all?"

"Well, she mumbled something about having no quarrel with me, if you call that something. And if you noticed, she was very, very polite to me when she served dinner."

"I didn't notice. Ima is always polite."

"All right, if you say so. But unless you want trouble here, just warn her to keep her distance when I'm around."

17

The Power of Obeah

At the police station in Wait-a-Bit the corporal was obviously not overjoyed to be receiving visitors. "Mowatt won't talk to you," he predicted, rising with an elaborate shrug from behind his desk. "But come along if you like."

"Both of us, I hope," Will said.

"Why both?"

"If Mowatt does talk, I may not understand what he says."

The Red Stripe could see the logic in that. He shrugged again and led them to the lockup.

Stepping past him, Will walked part way across the cell and halted as though stopped by an unseen barrier. In astonishment he gazed at the man seated before him. There was a cot in one corner of the room. There was a chair. But the fellow was using the floor.

Ken Daniels said softly, "Uh-oh. I half expected this."

Keith Mowatt was no longer the husky, defiant man Sam and Will had left here. Not the confident fellow who had strutted into Sister Merle's house wearing Juan Cerrado's dyed field boots. His skin now was the color of wood ash. He sat with his back against the wall and

146

his arms loosely draped over his drawn-up knees.

His shoulders nearly met under his drooping head, looking as though all the bone had been extracted from them. He showed no interest whatever in his callers.

"Go ahead," the corporal said from the doorway. "Talk to him."

Will advanced a step. "Mowatt, do you remember me?"

No response.

"Look at me, Mowatt. Mr. Norman and I had you brought here after we saw you wearing Mr. Cerrado's boots."

The head slowly came up, twitching, and Will saw the man's eyes. They resembled brown and white balls of glass with streaks of crimson in the white, and seemed unable to focus. After a long struggle they finally fixed their gaze on his face, but with no sign of recognition.

Will looked helplessly at Ken Daniels, and the bearded man stepped to his side. "Hey, Keith." His voice was light and teasing. "You 'member me, Ken Daniels? Drive a taxi in Christiana and Devon? You know me, man."

"It won't work," the corporal said behind them.

"You 'member how the corpie here did come get you at your house, Keith, and your woman Celia was there? How him did bring you here and question you 'bout Cerrado's boots? You 'member that, Keith? Think, man."

"It won't work," the corporal repeated. "We've done all this."

"What wrong with him, then?" Will demanded.

A shrug. "Maybe the hospital can find out. As I told Daniels yesterday, we're taking him there this morning."

Abandoning his attempt to communicate with the man on the floor, Ken said with a frown, "Did he just suddenly become like this, Corpie?"

"No. It was gradual."

"Beginning when?"

"The day after we brought him here. He was all right when he ate his supper and went to sleep that night. In the morning he wouldn't eat or talk, just sat on his cot looking into space. Next day he moved to the floor, and he hasn't stirred since."

"Not even to go to the bathroom?" Will asked. There was an odor in the cell indicating that Mowatt had relieved himself somewhere, but it was not strong.

"If he's done anything like that, it's in his pants. He never once asked for the toilet."

"In all that time?"

"As you can see, there's something wrong with him. With even that part of him, it looks like. You notice his pants aren't stained. He's worn that shirt from when he came here, too, and there's no sign of sweat on it."

"Try him once more, Ken," Will urged.

Ken leaned over the prisoner and grasped his shoulders, at which Mowatt sagged sideways and might have toppled over had the taximan not held him upright. The drooping head rose again and the glassy eyes focused on Ken's hovering face, but only briefly. Then they closed again and the head slumped back to its original position.

"Listen me, Keith," Ken said, seeming now to choose his words with special care. "Me think me know what is wrong here. Who it was came to see you? Your woman?"

No answer.

"Talk to me, man. Because it's a lie what she told you. Sister Merle can't do nuttin' to harm you."

The prisoner seemed not to hear.

"You must have to believe me, man," Ken persisted. "Sister Merle is not no real obeah woman, no matter what she say. If she is so, why she must had to employ Manny Bignall and Nevil Walters to kill the United Nations feller, huh? You hear what me saying? If she is truly able to punish you for wearing the boots, why she didn't kill Mr. Cerrado the same way?"

The man on the floor simply leaned back against the wall and sat there, a breathing scarecrow with his eyes shut.

The taximan straightened. "Am I right, Corpie? Did his woman come here?"

"As a matter of fact, no, she didn't. Nobody been here to see him. Not a soul."

Ken peered at the seated man again, then frowned at Will. "Seem like I was right when we had our talk about obeah, Mr. Will. A victim don't have to be told he been selected."

Will nodded.

Turning back to the corporal, Ken said, "Will the hospital be able to do anything for him, you think?"

The Red Stripe only shrugged.

There was no point in continuing, Will decided. With a nod to Ken he thanked the policeman and made for the door.

At the Land Rover he said, "You drive, will you, Ken?" and climbed in the other side, wanting to do some thinking. After a while he said with a scowl, "What do we do now?"

"I believe we should go to Gourie Forest."

"But the Christiana police said—"

"I know, but I doubt they will look in the cave." Ken jerked the wheel to let a bus go by, and because it was demanding more than its share of the road and traveling too fast, he softly cursed the driver. "There are supposed to be men around here who know that cave fairly well," he said then. "I don't know who they are, but I can ask and try to hire one."

"You mean we'll need a guide?"

"I am a coward in such places, Will. Besides, Gourie is said to be dangerous."

"How long will it take you to locate someone?"

The wide shoulders moved in a shrug. "In any case, we can't go to the cave until you tell your wife where you will be. Also, we'll need equipment of some sort, I suppose. Why don't I drop you at the house and come back for you after lunch?"

Will frowned at his watch. "It's only ten past eight."

"As soon as I can, then. But finding someone who knows the cave and will take us there may not be easy."

At the house, Vicky was up and having her breakfast. Will saw at once that Ima was keeping her distance as much as possible—was, in fact, acting as though she were somewhat afraid—and wondered whether the opal ring with its so-called powers might indeed have intimidated her. The ring was very much in evidence on Vicky's hand.

"Can you fix me something, Ima?" he asked. "Coffee and a couple of soft-boiled eggs, maybe?"

"Of course, Mr. Will."

"So it's 'Mr. Will,' is it?" Vicky said when he joined her at the table. "How long *have* you been here?"

"You heard her call me that yesterday."

"Did I? Perhaps I wasn't paying much attention then."

"And now you are?"

"Very much so, now that I know what she is."

Will peered across the table at her. "I'm surprised you didn't try to make friends with her when you found out she was a hounsi."

She shrugged. "Voodoo doesn't interest me. It's just another religion."

"You were possessed at a service once, if you remember."

"I was a neophyte then, merely groping. Did you talk to your man in Wait-a-Bit?"

He told her what had happened there, and that Ken and he were planning an afternoon visit to the cave. She would not want to accompany them there, he knew. In

Haiti he had explored a number of caves with Sam Norman, and she had always found other things to do. Not that he blamed her. Exploring wild caves in the Caribbean was a far cry from strolling through lighted tourist caverns in the States.

"I think I'll walk up to the village," Vicky said. "If Saturday is the big shopping day, it should be interesting. Can you give me some Jamaican money?"

He did so. She finished her food and went into their bedroom, leaving him alone at the table, as Ima returned with his breakfast. He took his time eating and had only just finished when Ken Daniels turned up again.

"I found a fellow in the market who claims to know the cave. He says we ought to have hard hats and carbide lamps. He can get the hats, he's a bauxite worker, but for the lamps he would have to go to Kingston and maybe wouldn't find any even there."

"Can't we use flashlights?"

"We'll have to, it seems. I gave him some money and he's looking for some now, as well as some rope, in Christiana. We're to pick him up in an hour at the post office."

"You need some breakfast," Will said.

"Thanks."

"Come tell Ima what you want." He led Ken into the kitchen, where the taximan said simply, "Me dyin' fe hungry, Ima," and the housekeeper smiled back at him. There was a small formica-topped table in the kitchen, with two chairs. They sat there.

While Ima produced a prodigious breakfast of warmed-over rice, fried eggs, and steaming tea with condensed milk in it, the taximan said quietly, "I learned something else, Will. Something that makes a trip to Gourie Cave a necessity, I think."

Will gazed at him and waited.

"When I talked to the fellow who is taking us in there,

Waldon McKoy, his name is, he told me the name of the one man in this district who really knows that cave. You know why we can't use him?"

"Why?"

"He's in the Wait-a-Bit lockup. Unless they've already taken him to the hospital."

Will looked at him in silence again, then said, "So now you believe we're likely to find what we're looking for in there."

"Mr. Cerrado, at any rate. Mowatt had his boots."

The handsome Haitian woman at the stove turned swiftly to stare at them.

"You think we'll find Sam Norman too?" Will asked, hating the sound of his own voice. Sam and he had been close friends for a long time, and had shared alot. At the prospect of finding Sam dead in a cold, wet underworld, he felt a coldness welling inside himself and a wetness blurring his eyes.

Into the kitchen now, interrupting his thoughts, came Vicky, and at sight of Ken she stopped short. Ken rose. Politely he said, "Good morning, Mrs. Platt," not this time offering his hand.

She nodded. To Will she said, "I'm going now. When shall I expect you back?"

By turning his head he silently passed the question to Ken.

Ken shrugged. "Day and night will be all the same in there. If we find anything to keep us going, I don't suppose we'll want to come out and have it to do all over again."

Vicky seemed indifferent. "Whatever you say. I'm sure I can amuse myself."

"We can drop you off in Christiana, Mrs. Platt," Ken offered. "We'll be going that way."

"Thanks. I prefer to walk."

Will frowned after her as she departed. Had the words "amuse myself" meant anything special? Probably not.

More than once, he was sure, he had read into her remarks meanings she had not really intended. He looked at his watch, then at Ken. "What time did you say we're to meet your friend?"

Ken's plate was almost clean. "We can leave now. If I know McKoy, he'll be there waiting." Popping the last heaping forkful of rice into his mouth, he pushed back his chair. "Thanks for breakfast, Ima," he said, then for the first time seemed to notice Will's shoes. "You don't have anything more suitable than those? Water boots, say? It'll be wet in there."

"Do cavers wear water boots? I don't think so." Will saw himself sliding and stumbling in loose-fitting rubber boots through a wet, black underworld, and guessed the taximan knew no more about caves than he did. "Forget it. I'm all right with what I've got. How about yourself?" He frowned down at the well-worn dress shoes on Ken's broad feet.

"I don't own any water boots, Will."

"Shall we stop and buy you a pair? On me?"

"No. Buy me a new pair of shoes if I ruin these." There was an imp in Ken's grin but it swiftly vanished. "If you're ready, let's go. Bye, Ima."

The woman at the sink did not answer, and on reaching the door Will looked back at her. She stood there with her long-fingered hands clasped under her breasts, her shoulders drooping, and tears on her cheeks.

Still a handsome woman but older now, Will thought. Much older.

18

A Special Grief

The man waiting on the asphalted slope in front of the post office was in his late twenties and wore no shoes at all. Only about five-two, weighing no more than one-hundred-twenty pounds, he had on faded khaki pants, an undershirt that would never be white again, and a knitted red and yellow stocking cap.

Tossing some gear into the back of the Land Rover, he climbed in and said almost nothing until, in Gourie Forest, they reached a picnic area and he ordered Will to stop.

Just ahead, the forest road disappeared to the right among tall pines. A path angled off to the left; another went straight on. At the point where the paths began stood a hexagonal open shelter with a concrete floor and a shingled roof, apparently a place for visitors to escape an unexpected rain or cook a meal.

Donning a proffered hard hat and following their guide down a sloping track to the cave entrance, Will found himself confronted by manmade stone steps leading down into darkness.

"The Forestry Department built these," Waldon McKoy explained, "because getting down into the cave was too dangerous. You could slip and break your neck." Handing out flashlights from his knapsack, he went carefully down the curving steps and waited for Ken and Will to reach him, then aimed his beam to the right where it revealed a boulder-choked stream some eight feet wide emerging from under a low roof of rock.

"That's the way the picnickers go, but they don't go in very far—just under the ceiling there and on to another entrance about fifteen minutes from here, where they climb out and say they've explored Gourie. Beyond that other entrance, though, there's a narrow passage that leads to a whole spiderweb of tunnels on two levels. Upper Gourie, it's called. The rest of the cave is to our left here."

As he turned, his light revealed a low-ceilinged tunnel into which the stream abruptly vanished after its journey through the roofless chamber in which they stood. "We have to climb over that big rock there. Then it gets pretty nasty, with a whole series of cascades and pools. There's a drop where you need a rope ladder, and a place where you have to crawl through a long, muddy sump."

He paused, eyeing them. *"Crawl,* I said, not wade, because there isn't always room to stand up. At the end of the sump you have to squeeze under a low-hanging roof with only a couple of inches of air space when the water's low, none at all when it's high. We used to think the cave ended there."

"It doesn't?" Ken asked, looking none too happy.

"No, it goes on and gets worse. This is one of the longest caves in the island, and if it rains hard outside while you're in here, this stream can rise up without warning and trap you." Again he paused to peer at their faces. "The known part of Gourie is almost three miles long. Only God knows how much more there is of it."

Will said, "If you had to hide a body in here, would you take it upstream or down?"

"Upstream." McKoy pointed to the right. "And I'll

tell you why. To get far enough downstream to hide anything like a body, you'd have to go beyond the place where the roof is so low. I don't think anyone in his right mind would try that, when this way would serve the purpose just as well. Nobody ever goes upstream past the other entrance I told you about. A body could be in there for years and never be discovered."

"Ken, what do you think?"

"He's the expert, not me. I'm scared right here."

"Let's go, then, McKoy. If we don't find anything upstream, we can always turn around."

With a nod, their guide stepped into the stream and led them into a cold, damp darkness where the only sound was the whisper of flowing water. Trailing him, with Ken Daniels bringing up the rear, Will shivered with more than the cold as the water splashed about his ankles and filled his shoes.

They wormed their way under the low-hanging roof into a broad passage where rock pillars loomed like stone spectres silently on guard. Twenty minutes later, after halting to play their flashlight beams into potential hiding places, they passed the exit used by picnickers, and the easy part of Upper Gourie was behind them.

A narrow slot to the left now led them into total darkness again, and McKoy said warningly, "We better go slow here. If anyone carried or dragged a body this far, they might have just dumped it and hoped nobody would come here with a light bright enough to discover it." He looked back. "You fellows okay?"

A few yards behind him, Will nodded and said, "We're all right. Keep going." Behind him, Ken Daniels merely grunted.

They trudged on. Will was wet to the knees now and shivering. A little awed, too, by the stillness that amplified even the smallest sound as they advanced. You kicked a stone and the echoes scurried like lizards along the walls of the tunnel. You spoke, and a choir of voices picked up the words, running them together and making them incomprehensible unless you had spoken slowly.

And although they had left the stream behind them at the last exit, where it flowed into the cave for its long run underground, there was everywhere a ghostly sound of dripping water, as though the dark walls eternally wept.

McKoy stopped. The long, narrow beam of his five-cell flashlight had fastened on a side passage ahead. "From here we have to be careful," he said. "Small tunnels go every which way, even up and down. Stay close to me, please. You could get lost and maybe not find your way back out." He turned along the side tube. "This goes to a big chamber with lots of hiding places. We should search it first, I think."

A wild-goose chase, Will thought. Even if the U.N. man had been lured from the Christiana market to his death, what killers in their right minds would have gone to the prodigious effort of concealing him in a place like this?

Still, maybe they had killed him *after* leading him here on some pretext he had believed plausible.

He plodded on, following the light ahead and the five-foot-two figure silhouetted against it. His own shadow jerked over the uneven floor ahead of him, created by the light in Ken Daniels's hand. The ceiling rose and fell. The walls dripped. The flight of stone steps by which they had descended into this underworld seemed far behind now.

McKoy halted. On reaching him, Will and Ken did too, and their combined lights slowly probed a nearly circular chamber some sixty feet across. "I don't think I'd go beyond this room if I had a body to hide," McKoy said. "Suppose I take the right hand wall and you fellows the left, and we meet where the passage continues over there on the other side."

"All right," Will said.

"Look in every cranny."

And hope to God, Will thought, we don't find what we're looking for. Yet it would be a relief, in a way, to find Cerrado, for by now he must be dead somewhere. If Sister Merle had engineered his disappearance from the market, why would she want to keep him alive? The one hope was that she had not wanted to kill Sam Norman too. He had merely blundered into her world in his attempt to help Cerrado, and so just might still be alive.

With the wall on his left and Ken at his heels, Will led the way forward, moving very slowly and shining his light into every crevice. The room had its share of those, some deep enough to be mistaken for tunnels. On the other side of it McKoy kept pace, his light moving over the wall there like a brush in the hands of a careful painter. The scuffing of two pairs of shoes and McKoy's hardsoled bare feet filled the chamber with a sound that seemed unreal and somehow threatening.

"Hold it." The voice was McKoy's, not loud but sharp. Turning toward it, Will saw that the guide had stopped and was holding his light steady. Its beam slanted downward at what looked like a dark vertical streak on the chamber wall. "Found something!"

Followed by Ken, Will hurried across the room and saw that the dark streak was a niche some twenty feet high and twelve feet deep, ranging from a yard in width at its base to mere inches at the top.

In it, on his back and with his feet toward them, lay a man wearing a khaki shirt, khaki pants and socks, but no belt and no shoes. His head was deep in the niche and twisted sideways, so that their lights could not reach his face. His knees were upthrust, as though he had been placed on the floor and pushed in by his feet.

"This is the man we are looking for?" McKoy asked, frowning at Will.

"I've never met Cerrado. Is it, Ken?"

"I think so. Let me pull him out."

"Maybe the police would not want us to touch him," McKoy warned.

"Well, then . . ." Ken dropped to hands and knees and gingerly worked his way into the niche to shine his light on the man's face. "Yes, it's Cerrado. Dead for days, I'd say." He suddenly voiced a sound of fright that came loudly from the niche and struck echoes from the walls of the main chamber.

"What is it?" Will asked quickly.

"I thought he moved. It was a beetle crawling out of his shirt front."

"Can you see how he was killed, Ken?"

Still on hands and knees, Ken played his light over the body, letting it rest finally on the dead man's neck. "He was chopped once on the neck, deep—with a machete, it looks like. And from behind. There's no blood on the floor here, so it must have happened elsewhere. His clothes are torn, as if he was dragged through the cave instead of carried through. Dragged some of the way, at least. Should I turn him over?"

"No. As McKoy says, the police may not want him moved. And the sooner we get to the police, the better. Let's go."

Ken crawled back out and stood up. "Should we look further for Mr. Norman?"

"Well—the rest of this chamber, maybe. It seems to me if they thought it a good place to hide Cerrado, they might have hidden Sam here too." But I don't want to believe Sam is dead, Will thought. I *won't* believe he is, damn it!

The searched the rest of the room and found nothing. Returning through the cave to the flight of steps by which they had entered it, they hurried back to the Land Rover.

"McKoy, you'd better come with us to the police," Will said as he drove out of Gourie Forest. "You'll have to guide them to the body."

"Add that to what *you* pay me," their guide said unhappily. "I'll get nothing from them for doing it, you can be sure."

"Of course."

At the Christiana station the police listened attentively to what Will told them, and asked questions. When told that Sister Merle's follower, Keith Mowatt, was apparently under an obeah spell, they demonstrated even deeper interest.

"Will you now question the two men Ken saw coming out of Gourie the day Cerrado disappeared?" Will pressed.

They agreed to do so.

"Let me make a suggestion, then. It might be wise to talk to them in such a way that Sister Merle won't hear about it. Otherwise you may have two more men in the hospital for no apparent reason."

A slender corporal in red-striped pants gazed at him with obvious curiosity. "You believe in obeah, Mr. Platt?"

"I can't answer that. I don't know enough about it."

"You seem to believe. I thought you Americans looked upon us as superstitious Africans for believing in such things."

Will studied the handsome young face and thought he detected a touch of the racism that prompted some Jamaicans to snarl at white-skinned visitors. "I'm an old Haiti hand, friend," he said quietly, "and have written books about voodoo. I happen to have a healthy respect for some of the so-called superstitions of Africa."

It could well have been this brief exchange that brought about a shift of attitude there in the police station. Something, at any rate, seemed to rid the room of its hostility. "We will go to Gourie and get Cerrado's body," the man in charge said. "You can take us to where it is, McKoy. Then tonight, when there will be less chance of our being seen, we will pick up Bignall and Walters and bring them in for questioning."

He gazed at Will with new respect. "I commend you for finding the body, Mr. Platt."

"Commend McKoy. But thanks."

"We'll keep in touch with you."

"And please keep looking for Sam Norman."

"Of course."

Leaving McKoy at the station, Will and Ken returned to the house. It was quarter to one. Vicky had apparently not returned from town, and Ima was in the kitchen where they could hear her bustling about when they came in.

"Stay for lunch," Will urged the taximan. "My wife is enjoying the mob scene in the market, I'm sure."

"Thanks."

"Don't thank me." Will glanced toward the kitchen. "I need help, Ken."

"Help?"

"Someone has to tell Ima about Juan Cerrado. She was fond of him. Perhaps sleeping with him."

Ken smiled. "Fond of him, yes. Sleeping, no."

"How do you know?"

"I have been trying to take that woman to bed for at least two years."

"That doesn't mean *he* didn't succeed."

Just then Ima came out of the kitchen. She looked from one to the other, reading their faces, and then asked, almost hesitantly, "Did you find anything in Gourie Cave, please?"

Will looked at Ken, who gazed at Ima's anxious face and said, "Ima, I'm sorry. I don't want to tell you this, but I have to. He is dead."

She stared back at him, her face expressionless. "Dead? Juan is *dead?*"

"Yes, Ima. Murdered."

Her tall, slender body began to sway from side to side like a clock's pendulum. Her hands trembled to her face and covered it. Through her long fingers poured a bawling like that of a wounded calf, filling the room, the whole house. She fled into the kitchen.

Ten minutes passed before her torrent of grief began to subside, and then another five went by before she stopped sobbing. Finally she came from the kitchen to confront them.

She stood quietly, her face now empty of expression and her long arms at her sides. "Who killed him?" she asked in a controlled voice. "The obeah woman, Sister Merle?"

Will said, "We think she arranged it, Ima. We have no proof yet."

"When you find proof, will you let me know?"

"Of course."

"Thank you. Lunch is ready now."

I wonder, Will thought at the table, *if any woman on the face of this earth will ever grieve like that on hearing I am dead. You were a fortunate man, Cerrado. I envy you.*

19

Trapped

Vicky, he soon learned, was doing more than exploring Christiana on her daily tours of the town. "I hear you've been asking about Sister Merle," he said to her at breakfast, five days after her arrival on the island.

"Meaning I shouldn't? Who told you?"

"Ken."

"Oh, your buddy. And how did he find out?"

"You questioned some of the taximen. They all know one another." He frowned at her across his uplifted fork, on which a peg of breadfruit was impaled. "What do you want with Sister Merle, Vicky?"

"I told you before. I'd like to meet her."

"My God."

"What do you mean, 'My God'?"

"That woman is almost certainly responsible for the death of Juan Cerrado." He had told her about finding the body in the cave. "And she's probably responsible for the condition of that fellow Mowatt, in the hospital."

Mowatt, at last report, was in a coma. Will had driven to nearby Spaldings to inquire about him and had talked to two doctors at the excellent little hospital there. So far their tests had failed to turn up anything to explain his condition.

"There's something else, Vicky."

Her reluctant gaze conveyed indifference, but she did look at him.

"Something I haven't told you. Saturday night, after we found Cerrado, the Christiana police arrested the two men who were seen driving out of Gourie Forest the day he disappeared. The police picked them up at night so the arrest wouldn't be noticed and Sister Merle wouldn't hear about it, because these are the men we think actually murdered Cerrado, at Merle's bidding."

Vicky was apparently more interested now. She stopped eating and sat motionless, watching his face as he spoke.

"The plan went wrong," he said. "The got Bignall quietly enough; he lives alone back in the bush. But when they went for Walters, he had a woman with him, and apparently she went straight to Sister Merle to report his arrest."

Vicky continued to stare at him.

"Now," Will continued, "Bignall and Walters are in the lockup, and they seem to have embarked on the same dark journey that took Mowatt from the Wait-a-Bit jail to the hospital. They won't eat or talk, just sit there gazing into space."

"Interesting."

"Don't call on Sister Merle, Vicky."

"But she sounds fascinating."

"Don't do it. This isn't voodoo, with drumming and dancing and lovely exotic ceremonies. It's dangerous."

"Margal," she said.

"Yes. The kind of dirty business Margal practiced. A dark magic involving mind control."

"But I'd like to know more about mind control. It's a coming thing, really big in Russia. Haven't you heard?" She actually smiled at him. "And you need all the help you can get, it seems to me. *You* don't seem able to find out what's happened to Sam Norman."

It was true. While the police had searched the rest of Upper Gourie, Ken and he had doggedly continued their questioning of anyone who would stand still long enough to be interrogated. There was scarcely a road within fifty miles of Christiana, paved or otherwise, that did not know the tread of the Land Rover's tires. And they had learned nothing. Absolutely nothing.

Finishing his breadfruit, which Ima had roasted over charcoal the day before and simply fried in butter this morning, Will stood up.

"Where to this morning?" his wife asked.

"Gourie again."

"You're going back to the cave?"

He shrugged. After days of getting nowhere in their search for Sam, Ken Daniels last night had suggested they employ Waldon McKoy again, this time to guide them into the part of Gourie not yet explored. "We can't drive around forever asking questions," the taximan had said, "and it's all but certain Bignall and Walters won't talk, any more than Keith Mowatt would."

Will said to Vicky, "Don't think I'm overjoyed at the prospect. But we're at a dead end."

"What time will you be back?"

"God knows. But please—don't try to visit Sister Merle."

She did not reply. A car had stopped at the gate outside, and she stood up without bothering to finish her breakfast. "That will be your friend now," she said. "Do me a favor and tell him to stop spying on me. I don't appreciate it."

Disappearing into the bedroom, she slammed the door behind her.

Will had already opened the gate in anticipation of Ken's arrival. He went to the front door now and watched the battered old Austin Cambridge roll into the yard. The taximan made several trips from his car to the Land Rover with caving gear—much more of it than they had carried before, Will noted with dismay. Then he called out, "Ready, Will?"

"Have you had breakfast?"

"Hours ago."

"One minute, then." Will turned and walked back through the living room to the bedroom. Vicky was seated by a window, silently gazing out at the road.

"I'm gone, Vicky." He was beginning to talk like a Jamaican, he thought with a welcome touch of amusement. In Haiti, his excellent French had quickly been corrupted by Creole the same way.

"Good luck," she said coldly.

"Please. Don't go to see Sister Merle. You could make everything more difficult. Even more dangerous."

She did not even turn her head to look at him. Knowing he was wasting his time, he angrily walked out.

Ken Daniels was waiting for him at the Land Rover, and when they reached the gate, Ima Williams was there to close it. She too called out "Good luck!" but with far more sincerity than Vicky had. Will thanked her with a wave.

"We are to pick up McKoy at his house this time," Ken said. "It's on our way."

"I suppose he thinks we're crazy to be doing this."

"Well, yes, in a way. If you remember, he said before that he didn't think anyone would try to carry a body into the lower cave." The taximan fell silent while Will steered the bulky vehicle between double files of children en route to school: boys in khaki, girls in yellow and brown. Then he said, "I've got a rope ladder. You remember he said there's a place where we'll need one to reach a lower level."

"Ken, they wouldn't have carried Sam Norman's body down any rope ladder."

The taximan swiveled on the seat to scowl at him—a long, intense scowl that to Will was most eloquent. It said, he was certain, that Ken Daniels was now a close friend and just as concerned about the fate of Sam Norman as he himself was. True, Ken was being paid for his help, but this was not a man who would stick so close and work so hard for money alone.

"Will, he could have gone down a ladder under his own power if they told him he might find something down there," the bearded man said. "He was looking for Mr. Cerrado, remember. They could have lured him deep into the cave, even down a ladder, and then killed him. Or—"

Will said through dry lips, "Or what?"

"Or pulled the ladder up and just left him there alone in the dark, to die. I hate to say it, but that would have been easier."

Will could not think of an answer.

A mile beyond the town their McKoy was waiting at the road's edge in front of a small cottage. Barefoot again, he wore ragged khaki pants and shirt, and from one hand dangled a well stuffed knapsack.

With a polite "Good morning" he climbed into the back of the vehicle, then was silent until the Land Rover had growled its way through the pinetree whisperings of Gourie Forest to the cave entrance.

"We will be here longer this time, I think," he said then, dropping to the ground. "I brought along some bammies in case we get hungry in there. You eat our Jamaican bammies, Mr. Platt?"

Will recalled a time he had bitten into a flinty round biscuit and nearly shattered a tooth. Were all bammies like that? "If I have to," he said grudgingly.

McKoy grinned, then divided up the gear and handed out the hard hats. This time at the bottom of the stone steps he turned left and led a difficult climb over the slanting rockface there. Will followed, and again Ken Daniels brought up the rear.

We're wasting our time, Will thought dourly, unless Ken is right and Sam was lured into doing this under his own power.

As he struggled on, the feeling became stronger. No

one could possibly have carried or even dragged a body through this labyrinth. Floating one would have been easier. A glimmer of daylight on the left caused their guide to say quietly, "Another entrance. Small one. After this there is no way out."

Will peered long and hard at the light as they passed it, and turned to look back as it fell behind. Then the darkness engulfed them again.

The stream seemed higher and swifter than it had been in the upper part of the cave. Was that normal, or had the rains of the past couple of days increased its speed and volume? At times it filled the tunnel and made wading necessary; then the cold climbed Will's legs and seemed to reach the pit of his stomach.

Adding to the chill was the thought that Sam Norman could have stumbled through here before him, en route to an execution.

He trudged on behind McKoy, who now was a silent, plodding shape silhouetted against the wavering glow of his light. The walls and roof of the cavern seemed spotted with fungus—which turned out to be bats. Those awakened by the lights released their hold and went whirring and squeaking past in search of new darkness.

Why, he wondered, was there no guano underfoot? Did the stream rise often enough to keep it from accumulating?

The stream now had become a series of deep-looking pools connected by noisy cascades, getting around which involved clinging to any handy outcrop of rock. Clawing his way along just above the rush of water, peering down into it when his light happened to touch its swift, swirling motion, Will felt trapped and frightened.

When he'd explored this kind of underworld in Haiti with Sam, he had felt no fear, he recalled, only an intense exhilaration which made any ordeal a grand adventure. This was different. This cavern was a haunted place in which every forward step seemed more perilous than the last.

Ahead, McKoy had stopped and was shining his light back to help Will cross a shelf of rock covered with a skin of swift water. Both their lights aided Ken Daniels over the danger. The darkness ahead was filled with a thunder of sound.

To be heard above the roar, McKoy said in a loud voice, "We will need the ladder now if you think we ought to go on. Look." Turning, he aimed his light ahead.

Its glow, far less brilliant than the carbide glare such dungeon darkness called for, revealed the lip of a cascade noisier than any of those behind them. "It falls about thirty feet straight down, but we can belay to that outcrop there," he yelled, pointing to a ledge on their left at the brink of the drop. "What do you say?"

They went forward to the edge, where Ken Daniels peered into the noisy depths and shuddered. Will, too, leaned forward to look down.

Far below, the stream crashed into a boulder-strewn pool and then sped out of sight into darkness.

Will had a mental picture of Sam Norman sliding down a rope here, and of those above snatching the rope from his grasp after he reached the bottom. As the picture developed more sharply, he saw Sam standing abandoned at the foot of the fall, helplessly gazing up, knowing he was doomed to wander alone in darkness until he died.

"Well, Mr. Platt?" McKoy said.

"He may be down there. Let's go."

"Even if he is there, can he possibly be still alive?"

Five days, Will thought. Or was it six? But—and he said it aloud—"Sam may not have been brought here the day he disappeared. We don't know. And even if he had no food, he'd have had water. Let me go down there alone and see what I find. You two wait here."

"What can you find?" McKoy protested. "Mr. Platt, that passage leads down to a deep, muddy pool, very nasty, very dangerous. To go beyond it you will have to crawl under a low ceiling with your head under water. After that—"

"If they brought him here to kill him, it isn't likely they went beyond this drop. There'd be no need."

"Then what—"

"I know Sam. If they tricked him into going down a rope here, or forced him to and abandoned him, you can be sure he left a message of some sort, even if they stripped him naked and he had to scratch it on the wall with a stone." Will reached for the rope ladder hanging from the guide's shoulder. "Come on, let's get this into place."

It seemed safe enough when McKoy finished rigging it. It was long enough, too. Will winced a little when first trusting it with his weight, but the thin yellow nylon rope was strong.

Slowly he descended, with his feet feeling for the rungs and his flashlight jammed into his pocket. Over his head Daniels and McKoy lay on the lip of the drop, aiming the beams of their lights into the depths.

The sound of the waterfall became a deafening thunder. The mist rising to engulf him sparkled in the light-beams. The ladder became wet and slippery, spoiling his rhythm; then it began to sway from side to side over the rock face until, at the end of each swing toward the cascade, he felt the torrent trying to tear his left hand loose.

Hang on, Platt. You can do this.

It seemed to take forever but his feet at last touched solid rock and the pendulum stopped swinging. With a grunt of relief he released the ladder and stepped away from it—onto a smooth, spray-slick slope that whipped his right foot from under him and sent him plunging into the stream.

Above, either Ken or the guide yelled at him to be careful, and he was a little surprised that he could even hear the yell above the fall's thunder. Struggling to his feet after the swift current had swept him downstream a few yards, he regained the bank and frantically tried his flashlight.

It still functioned, thank God.

He made his way back along the stream's edge to the foot of the cascade and looked up. The men above called to him—this time he could not make out the words—and he waved to tell them he was all right. As he began his search for a message, their lights played around him, seeking to aid him.

There was no scrap of paper with words on it. Nothing scratched on the cavern wall. And it had to be on this side if it existed at all; a man marooned here would never have tried wading through the torrent to reach the wall on the other side, where he would have had to stand in water, in any case, to scratch a message.

Nothing. He repeated the search, going as far as fifty feet downstream from the cascade. Nothing at all. Of course, Sam might have tried to find a way out. Might have gone on downstream in search of another entrance, not knowing there were no others.

Will returned to the cascade and signaled the men above with his light. "I'm going downstream!" The yell seemed loud enough to him despite the water's roar, but Ken Daniels shouted back, "What?"

"I am going downstream to look for him!"

"Be very careful!" McKoy warned. "Watch the sump!"

It was different, plunging into that unknown darkness alone. He hadn't realized how much the company of Ken and McKoy had meant to him before. The thunder of the waterfall became fainter and fainter behind him as he picked his way through descending twists and turns of tunnel with the stream gurgling along beside him.

His light, of course, kept sweeping the cavern floor for

the message he sought but hoped not to find. Or—worse
—for the body of a trapped man who in the end might
simply have collapsed from exhaustion and died here.

A sharply descending section of roof caused him to
stop and kneel; he played his light ahead through an
opening barely four feet high to see what he might be
getting into. The tube was only a few yards long; then
the roof sloped up again. But the probing light did
something to a vast black stain on the walls beyond.

The stain suddenly detached itself and hurtled down
to pour through the tunnel, a hurricane flutter of wings
and a mad symphony of squeakings accompanying it.
As it reached him, he hit the cave floor and covered his
face with his hands, gasping for breath in momentary
panic.

Then it was past him and he rose again, trembling
from head to foot, and watched the bats until they vanished beyond the reach of his light. Shaking his head, he
went on.

And came to the barrier McKoy had warned about.

A sump, he had called it. A deep, muddy pool which
in this case filled the passage from wall to wall. No way
around it; you had to go through. He shone his light
ahead and could not see the end of the dark water,
though the light was an excellent instrument with a long
beam. Well, if he had to wade . . .

But it was not simply wading. It was trying to keep
himself erect on an invisible carpet of mud that would
not stay still. For the first few yards the water deepened
as he expected, rising slowly to his waist. No problem
unless it rose too high. Then the floor played tricks.

His feet, moving ever so slowly because he sensed the
risk, encountered hidden holes that sent him lurching off
balance, ledges that turned an ankle when a foot came
down on the edge of them. And still the sump continued.

Then, ahead, the roof of the passage sloped down into
the water and he recalled McKoy's warning that he

would have to crawl through a low spot with his head submerged.

Would Sam Norman have tried to do such a thing, not even knowing it could be done? No. Never. Any man who had not been told otherwise would have to believe the cave ended here. Those who had continued past this point had been dedicated spelunkers with special equipment.

There was no point in trying to go farther. Sam was not here. Had probably never been here.

He turned and started the slow, dangerous return journey through the sump, wishing he had eyes on his feet to detect the booby traps in the mud. Then he heard something he had not heard before in this eerie place—a snarl of swift water in the near distance.

Halting, he played the flashlight's beam along the gliding surface of the pool. Nothing. The water scarcely moved. But the sound was there beyond reach of the beam. Louder now.

Frightened, he pushed on again, this time too fast. The booby traps were waiting. A turned ankle brought a gasp of pain from his lips as he staggered off balance and barely caught himself.

Platt, for God's sake take it easy! This is a long pool. You have to wade it, not run it. And that sound could be something that was there before. You just didn't hear it.

But the sound was louder. Water growling, snarling, hissing like snakes in a pit.

He stumbled on, holding his flashlight at arm's length to gain the last few inches of its range. Ten steps, twenty, thirty, his feet feeling their way through the pool-bottom carpet of thick mud. Then his light reached the end of the sump and he saw what was happening.

Waldon McKoy's words exploded like thunder in his head. "If it rains hard outside while you're in here, this stream can rise without warning and trap you."

Caution be damned now! Sucking in a breath, Will

threw himself forward. His legs worked like pistons, arms flailing the air to help him maintain balance. Long before reaching the place where he could pull himself from the pool onto the open floor, he felt the rush of water against him, as if alive, trying to force him back. It caused him to stumble the last few steps with his arms outflung and body pitched forward. When he emerged from the sump he was all but horizontal, crawling up the stone slope to a place where the stream could not reach him.

But the stream was rising. He could see it creeping up the sloping floor, boiling over small boulders and climbing the sides of big ones. He could not stay here!

The sound of racing water filled the passage now. He pushed on through it, afraid to run, but moving as fast as he dared. How high the water would rise would depend on the varying width of the passage. But this was a river cave. The passage was nowhere wide enough to spread a swollen stream out and pull its fangs.

And he had seen Jamaican rains. He had seen five, six inches of rain fall in an hour to wash out substantial bridges and bring the island's earth slithering down mountainsides to bury country roads under tons of mud. At the thought of what a daylong rain might do to the stream now threatening him, he felt ice in his blood.

But he was making progress. Despite the danger underfoot, he had reached the place where the roof dipped low and his light had dislodged the barrage of bats. If he could just get past the dip to the stretch of wider passage beyond. . . .

He could not.

Swift, thundering water filled the entire opening now, boiling out at him as though the tube were an overfilled storm sewer. He knew it was only a few yards in length, but to crawl into it would be suicidal. He would not be able to travel a yard before being battered senseless and hurled back again to drown.

Approaching to within ten feet of the tube, he stared at it with a feeling first of shock, then of helplessness. And then of terror, for the water hurtling toward him increased in strength and volume even as he watched it.

He had stopped on a ledge wet only by spray. Now before he could step to a higher perch, the water leaped at him like a living thing and swirled about his shoes.

How high would it climb? To the ceiling?

He looked about him in near panic. The river filled half the passage here, leaving only four yards or so of sloping floor not yet inundated. The roof was a thing of dips and domes, in some places no more than eight feet above his head.

Wading through white water at the edge of the rioting stream, he battled toward a part of the floor that rose steeply through a nightmare of boulders to the highest section of ceiling. Doggedly he climbed until exhaustion stopped him.

Still only half way to the top he reached a formation that could have passed for a saddle on a stone horse, and sank onto it. Sore, winded, numb with terror, he knew he would have to rest before continuing the struggle.

Relentlessly the water pursued him.

20

The Gèdés

For the third time since learning her beloved Juan Cerrado was dead, Ima Williams stood in her nightgown, beside her bed, determined to avenge him. The hour was eleven P.M. and the door of her room was closed. Though Mr. Will's wife was in the house, she anticipated no intrusion.

On the dresser to her right were an aluminum pie plate filled with flour, a box of white candles, and a crudely made earthenware jar.

The jar was a govi from the altar of a voodoo hounfor in which she had served in Haiti, and had been a parting gift from her people when she left twelve years before. About ten inches high, it had an earthenware lid with a small knob in its center for a handle.

One side of the jar bore blotches of white paint on a field of black. The other bore similar daubs of black on white. In an inch-wide band around the middle were assorted voodoo symbols: X's, a cross, horizontal bars with a vertical stripe through them.

This particular govi held the spirit of Gèdé Nimbo, the god of death and a son of Manman Brigitte, to whom Ima now addressed herself.

A certain ritual had to be followed. First she crossed

herself by touching her right hand to her forehead, then to her breast, then to her shoulders. Next, taking the plate from the dresser, she proceeded to dribble the flour through her fingers onto the polished mahogany floor drawing a design similar to the one on the jar: a vèvè of the god of death, a magic symbol that would insure his presence and his attention.

When the design was finished, she gently blew some of the flour from her fingertips to the four points of the compass before returning the plate to the dresser.

Now from the dresser she took the govi and placed it on the floor in the center of the vèvè, where she ringed it with lighted candles set upright in small puddles of their own soft wax. Falling to her knees, she pressed her lips to the decorated floor as a gesture of respect. Then, rising, she turned to the bed.

On the bed was a bowl-shaped iron cook pot of the kind used by most peasant families. Its contents had taken her most of her spare time that day to collect. It held lime juice and oil pressed from castor beans, and scrapings of soot from a kerosene lamp, and—the really difficult ingredient—parts of the gall bladder of a bull, for which she had had to take a taxi to the village of Mollison to visit a butcher she knew.

Now she lifted the iron pot from the bed and placed it on the flour drawing, next to the painted jar.

Only one family of loa would be interested in such an offering. It was for the Gèdés. Not just for Gèdé Nimbo this time, but for all of them: L'Oraille of the thunder, Zeklai of the lightning, and the more than thirty others in the family of death.

At last, with the ritual completed and everything in place, Ima reached to the bed for her cocomacaque stick and, facing the design on the floor, held the stick out in front of her at arm's length.

"Manman Grande Brigitte, come and help me!" she cried out in a voice that filled the room. "I have made a vèvè for your son Papa Gèdé and would make one for you too if I knew how. But I am only a simple hounsi, ignorant in some things, and you must not expect too much of me. Manman, listen to me, I beg you. The man I love is dead, murdered by that evil witch, Sister Merle. He must be avenged!"

She paused, and the room filled with stillness except for the sputtering of one of the white candles. Fixing her gaze on the govi, she waited for it to move. And it did, though perhaps only because in leaning forward she shifted her weight on the floor and caused a loose board to quiver.

"Take this, Manman!" she cried then, kneeling suddenly to slap the cocomacaque down in front of the jar. "Maîtress Erzulie herself has blessed it for me! Take it and destroy that horrible woman, I beg you!"

She rose. The candles flickered and the room was alive with their soft, shifting glow. The govi had stopped moving. With her hands at her sides, Ima awaited a reply.

Suddenly her hands clenched and an expression of agony changed the shape of her face. She cried out in a strangled voice for help. With the heels of her hands pressed fiercely against her eyes and her fingers gouging her forehead, she staggered back against the bed.

She began to tremble. Then to writhe. Then to moan. And her bare feet beat a tattoo against the mahogany footboard of the bed in a way that must have filled them with pain.

For two or three minutes she struggled bravely to fight off the force that assailed her, but it would not be denied. Gradually her resistance weakened until her struggles ceased.

The door opened then. Into the room came Will Platt's wife, in *her* nightgown. Skirting the vèvè and voodoo paraphernalia on the floor, she silently approached the bed and looked down at the unconscious woman lying there.

For a long time she merely gazed at Ima in silence. Then with just the ghost of a sneer she said quietly, "Now you know which of you is more powerful, don't you? Foolish little creature, didn't you know I would warn Sister Merle that something like this would happen? And that the two of us, working together, would be able to stop you?"

Receiving no answer, she turned away—pausing on her way to the door to blow out the white candles.

21

"I Left Her Sleeping"

I'm going to die here in Gourie Cave, Will thought. *The water will continue to rise until it fills the passage, and I'll drown up here with my mouth pressed against the ceiling for one last breath.*

He could accept the prospect now without panic. There had been so much time for him to study the situation and weigh his chances. How much time? He lifted his wrist to look at his watch again. Its glowing hands stood at ten minutes to eleven.

At night.

It could not be as dark outside as it was in here, though. There would be stars unless the rain that had caused the flash flood in the cave was still falling. The air would be fresh. There would be blessed silence, or at least only a whispering of tall pines, instead of the everlasting suck and gurgle of the stream here.

He switched on his flashlight to look down at the water for a moment. Only for a moment. Hours ago he had realized that if the water did go down in time for him to continue upstream, the light represented his only hope of ever reaching the ladder.

He must save the batteries as much as possible. The instrument was a good one, though, or it would not be

180

working as well as it did after its dunking earlier. His watch, too, had been submerged but was still running. His luck was not all bad.

Were Ken Daniels and Waldon McKoy still waiting for him at the top of the ladder?

The water was only inches below his perch now, and the ledge on which he sat was the nearest he had been able to get to the ceiling. He could reach the ceiling with his hands. If he stood up, he would knock his head against it. How many hours had he been waiting here while the water relentlessly climbed to drown him? His aching body, numb with cold, thought it a lifetime.

But something different seemed to be happening to the water now?

He held the light on it longer than he wanted to, to be sure his eyes were not playing tricks. Just below his dangling left foot began a smooth stone slope that had twice thwarted his efforts to reach the ledge on which he sat. The water climbing the slope was only a few inches below the sole of his shoe, and for hours he had been able to judge the speed of its climb by watching it rise past selected points of reference. Now he was seeing a thin dark line of dampness *above* it, like wetness on a beach as the tide ebbed.

The water was receding! It had come so close to reaching his foot and starting its deadly climb up his body, and now it was retreating!

He had never been that close to death before, and stepping back from the threshold was a wholly new experience, even if he could not be certain yet that he had been saved. His emotions broke from control and ran riot.

First came noisy elation as he voiced premature yells of triumph that rang through the cavern like gunshots, creating a babel of echoes. "I'm going to get out of here! I'm going to live! I'll make it!" Then he took an interest in the near paralysis of his body and began to massage as much of his legs as he could reach without danger of losing balance. He would need all the strength and agility he could restore when the time came for him to attempt his escape. While massaging, he prayed silently for patience, for wisdom, for luck.

Then came the fear. Fear that when the water at last dropped enough for him to struggle upstream under the low roof of rock that had stopped him before, he might reach the ladder and find it gone. How could it still be there, dangling from a mere outcrop of stone, when the stream at the brink of the drop would have widened into a fury and engulfed it, almost certainly tearing it loose?

Don't think about that, Platt. Concentrate on getting your legs in shape, on watching the water go down, on being ready when the chance comes.

He used the flashlight sparingly, to conserve its already weak batteries. Timing himself with his watch, he thumbed the switch only at thirty-minute intervals and kept the light on only long enough to be sure the water was still receding. The process became an exercise in discipline. After a while he forced himself to wait thirty-five minutes, then forty.

Thus the time passed and the stream descended to its original channel. The opening under the low-hanging stretch of ceiling became visible again, though from his perch high up on the passage wall he could barely reach it with the beam of his flash and for a while was not quite sure. Then as the sound of the stream's flow decreased in volume, its level fell more swiftly. The time was right for him to make his bid for freedom.

He quit his perch and picked his way with infinite care down the boulder-packed slope to the water's edge, as much concerned for the safety of his precious flashlight as for his own. The light had to be left on now, and the weakness of its beam alarmed him. Could he make it last? As he approached the tube that led to the wider, safer passage above, the glow dimmed even more and he plunged ahead almost at a run.

He stumbled into the water now, first knee deep, then waist deep in order to clear the arch above. The current was still stronger than he had anticipated. Water growled against his thighs, hurling him back. Aghast, he saw that he had only a few inches of breathing space ahead where the roof dipped jaggedly down to stop him.

He filled his lungs with the cave's cold air and ducked under, holding his flashlight against the ceiling to keep it dry. Stumbling on a few steps, he surfaced again to find the danger behind and relief driving him on with new strength. Another five minutes of determinedly battling the current, and he was clear of the tube altogether, staggering up out of the stream onto the cavern floor.

Moments later he heard faintly the sound of the waterfall ahead, a sound that grew louder with his every step until it filled the cavern. And suddenly, as he rounded a bend in the passage, the beam of his failing flashlight showed him the cascade itself, more powerful now, arching far out into space before plunging down into the pool—an awsome sight in this underground world.

But he spent no time or light on it. Both his gaze and the dimming beam passed swiftly to the vertical wall of stone where the ladder should be.

There was no ladder now.

"Oh God," he heard himself say, and staggered two steps toward the blank wall and sank exhausted to his knees.

"Will! Up here!"

The roar of the waterfall muffled the voice but he recognized it. Ken Daniels. Still dazed, he looked up and saw a round yellow eye at the top of the cliff owlishly returning his gaze.

"Will, are you okay?"

Reeling with weariness, he struggled to rise from his knees and finally succeeded. "Yes, I'm okay. But the ladder—"

"It's gone. We have a rope."

Rope, rope, rope the echoes repeated, bouncing the beautiful word back and forth as it penetrated his anguish. Not even the thunder of the cascade could rob him of it. And then, "Here!" Ken yelled, and a long, thin, yellow snake uncoiled down the face of the rock.

Will stumbled forward to grasp it.

"Tie it under your arms to leave your hands free!" Ken yelled down at him, spacing the words so the echoes would not run them together. "Give us all the help you can."

He was no expert with knots, but the one he fashioned against his chest after looping the rope around his body would not come undone. He was sure of that. They tested it from above, found it good, and began with infinite care to draw him up the cliff face.

His fingers clawed the wall to add lift. The toes of his sodden shoes sought nooks and crannies from which to push. His flashlight was in his pocket again. The only light was the owl's eye—from a flashlight apparently wedged in a crevice now—peering down at him and seeming to grow a little brighter as he rose toward it.

His groping hands found the edge. It had been dry when he went down the ladder at this spot; now it was slimy. While one set of fingertips sought vainly for a hold, the other discovered a crack and curled into it. With what could have been his last all-out effort before collapse, he hauled himself over the brink.

Daniels and McKoy dropped the rope and knelt to grab him.

They dragged him a safe distance from the edge and helped him to stand. Briefly they shone their two waning lights on him to check for injuries. The darkness flowed back and Ken said, "Where were you when the flash flood came through?"

He took his time telling them. There was no need for haste now, so long as the lights were not in use, and he needed a rest before undertaking the still rugged journey to the entrance.

"You are a lucky man," McKoy said.

"I agree. Watched over."

They had been sitting at the edge of the drop awaiting his return, they told him. McKoy had removed his knapsack from his back and laid it beside him to rest his shoulders. They were talking loudly because of the waterfall and so perhaps did not hear the coming of the flood as quickly as they might have.

It caught them so nearly by surprise that there was no time for McKoy to snatch up the knapsack when they scrambled to their feet and raced to a less exposed place near the cavern wall. It was carried away by the tidal wave that came boiling through the passage.

"There were spare batteries in it," the guide said with a grimace in his voice. "Now all we've got to lead us out of here are the ones in our lights and they're all almost gone. We tried not to use ours much, but it's been a long time and we had to keep an eye on the water level. At one point we were only a few feet away from being washed out of here, over the brink."

"Where did you get the rope that saved me?"

"You know"—McKoy's voice in the dark seemed to hold a note of awe—"you could be right about being watched over, Mr. Platt. When we first got here, that piece of rope was in the knapsack. Later I got to thinking you might have some trouble at the top of the ladder when you climbed up here. So I took the rope out of the sack and carried it over to the wall and tied one end of it to an outcrop there. The other end I just took to the top of the ladder, meaning to hand it to you when you needed it."

"I'll be damned."

"More likely you been blessed, Mr. Platt."

Will thought about it and silently nodded, though with the flashlights not in use the nod was for himself alone.

"We'd better get going," McKoy said. "I don't foresee any special trouble, but it's still a long way we have to go and—my God, you fellows know what time it is It's ten minutes to three. I wish I'd taken those bammies out of the sack when I took the rope out. I think we should use only one light at a time where we can, and only two if we need more. That will keep one in reserve. Okay?" Not expecting an answer, he did not wait for one. "Let's go, then. close to me. Mr. Platt, you walk in the middle again in case you need help. You've had a rough time."

For Will it was like repeating a journey only parts of which he remembered, and even those he recalled but dimly. The stream was higher, the stone ceiling seemed ominously lower; where they had walked at the water's edge before, they were now forced to climb high against the walls and pick their way through new obstacles.

It was a scene from Dante, Will thought. One pale light, not strong enough now to reach even eight feet ahead. Three men struggling to stay close enough to use it for a common eye, in an underworld made wet and muddy by still receding floodwaters. A mocking sound of flowing water that never ceased. Sodden shoes—except for barefoot Waldon McKoy—that kissed and squished at every stumbling step. The cold that crept up the legs and chilled the gut and made even breathing an effort that demanded too much energy.

"Here it is," McKoy said. "Whoever looked after you back there is still doing it, Mr. Platt. Now let's get out of this place."

His light just barely touched what appeared to be an earthslide to their right, filled with boulders. Through the boulders a cluster of more distant lights—stars—winked in a tiny patch of black sky. They scrambled toward it, Ken Daniels yelling in triumph at the top of his voice, and clawed their way up through rocks and earth and scrub until they stood together, bodies touching, in a cathedral of pine trees.

The flashlight in Waldon McKoy's hand slowly gave up the ghost.

"What time is it, Mr. Platt?" the guide said.

Will read the luminous dial on his wrist. "Five to four, Waldon."

"It's been a long day and night," Ken Daniels said.

There were clouds in the night sky but the scattered stars provided light enough for McKoy to find a way through the forest. No rain fell now. The three of them trudged along over a wet carpet of pine needles with the treetops sighing overhead and their own talk filling the ground-level stillness. They talked mostly to let out the pent-up fears and tensions, though, and had lapsed into silence again by the time they reached the Land Rover near the cave entrance.

Behind it now stood a second vehicle.

When they were close enough to identify it, Ken Daniels said, "Well, what do you know. The police Rover from Christiana. Someone in it, too." He yelled, waving an arm to attract attention.

The vehicle's lights came on, and two persons dropped to the road. One, Will saw, was a woman. Vicky? No, not Vicky; it was the housekeeper, Ima Williams. The man with her wore a uniform.

With Ken and McKoy he hurried forward, and Ima ran to meet them. The policeman followed more slowly, gazing at them in disbelief. To McKoy he said, "Where you coming from, man? You supposed to be in the cave, this woman tell us."

"We came out the entrance below here." McKoy turned to frown at the nearby steps. "Is someone gone down there searchin' for us?"

"Two men."

"How long they been gone?"

"We only just got here."

"Blow your horn, then. Maybe they will hear it."

The policeman returned to the Land Rover and filled the forest with the goat-bleat of its horn. Will Platt turned to Ima.

Something was wrong, he saw at once. She was more

than worried or alarmed. Her handsome face told a silent story of some ordeal that had exhausted or even aged her.

He reached for her hand. "Ima, what's happened to you?"

"Nothing, Mr. Will."

"But you look—"

"I am fine. It is just the hour."

He would have to question her later, he decided. This was not the time for it. "Anyway, bless you for being concerned. Is my wife all right?"

As she gazed at his face, hesitating, there was a strange look in her eyes. A look of fear? "Yes, Mr. Will, she is all right."

"Where is she? At the station?" The two women had probably walked to the station together.

"I left her in bed, Mr. Will."

"In bed?" He could not believe it. No matter how Vicky felt toward him—

"She was out all day. When she came home after eight o'clock, she said the supper was cold and she didn't want any. She sat at the diningroom table for two hours, writing in a notebook, then went to her room. I went to bed about eleven." She paused, as though to let her thoughts bypass something she was not prepared to tell him. "When I awoke at three o'clock and discovered you had not returned," she finished, "I walked up to the police station.

The look in her eyes made Will certain she was holding something back. Was it something about Vicky? Hearing Waldon McKoy yell, "Here they are!," he was almost glad to turn back to the business at hand.

Trudging up the steps from the cave entrance, the two policemen who had been in Gourie looked as though they had been let out of jail. Will didn't blame them. To be ordered into Gourie at four in the morning after a hard rain . . . not even the rigorous training they received at the Port Royal police school could have prepared them for such an assignment.

He walked over to thank them for what they had tried to do. Then, as weary as he had ever been in his life, he went to the U.N. Land Rover and leaned against it.

Ken, McKoy, and Ima Williams joined him. "Should I drive?" Ken asked.

"Maybe you'd better."

The taximan peered at him. "Is something troubling you, Mr. Will?"

"No. I'm fine."

Something *was* troubling him, of course. And it was not the knowledge that the woman to whom he was married hadn't even worried when, after twenty-odd hours and a torrential rain, he still had not returned from the most dangerous river cave in the island.

What troubled him was a question, or rather two of them. Where had Vicky been all day? And what had happened between her and Ima when she returned?

22

Sister Merle's Pupil

Vicky was seated on her bed when he walked into their room. In her sexy pink nightgown she eyed him with sleepy accusation. "Your jeep or whatever you call it woke me up. You've been gone rather long, haven't you?"

He glanced at the clock on the chest of drawers. From eight A.M. to four-thirty the following morning was "rather long"? "Yes."

"Did you find your buddy Sam?"

"No, we didn't find Sam."

"That's too bad. But it was really a long shot, wasn't it? You only looked there because there was nowhere else left to look."

He began to undress, aware that his clothes were still wet and his shoes ruined. "Do you know the police came to find us?"

"What?"

"Ima walked up to the station."

"For heaven's sake. When?"

"About an hour ago."

"In the middle of the night? And after—" A frown touched her face. "I can't believe it."

"After what?"

"Well, I'm sure she sat up late, waiting for you to return."

That isn't what you were going to say, Will thought, but let it pass. "I was very nearly trapped in there by the rain." he said. "You do know it rained?"

"Of course."

Naked now, he sat on the edge of his bed, facing her. It always embarrassed her to see him naked, he suddenly realized. "You know something about caves," he went on relentlessly. "Enough, at least, to be afraid to enter one yourself. Couldn't you picture what a downpour like that might do to us?"

"I didn't think about it. I had other things on my mind."

"Such as? What were you writing in the notebook all evening after being gone all day?"

His nakedness did not protect him from a flashing look of anger. "She told you that?"

He shrugged. "I asked her if you were worried about me. She said no, you were writing in a notebook."

"I was writing down"—the words came sharply, with defiance—"what Sister Merle said to me."

"So you went there."

"Certainly I went there! Will, I won't be put through an inquisition at this time of night. I'm going to sleep."

He sat there in silence while she turned her back to him, then he put out the light and went to bed himself. He was tired, his body was one dull ache, yet he could not sleep.

So, after all his warnings, she had hired some hungry taximan to take her, perhaps not for the first time, to that devil-woman in the Cockpit—that obeah bitch who was almost certainly responsible for Juan Cerrado's death and Sam Norman's disappearance.

What kind of woman had he been married to all these years?

* * *

It was nearly two in the afternoon when he awoke. The other bed was empty, of course. A warm shower rid his body of some of its aches and, dressed, he went through the house looking for Vicky. He must talk to her again about what she was doing.

But the house was empty.

Ten minutes later, while he was rummaging in the fridge for something to eat, Ima Williams came in carrying her brightly colored shopping bag.

"How are you feeling, Mr. Will?"

"As if I spent the night in a cave."

She was not amused. "I've brought you some pears." Opening the bag, she showed him a dozen or more plump green avocados. "They're good for you at a time like this, and easy on your stomach."

He sat at the kitchen table and watched her peel and halve two of them at the counter. When she brought them to him, he said, "Do you know where my wife is?"

"She went out before nine o'clock, Mr. Will."

"Did she say where to?"

"No."

"I suppose you know where she went yesterday."

Ima shook her head. "No, Mr. Will. That is, not for sure."

"She called on Sister Merle. And I think if we question some of the taximen, we'll find she has been there before."

The housekeeper stood still as a dark statue, gazing at him. "Mr. Will, I suspected she had been there."

"Did you? Why?"

"Last night something happened to me. I was talking to the loa and Sister Merle came between us. And then, Mr. Will, when I thought I was going to die, my door opened and your wife came into my room. She stood beside the bed where I was lying, and she said something to me. Something like—didn't I know she would warn Sister Merle about me."

"So my wife is already a pupil of that damned woman," Will said bitterly. "Do you suppose she has gone there again today?"

"If Sister Merle commanded her to."

He stopped a spoonful of avocado at his lips and scowled at her. "What do you mean by that, Ima?"

"Mr. Will, you have been giving that woman trouble. Keith Mowatt is in the hospital. Emmanuel Bignall and Nevil Walters are in the lockup. I think she must have been very glad when your wife came calling, and would want her to come again. Yes, I am sure of it. She must hate you very much for all the trouble you have caused her."

He did not want to be drawn into that, he decided. "Have you seen Ken today?"

"Not yet. I suppose he is as tired as you must be." Ken, on their return to the house just before daylight, had refused to use Sam Norman's bedroom and gone home in his taxi. "But I think he will come this afternoon," Ima went on. "After all, you still have not found Mr. Norman."

In less than an hour the taximan arrived, with an even longer face than Will had expected. Coming into the house, he said at once, "Will, do you know where your wife is?"

"I suspect."

"You know she went there yesterday? And before?" Will nodded.

"This is bad," Ken said. "I don't like it. Sister Merle is a clever woman. Clever enough, maybe, to find out from your wife what we are doing or planning."

"I agree," Will said. "So from now on I'll make sure my wife doesn't learn anything. But I can't keep her away from there. She has a mind of her own."

They sat for a time, discussing what to do next in the search for Sam Norman. Their one remaining hope, Ken felt, was to talk to the two men in the Christiana lockup, if the police would permit it.

"*Will* they permit it, Ken?"

"We can only ask them. After what happened in the cave, they at least know we are doing our best."

Will thought about it and nodded. "All right. When should we go?"

"I think in the morning, when we are fresh. Because we will have to talk to those men in a special way, Will. They are going to be like Mowatt, sitting there waiting to die. Mowatt *is* dead, by the way. Have you heard?"

It took a little while for Will to stop staring and shake his head.

"He died last night while we were in the cave," Ken said. "The taximen in Christiana were talking about it when I stopped in town just now. One of them had just come from taking a fare to the hospital." He stood up. "Be thinking about what we ought to say to those two, will you? It may be our last chance. Shall I come by for you about seven?"

"I'll be ready." Will walked with him to the door. "By the way, how did you find out where Vicky went?"

"The same taximen. She talked one of the drivers into taking her to Sister Merle. How many times she has been there I don't know, but today he took her again. Sidney Lewis, his name is."

"What's he like?"

Ken shrugged. "Just another fellow trying to make a living in these hard times."

Two hours later Will was sitting on the veranda with a drink, waiting for the housekeeper to tell him supper was ready, when Vicky arrived at the gate in a taxi only a little less ancient than Ken's.

He saw her pay the driver, then stand by the car talking to the fellow for a moment. He solemnly nodded before starting the car again.

Vicky opened the gate, closed it behind her, and came to the veranda with a strut that plainly said her day had been a success.

"Hello," she said. "Am I late for supper? I'm starved."

"No, we waited for you." He looked her over, noting the red earth stains on her sturdy shoes, the sensible denim pants and cotton blouse she wore. It was nearly the same outfit she had worn in Haiti when he found her possessed at the voodoo service. Had she told Sister Merle about her Haitian adventures?

"You've been to the obeah woman again," he said quietly, trying not to sound accusing.

"That's right."

"Want to tell me about it?"

"I'm dying to tell someone."

She had to postpone the recital, however. Ima came at that moment to say supper was on the table.

In the end Vicky told him little, really. Apparently she had learned something of what obeah was basically about—the sorcery involved, the conjurations, the various charms and spells. She told him that much out of pride, he was sure. But when he attempted to delve more deeply, her vagueness baffled him.

"What has she told you about mind control, Vicky? You said you were really interested in that."

"We haven't discussed it yet. Not in depth."

"Yet? You mean you're planning more trips to that house?"

"Of course. I'll be bored to death here if I don't do something stimulating."

"I see." He didn't care any more, he realized. Now that he had made up his mind about his future with her, what she chose to do with her time was of no interest to him. "Vicky, there's something I have to tell you."

"At least," she said, obviously not listening, "Sister Merle is a woman you can learn from." Poking with her spoon at the soup in her bowl, she frowned and added, "What *is* this concoction?"

"It's a country chicken soup."

"*This* isn't chicken," she complained, holding her spoon out to him with a bit of meat on it.

"No, it's pig tail. They use pig tail and chicken feet.

Where did you have your lunch?"

Making a face, she pushed her soup away. "At Sister Merle's."

"Oh? What did she serve you? Something appropriate to the occasion?"

"She served corned beef out of a can, some bread, and some kind of tea."

"Bush tea?" Some such infusions in Jamaica were known to have curious properties.

"What is bush tea?" Vicky said.

"It's—oh, let it go. I said I have something to tell you."

Turning on her chair, she frowned toward the kitchen door.

"When we get back to Florida, Vicky, I want a divorce."

"The tea did taste bitter, sort of," she said. "It gave me a lift, though."

"Vicky."

"What's keeping that stupid woman? First we get a soup that turns my stomach; now we don't get anything at all!"

He leaned toward her, trying to recapture her attention. "Vicky, are you listening to me at all?"

"No. I'm hungry."

He spoke very slowly now. "I said when we get back to Florida I want a divorce."

"A what?"

"A divorce, Vicky. An end to our marriage. Freedom."

Turning at last, she gazed at him in hostile silence for a few seconds, then shrugged. "All right," she said. "Maybe you'll even find someone who likes pig tails and chicken feet. That ought to make you ecstatic."

23

The Finding

Emmanual Bignall and Nevil Walters had refused to talk. Now both were in the hospital where Keith Mowatt had died.

Vicky, for six days a daily visitor to the house in the Cockpit, was behaving almost as strangely, Will decided, though he saw too little of her to be sure of his judgment.

Since the word *divorce* had come into their limited dialogue, he had moved into Sam Norman's unused bedroom. He met his wife at breakfast if she happened to be up. But he no longer told her what Ken and he proposed to do that day. "I don't think I want you telling Sister Merle," was his usual blunt reply when she was interested enough to ask.

Most of the time he also said something like, "For God's sake, Vicky, don't visit that woman again! It's doing you no good!"

Then he would pick up Ken—he was doing that now instead of having the taximan come to the house—and, of course, Vicky would ignore his pleas and spend her day with the obeah woman.

He ought to take her back to Florida, he thought, before what was happening became irreversible. But he couldn't, not with Sam still missing. Anyway, he didn't know *what* was happening to Vicky and how much of it was genuine. Dissembling had always been something of an art with her. What she was doing now could easily be, at least in part, a way of getting even for his daring to want a divorce.

On one of the few occasions that they did still try to talk, Will told her what he'd been thinking about their marriage. "If I hadn't gone after you so determinedly, Vicky, I don't believe you would have married anyone at all. The mistake was mine, pressuring you into doing a thing you had no real desire to do. I'm sorry. God knows I've paid for it."

They were having a nightcap in the living room at the time he said this. The electricity was off—a not uncommon occurrence in Christiana—and the only illumination was from a kerosene lamp that Ima had brought to them. As it happened, the light only dimly reached the chair in which Vicky sat, and her face was in near darkness. When she looked at him, he was fascinated by her eyes.

For some reason he found himself back in that house in the Cockpit where Sister Merle, too, had stared at him with eyes that seemed abnormally bright and piercing.

"Do you really think you've paid?" she said.

"What?" Shaken by the way she stared at him, he had forgotten his remark.

"You haven't, you know," she said. "Ah, no, Will Platt—you haven't."

There were other indications that her visits to the obeah woman were strangely affecting her. She was drinking a lot these days, and he noticed she was taking her liquor, usually rum, almost straight. At times she spoke to him in a way that surely would have shocked the good ladies at Lakeside Manor back in Florida. In fact, her choice of words even shocked him, making him wonder if a veneer of some kind, perhaps one that was generations old, were being slowly worn away to expose something surprisingly violent underneath.

And she was actually using, or practicing, some of the things she learned from Sister Merle. He heard her at night, sometimes as late as three or four in the morning, talking to someone in her room. She had to be alone in the room unless she had let some stranger into the house, but she certainly was talking to someone.

Most of the time she spoke in a voice so low he could not distinguish the words, even when he went to her door and stood there listening. But one night he distinctly heard her address someone as Mordecai.

"Mordecai, arise!" she cried out. "Turn to the north, south, east and west. Come to me with . . ."

He thought he heard the phrase "power of demons," but her voice had suddenly become a mumble and he could not be sure.

She was up to something almost every night, and one day when she was out, curiosity or fear drove him to invade her room in search of some answers. He found no answers, but did encounter a puzzling smell of sulphur and discover under some clothes in her dresser an array of small, screw-top jars with cryptic handwritten labels on them.

He did not disturb the jars or challenge her about them. But he was apprehensive.

And then there was the night he awoke at four in the morning and felt he was in some kind of danger, so lay there motionless, listening, waiting for some sound or movement to tell him where and what the danger was.

He became aware that his door was open and someone was standing there. His eyes continued their slow adjustment to the tropic dark, and the someone became Vicky in a dark, long-sleeved dressing gown, looking in at him, her eyes abnormally bright, unblinking.

For all of three minutes she stood there on the

threshold. Then her figure faded and the door closed with an almost silent click.

"Vicky," he began, the next morning at breakfast, "did you come to my room last night?"

"Did I what?"

"Did you come and open my door last night, and stand there looking in at me?"

Her laugh was ugly, and then her voice dripped sarcasm. "Now really, Will—we're planning a *divorce*."

Of course, it could have been a dream.

And of the missing Sam Norman—nothing.

Ken and he had been to Silent Hill twice. Had spent hours searching the now abandoned shack of obeah-man Emmanuel Bignall in hope of finding some overlooked clue to tell them Sam had been there. The shack had nothing to reveal.

Then late one afternoon, when they were returning to Christiana after still another fruitless search of the area, Ken Daniels lifted his foot from the gas pedal and said, "Will, look."

Dead tired, Will had been dozing. He opened his eyes. Trees on both sides darkened the road ahead, but he saw a drunken man staggering along its edge.

"Look at what?" he mumbled without interest. It was a Saturday, when in rural Jamaica quantities of rum, beer or stout were consumed, and being unsteady on one's feet was not enough to set one apart.

"That's a white man, Will," the taximan said, slowing the vehicle to a crawl. Reaching out, he turned on the lights.

The man ahead may have been too intoxicated to have heard them coming, but he lurched around when the lights went on. For a moment he stood rooted on widespread legs, his body and limp arms swaying, his face white in the headlamps' glare. Then with what had to be a desperate effort, even if a drunken one, he threw himself out of the lane of light and into a wall of vege-tation beside the road.

"It's Sam!" Will shouted hoarsely. "Ken, it's Sam Norman!"

Ken brought the Land Rover to a jolting stop where the man had vanished, and Will leaped out of it. "Sam!" he yelled, plunging into a tangle of neglected, gone-wild coffee trees. "Sam, wait! It's Will!"

Ken Daniels tore into the tangle behind him.

It was dark here. The coffee was ten feet tall with half its limbs dead and brittle. A maze of broken branches littered the ground. A jagged limb dug into Will's thigh and he stumbled to one knee. Behind him the taximan sounded like a charging bull but caught up to him and stopped to help him. For a moment there was silence except for the sounds made by the man they were pursuing.

He must have thought the pursuit had been abandoned, for suddenly he too was silent.

"Sam!" Will called. "Can you hear me? It's Will Platt!"

No answer.

"For God's sake, Sam, come back. We only want to help you!"

A sound of slow footsteps, unsteady but approaching. A voice, barely audible though certainly close by. "Will? Is that you?" Not a drunken voice. The speaker was in pain, and weak.

"Over here, Sam. There are two of us, so don't be alarmed."

The footsteps came closer. Will heard the snap of a branch not more than a yard or two away. Then he saw the man stumbling toward him and heard Sam gasping his name, and stepped forward with his heart pounding and arms reaching.

Sam collapsed against him, too exhausted to speak again.

Not until they had left the abandoned coffee walk and were approaching the car, Ken on one side of the stum-

bling man and he on the other, did Will get a close look
at Sam's face. It seemed years older than when he had
seen it last. Even the growth of hair that all but covered
it could not hide the signs of suffering.

"Sam, are you hurt?"

"He shot me, Will."

"Who? Where?"

"Bignall. At his house. But I got away."

"Wait," Will said to Ken Daniels, and they stopped.
But the hurt man shook his head.

"Not now. It's only my leg. Get me home first."

When they were helping him up into the Land Rover,
Will realized how much weight he had lost and how
weak he was. His clothes were the ones he had worn
when he went to Silent Hill that day to question Bignall,
but they looked now as though he had crawled in them
for miles through thorny scrub and over the region's red
clay, and no longer came even close to fitting him.

Questions tumbled over one another in Will's mind,
but he said only, "Sam, this is Ken Daniels. He's been
helping me look for you. No man could have worked
harder."

"Thanks, Ken," Sam said.

On the way home, Will steadied him with an arm
around his shoulders while Ken drove.

24

Sam's Story

At the house they led Sam to the sofa and, after making him comfortable, looked at his leg. Ima Williams watched wide-eyed. Vicky had not yet returned from her daily session with Sister Merle.

"He was a rotten shot," Sam said. "At twenty feet this was the best he could do. But it's kept me immobilized all this time."

Ima said in a near whisper, "Mr. Sam, can I get you some food?"

He smiled up at her. "When I've had a bath, Ima."

"I will get the tub ready."

"Bless you. Then something easy to swallow, like soup, maybe. I haven't done much eating lately."

Finishing an examination of the leg, Will said, "This isn't infected, Sam." Despite Sam's generally unwashed condition, the leg was clean and the wound in the calf nearly healed.

"It's a long story," Sam said.

He told it after soaking in the tub for an hour and downing three bowls of the gungo-pea soup Ima served him. Back on the living-room sofa with an almost comical expression of contentment on his face, he began.

"When I got there and told Bignall what I wanted to

see him about, he invited me in. I suppose you've been there by now, looking for me, so you know what that shack of his is like."

"We know," Ken Daniels said.

"I told him we'd heard that Juan Cerrado left the market that day with him and another man, in a yellow Prefect, and I wanted to know where they took him. 'Well, now, I will tell you,' he said, and he pulled that old bed aside and reached behind it and produced a shotgun. There wasn't a thing I could do. He just sat down and aimed the thing at my chest. It was a single shot twelve gauge, pretty old. They use them a lot here to shoot rats."

"And hawks," Ima Williams said. "The hawks kill our fowl."

Sam smiled at her and said, "That's right." Then he said, "He was proud of himself, I guess. He kept me there a long time, boasting how he and the others lured Cerrado from the market to his death."

Suddenly realizing he might have casually said something shocking, he sent a startled look at Ima Williams. "Did you know Juan is dead?"

"Yes," Will said. "Ken and I found him in Gourie Cave."

Sam seemed relieved. "It seems Bignall and Nevil Walters approached him in the market and said they wanted to talk to him. They took him outside to Walters's car. Walters was a farmer, they told him, on Juan's side in his fight with Sister Merle, and they just happened to know that Merle was planning to kill him and had already killed another man who dared to challenge her. The other fellow's body was hidden in Gourie Cave, they told him, and why didn't they take him there and show him, to prove it, so he could go to the police and have her arrested."

"He should have known better," Ken Daniels said, sadly shaking his head.

"Probably. But he was keen on getting that woman off the farmers' backs, remember. It meant a lot to him. Anyway, he let them drive him to Gourie Forest, and Keith Mowatt was waiting there to guide them into the cave. And when they got him in there where no one would be likely ever to learn what happened, they killed him."

"At which point," Will said, "Mowatt couldn't resist taking his boots and belt."

"That's about it."

"Tell me something, please," Ima Williams said, stepping closer to the couch on which Sam lay. "Was Sister Merle the one who planned this?" Her voice was brittle. Will had a feeling that if she had spoken even a little more loudly, it might have broken into fragments like a thin glass hurled against a wall.

"She planned it, Ima. Right down to the last detail. All they did was carry out her orders."

"Thank you. Excuse me, please." Stepping back, Ima turned swiftly and hurried from the room.

"Did she take it hard when you found Juan?" Sam asked, looking up at Will.

"Very hard, Sam. I remember thinking no woman would ever grieve that way over me."

"Tell us how you got away from that house in Silent Hill after Bignall told you these things," Ken Daniels said.

"I was lucky. I took a chance and it worked. He was do damned proud of himself, he let the sound of his own voice lull him off guard," Sam explained. "I picked what seemed a good time and made a grab for the gun. Didn't get it—he wasn't that much off guard—but I did succeed in knocking it half way across the room. Then I ran.

"Maybe I should have tried to beat him to the gun, but I don't think so. He's a big fellow; he most likely would have clobbered me before I reached it, if he didn't reach it first. Anyway, I ran, and he got a shot off from

the doorway before I was out of the clearing. But, as I
say, he's a lousy shot. Thank God it wasn't a double-
barreled gun."

"Then what?" Will asked.

"I made it into a yam field with him after me, and
then he made a mistake. He turned back—I think probably to get some shells for the gun. At the end of the
field I ran into a wall of candelabra cactus that should
have stopped me—you knew the stuff in Haiti, Will—
and my luck held. A pig or something had burrowed
under it. I went under, too, and pulled some trash in
behind me to hide the opening."

Sam paused to get his breath. "It threw Bignall off.
For half an hour I heard him searching the field for me
while I lay there on the other side of the cactus expecting
to bleed to death."

"And he finally gave up?" Ken asked.

"No, but I guess he convinced himself I wasn't in that
part of the field. He went charging off out of sight, and
I got up and found I could still walk, and walked for at
least an hour. That's pretty wild country in there. When
I finally came to a house, I'd had it, really had it, and the
house was a shack like Bignall's only worse, and the
people were an old fellow at least eighty and his woman,
even older than he was. I still don't know their names."

Will was remembering what Ima Williams had told
him after asking her voodoo loa to let her see what had
happened. How Sam had been shot but was with two
old people who were helping him. "They took you in?"
he said.

"They took me in. But then I made a damn-fool mistake. I told them who shot me and asked them to go for
help."

Ken Daniels slowly moved his head up and down.
"And of course they knew Emmanuel Bignall was an
obeah man and were afraid to do that because he might
find out about it."

"That's what happened."

"But," Ken went on, still nodding, "they were decent people who couldn't force themselves to turn you out, so they looked after you."

"After I promised never to tell anyone what they'd done," Sam said. "And, as I say, I never did learn their names, so I'm not breaking the promise even now, am I? I just called them Ma'am and Mister."

As he talked, Sam began shaking his head in wonder at what had happened. "They were such good people. She washed my leg three or four times a day, even though she had to walk half a mile to a spring to get water. They shared their food with me—what they had of it, mostly yams and sweet potatoes and cornmeal porridge. She even wanted to wash my clothes, but I wouldn't let her. I had a horror of being naked and having Bignall or one of his cronies walk in on me."

"Did they finally let you leave?" Will asked. "Or did you just walk out when you had the chance?"

"Would you believe they went to a wedding? It was the craziest thing. I was stretched out on the old bed they were letting me use. The lady came in and got down on her knees and fished a hundred-year-old suitcase out from under that bed, and opened it, and took out a long white dress for herself and a white shirt and dark suit for her old man, and she showed them to me as if she were showing me the latest Paris fashions. 'We're going to his granddaughter's wedding in Borobridge,' she said. 'You just stay here nice and quiet now and we'll be back by noon tomorrow. I'll be leaving you some roasted breadfruit and plenty of water, and you won't have a thing to worry yourself about.' "

"So they left, and you did too," Ken said.

"Right. But I'm going back there, believe me, with money for those two, and presents. They're the old, good Jamaica. This new Jamaica can't hold a candle to them."

"Why did you run into the coffee walk when we came along?" Will asked.

"I'm not sure. I think because you turned your lights on me."

"I don't understand."

"I'd been lying in that shack for days, a prisoner because of my leg. Now I was out of there, trying to get home as quietly as possible, and suddenly there's a car behind me. All right, cars do use that road, and I think I would just have stepped off the shoulder and let you go by if you hadn't turned your lights on. That scared me. Bignall is still trying to find me—you can bet on it—and his pal Walters has a car."

"Bignall and Walters are in the hospital in Spaldings," Will said. "Keith Mowatt is dead." He told Sam about that part of the story.

As he finished, a taxi stopped at the gate outside, and Vicky came into the house.

Sam was surprised. A number of things had been left unsaid, Will realized. Sam and Vicky had known each other in Haiti, of course, but had never been fond of each other.

Vicky touched Sam's outthrust hand now and said she was glad they had found him, glad he was safe. Sam thanked her. An awkward silence followed.

Vicky broke it by saying, "Can I promote something to eat, do you suppose? It's almost eight o'clock, and I had no lunch today."

"Ima must have something ready," Will said.

Vicky went to the kitchen but returned after a moment, looking annoyed. "Where is she? There's some kind of stew being kept warm on the stove, but she isn't there."

"Try her room," Will suggested.

"You try her room. I don't know her that well, thank you."

You didn't hesitate to go there in the middle of the night and threaten her, Will thought, but with a shrug he rose and went to check. Ima's door was ajar. He knocked, and on receiving no answer, pushed it wider. She was not there.

She walked about the yard sometimes, he remembered. She was the kind of person who, finding a bean or pumpkin seed, or any other seed large enough to be picked up, would carry it home and plant it, even though she might be working elsewhere when it was ready to be harvested. He walked out into the back yard and called her name, but got no answer.

Strange, with supper on the stove. He walked out to the gate and looked along the road, but of course the road was dark now. Returning to the living room, he said, frowning, "She seems to have gone somewhere. Vicky, you probably need a shower after being at that place all day. I'll put some food on the table. Sam, can we count you in?"

"I've had mine for now," Sam said. "I'm for bed."

"Hold on a minute. Let me see if—" Will went into the room he had been using and, yes, Ima had moved his things out of it and put fresh sheets on the bed. She must have done so while Sam was bathing.

In the kitchen he sampled what Vicky had referred to as "some kind of stew" and found it to be stew peas. Perhaps for Vicky he had better give it some phony exotic name, with a wink at Ken when he did so. He turned the light up under it and went out to set the table.

Sam, on the way to bed, stopped to put a hand on his shoulder. "Will, old boy, Ken Daniels has just told me some of the things you and he did, trying to find me. Like going into Lower Gourie and nearly being trapped there. Believe me, I'm grateful."

"I wish we could have found Juan before it was too late, Sam."

"We tried. When will you be going back to the States?"

"When will you?"

"I'd better rest a few days first. But you and Vicky

don't have to stay. Ima can look after me."

"I'll make arrangements, then."

But it was not to be so simple.

"I can't go right away," Vicky declared when he brought the subject up after supper. Ken Daniels had eaten and departed. He was alone with her in the living room.

He wished he were in bed. The evening had turned unusually warm and humid for this high part of the island, and in the yard the whistling frogs sounded like scores of tiny hammers striking crystal anvils. It was a noise he could happily do without at this point. At the same time, he was reluctant to turn in, knowing that Vicky and he would again be sharing a bedroom.

"What's to keep you here?" he demanded, frowning at her.

"I have to call on Sister Merle again. Once, at least."

He was incredulous. "For God's sake, Vicky, you heard what Sam said. That woman definitely planned the murder of Juan Cerrado and—"

No, she hadn't heard Sam say that, he realized. She had come in too late to hear it. He told her what Sam had learned from Bignall about Cerrado's death. "But I suppose you don't believe it," he concluded angrily. "You don't want to believe it."

"I still have to see her at least once more," Vicky argued.

"Why?"

"She has something of mine that I have to get back."

"What does she have that's so important?"

"My ring. The opal you bought me that time in Pachuca."

"Why in hell did you leave *that* with her?" Will asked in a fury. "It's one of your most cherished possessions!"

"She wanted to study it."

"What do you mean, study it?" He could be losing his mind, he thought wearily. He was so tired, and the damned whistling frogs just wouldn't shut up. "How can you study a ring?"

"You can if it possesses occult power and you're an obeah woman," Vicky snapped back. "You've studied voodoo objects, haven't you? When I first went there, she noticed it on my finger and asked me where I got it. Later she asked if she could keep it a few days and wear it. What's wrong with that?"

"All right." He took in a deep breath and noisily let it out as he stood up. What he wanted now was a drink of something. "I'll take you there tomorrow and you can get it back."

"You don't have to take me. My taximan—"

"*I'll* take you. That damned woman has killed Juan Cerrado and Keith Mowatt, and has two other men dying in the hospital. I'm not trusting this to some taximan I don't even know."

"I thought you wanted to be rid of me," Vicky countered.

"I want a divorce, not a funeral."

At the sideboard in the dining room he poured himself half a glass of rum and drank it down, remembering, in spite of himself, the body they had found in Upper Gourie. Then, hating Vicky passionately for having made still another trip to that house in the Cockpit necessary, he walked through the kitchen to see whether Ima Williams had returned yet. She could have come in through the back door while Vicky and he were talking.

Her room was still empty.

25

The Opal Again

Ima's room was still empty when Will went to check
it in the morning. He was worried; it wasn't like her to
go out without a word to anyone. But then she was still
no doubt grieving for Juan and might have felt the need
to be alone.

In any case, Will was determined to take care of the
remaining business with Sister Merle. A quick look into
Sam Norman's room showed him soundly sleeping, unlikely to wake for some time. Will left a note on the
bedside table.

A few minutes later Vicky and he were on their way to
recover her ring.

"When are we leaving for Florida?" she asked as the
Land Rover growled over the Sunday-empty road.

"I'll phone the airport this afternoon. We should be
able to get out tomorrow."

She shrugged and was silent.

Beyond Wait-a-Bit he found the red clay road into the
Cockpit and turned down it, driving past Sister Merle's
to the turnaround. It must have been what her taximan
had been doing, for as soon as he stopped, Vicky got out
and began walking back.

In no hurry to catch up to her, he followed ten yards

or more behind, angry with her for so foolishly having made this final visit necessary. He had no desire to confront a woman who had planned the cold-blooded murder of Juan Cerrado. She was Jamaica's problem, not his.

Knowing the way well, Vicky turned down the steep path to the house and set a fast pace. He refused to be hurried. Like the night before, the morning was sticky hot, and in this all but shadeless place he was already soaked in sweat.

The house came into view below, its aluminum roof glittering in the sunlight. Vicky was in the yard, striding toward the door. The door was open, he noticed as he continued his descent. Strange. Vicky knocked and waited. He saw her go inside.

Almost at once, in a voice so shrill it was nearly a scream, she called to him. "Oh, my God, Will! Hurry!"

He ran the rest of the way down the trail and into the house, where he found his wife in a bedroom, on her knees beside a bed. On the bed, clutching Vicky's wrists, lay the obeah woman.

Blood bubbled from her mouth as she noisily struggled for breath. Blood made a crazy crimson and white patchwork of her nightgown and the bedsheets. Streams of blood had spilled onto the floor to form a dark, shining pool.

He stepped past the pool to Vicky's side and looked down at Sister Merle's contorted face and knew she was dying. She had to be dying. Her nightgown was pierced in half a dozen places where a knife or some other sharp thing had been plunged through it into her body. Her eyes were bright enough as they stared up at Vicky's hovering face—almost too bright to be real, and they never once blinked—but her grip on Vicky's wrists weakened even as he stood there.

Suddenly a gale of breath exploded from her lungs, spraying blood over Vicky's face.

Vicky shot to her feet with a loud cry and stumbled back to the wall, shuddering with revulsion as she frantically rubbed the red spittle from her eyes. The dwarfish body on the bed heaved up to a sitting position. A hand shot out to point at Will, and he saw the opal ring darkly glittering on one of its stubby fingers.

The woman yelled something. His name was part of it —his full name, Will Platt, screeched out in a blast of venom and hate—but the rest was unintelligible. Perhaps it was not even English. It was full of threat, though; of that he had not the slightest doubt.

A curse, perhaps. Some grisly obeah curse. Then the woman fell back, heaved and writhed for a moment, and became still.

He had not run from her as Vicky had. Still standing beside the bed, he leaned over her and satisfied himself that she was dead. Without turning his head, he said, "Do you still want your ring?"

She did not answer. He turned to look at her, and she nodded.

He took the ring from Sister Merle's finger and thrust it into his pocket. "Go on back to the car," he ordered.

"What are you—"

"Go on back to the car!" he repeated sharply. "I want to make sure no one will know we've been here. We're not going to report this. It's none of our business. But if we say anything, they'll make it our business. They could keep us here in Jamaica for weeks. Go on now!"

He watched her walk unsteadily through the front room to the door, and through the doorway into the yard. When she started up the steep, twisting footpath to the road, he turned his attention to the problem at hand. It was true, he didn't want to leave anything that would tell the police Vicky and he had been here. But there was something else.

The death weapon. It just might still be here.

He searched the bed as well as he could without

touching the bloody sheets, but found nothing. He walked about the room, being careful to avoid the pool of blood that would have caused him to leave footprints. He knelt and peered under the bed.

It wasn't here, obviously. He turned to go. Then he saw it.

It lay almost dead center in the red puddle, but was so covered with blood itself that it had been all but invisible. Maybe its coating of the dead woman's blood explained why Sister Merle's killer, having dropped the thing, had not attempted to retrieve it.

Using just the tips of thumb and forefinger, he gingerly took it by the very end of its pointed blade and stood up with it.

A paring knife. A hollow-ground stainless-steel blade riveted into a brown hardwood handle. He made no attempt to wipe it off, simply wrapped it in his handkerchief and thrust it through a beltloop of his trousers, where his shirt would hide it.

A quick last look at bed and floor convinced him Vicky and he had left no evidence of their visit. Swiftly, then, he climbed to the road and ran along to the turnaround, where he found Vicky waiting in the Land Rover.

"Now remember," he warned on the way home, "we haven't been anywhere near that house today, if we're asked. The last time you saw Sister Merle was yesterday, when you paid your usual visit."

"What if we were seen this morning?" she asked nervously. "This Land Rover is known, isn't it?"

They were passing the Wait-a-Bit police station, and he glanced at it. The door was open; the yard was empty. She had a point, though.

"If anyone questions us, I was showing you a low-cost housing development down the road at Stettin. There is one—Sam pointed it out the day he drove me from the airport—and you're interested in that kind of thing."

"I hope we're not asked," she said fervently. "After what we've just seen, I won't remember what to say." She turned on the seat to look at him. "Will, who could have done that to her?"

He shrugged. "Many must have wanted to. What you're really asking is who was brave enough." ·

"Brave!"

"Yes, Vicky, brave. Courageous. Intrepid. Can't you appreciate what it must have taken to walk in on that woman and attack her, knowing what she's just done to men like Mowatt, Bignall, and Walters?"

She was silent. After a while she said, "May I have my ring?"

He took it from his pocket and handed it to her without shifting his gaze from the road. "Hadn't you better wash it before you wear it? There's probably some of her blood on it."

"Of course." The ring went into her handbag. "But who *do* you think killed her, Will?"

"I haven't the slightest, and couldn't care less," he snapped back.

Sam was having breakfast when they reached the house. "I want a shower," Vicky said, and went to take one. Will sat at the table and told Sam about Sister Merle.

"You're right to keep quiet about it," Sam said. "Not that you'd be suspected of killing her, but these Jamaican cops are thorough. Don't underestimate them. They'd really question you."

"Has Ima returned?"

"She fixed this breakfast for me. She's out back now, washing the clothes I was wearing when you found me."

Will went into the kitchen. Through the open door he saw Ima sitting by a standpipe, industriously using her knuckles and a bar of brown soap over a huge galvanized washtub. Without attracting her attention, he went to the sink and ran hot water into it, adding liquid detergent.

Then he took the handkerchief-wrapped knife from his belt loop, and scrubbed it clean of blood. After letting the water out of the sink, he scrubbed that, too, before turning to a knife rack on the wall above the kitchen counter.

There were slots in the rack for six different kinds of kitchen knives, and all were full but one. He slid the knife into the rack and it fit perfectly. He was half way across the kitchen when Ima came in from the yard.

"Well, hello," he said, feigning surprise. "Where have you been all night?"

She would have an answer, of course. She was intelligent. And she certainly would not say it was a long walk to Sister Merle's and back.

"I'm sorry, Mr. Will," she said. "A friend of mine was sick, and I stayed with her."

He nodded.

"I didn't expect you and your wife to go out so early this morning," she said. "I'm sorry I was not here to make breakfast for you."

"It's all right, Ima. No problem."

"Mr. Sam says you left him a note saying you were going to visit Sister Merle."

"Yes. She's dead, Ima. Someone has finally destroyed her."

She turned her head—perhaps she could not help it—to glance at the knife rack. He did not see her eyes widen, but they were certainly larger than normal when she swiftly turned back to look at him. Her expression was one of terror.

But as she gazed at him the expression changed. She came toward him and put her beautiful, long-fingered hands on his shoulders and touched her lips to his cheek.

"Thank you," she whispered. "But, Mr. Will—"

"Yes, Ima?"

"You must be careful. That woman hated you with a terrible passion because you caused her so much trouble."

"But she's dead now," Will protested, puzzled.

"Mr. Will, who knows what death is? Dead people often return. All the Gèdés are dead loa—I am sure you know about that—yet when they are called to a service, they come. Please, Mr. Will, be on your guard. That woman will seek revenge."

He remembered the curse shrieked at him by Sister Merle as she died. Scowling, he said, "Won't she want revenge on you, too?"

"Of course. But I have the loa to protect me." She paused, then touched him on the arm. "There is someone else you must be careful of, Mr. Will. Someone close to you."

He knew what she was getting at, but asked anyway. "Who?"

"Your wife. Those two were like this." Holding up her right hand, she crossed one finger over another. "And who can say what your wife may have learned there in that house of evil? Perhaps she learned very much."

He nodded. When he realized she had no more to tell him, he said quietly, "What will you do now, Ima? I'll be returning to the States tomorrow. Sam will be leaving when he's rested."

"It will be no problem, Mr. Will. When I am no longer needed here, I can find other work."

"I'm sure you can, a woman like you. And Ima—"

"Yes, Mr. Will?"

"I'm sure Juan Cerrado will rest better now. Everyone in this part of Jamaica should thank you."

The following afternoon Ken Daniels drove Will Platt and his wife to the Montego Bay airport in his taxi, and they boarded a plane for the eighty-minute flight to Miami.

Only eighty minutes, Will mused, from obeah and

black magic to condominiums and shopping centers.

Vicky, he noticed, was wearing her opal ring again, and was strangely quiet.

BOOK THREE

The Face-Off

26

"I Need You, Sam"

Lynne Kimball's concern for Will after the strange events of the evening brought it home to him that, for the first time in his life, he was truly loved. They stayed together—for what remained of the night—in Lynne's apartment, but slept little, speculating about the eerie visitor and its horrible, evil aura. And wondering what to do.

The footprints were dry when Will went back up to his apartment in the morning. A close examination of the carpet puzzled him, however. Any foot heavy enough to have made such distinct prints—such *wet* prints—should have left impressions, he told himself. There were no such impressions. It was as though the intruder had never existed.

He searched the entire apartment, determined not to overlook any clue. He examined every inch of the veranda, through the screen of which the thing had entered.

Nothing.

What now?

Lynne and he had talked for hours, getting nowhere. She thought he ought to go to Jurzak, that relentless homicide investigator from the sheriff's department. "Tell him the truth about you and your wife," she had

223

begged him. "Sooner or later he's going to find it out anyway."

"I can't."

"Why can't you? Wanting a divorce is no crime."

"Lynne, I've been stupid. I've already denied there is anything between you and me. Already told Jurzak I'm a happily married man trying desperately to find my wife."

"Will, you'll just have to admit you were lying. We need help now!"

She was right about that, of course. He needed all the help he could get. But not Jurzak's. Jurzak hadn't the kind of mind to understand the nature of the thing in the lake. There was only one man who might be able to help at a time like this.

Sam.

Six weeks ago Vicky and he had left Sam in Christiana. A week later Sam had telephoned from Massachusetts to say hi pal and thanks for everything, he was home safe and rapidly recovering from his ordeal. Will recalled how Vicky, after attentively listening to his end of the conversation, had said, "That ought to make you happy, a call from good old buddy Sam."

He had put the phone down and turned to gaze at her, trying for what must have been the twentieth time in the past week to read her mind. With every passing day she seemed to behave more strangely.

"Vicky, what's wrong with you? You can't be jealous of Sam?"

"Why should I be jealous of anyone? We're getting a divorce, remember?"

That night she had come to the doorway of his room at two in the morning and stood there in her nightgown, silently staring in at him the way she had done in Jamaica. With that same strange glow in her eyes. For five minutes she stood there, a hand gripping each side of the doorframe and her body faintly swaying back and forth while her gaze remained fixed on him.

He had been awake when she appeared. Had been lying sleepless since one o'clock, his mind full of questions about her behavior since their return from the island. Then, just when he was about to let her know he was awake by challenging her, she padded silently on bare feet back to her own room and quietly closed the door.

And the following night . . .

No one, but no one, knew about the events of the following night. Or ever would. But if he telephoned Sam now and told him what had been happening here at Lakeside Manor for the past few weeks, Sam would come to help. Of course he would. Just as I went to Jamaica to help him when he was in trouble, Will thought.

He stopped pacing the apartment and frowned at his watch. Seven forty-five A.M.—a good time to call. Sam probably wouldn't have left for work yet. He strode to the phone, snatched it up, and dialed the number.

After the footprints, after the long talk with Lynne about summoning Jurzak, after all the thinking about the problems and the options, it was good to hear Sam Norman's familiar voice again.

"Sam, I'm in trouble."

"You this time? Well, I owe you. Shoot, pal."

"It's too long a story to tell you on the phone. But since Vicky and I got back here, all kinds of things have been happening. I don't suppose the mystery deaths of Heron Lake, Florida, have hit the papers up your way yet, but they may if they continue. Not to mention the news magazines and tv networks."

"Mystery *deaths* did you say, Will?"

"A man, a woman, two dogs. And last night I might have been the next victim had I been in my apartment. The thing left wet footprints all through the place, searching for me."

"*Wet* footprints?" Sam echoed.

"It's coming out of the lake here, Sam. And it's nothing human, nothing even solid—just a thing of mist or vapor. I've seen it. How soon can I expect you?"

"Where do I fly to?"

"Orlando."

"I'll get onto it and call you back. A thing of mist, you say? Will—how is Vicky?"

"She left me right after we got back from Jamaica, Sam. Walked out without a word. I've been trying to locate her."

Sam's long silence was not unusual. He was a man who normally let a conversation hang while thinking. "All right," he said finally. "I'll check the flights and get back to you."

The following afternoon Will drove to Orlando to meet him, and was pleased to see that the Jamaican ordeal had left no mark on his friend. On the drive back to Heron Lake he showed a disinclination to waste any time, firing questions as fast as Will could field them.

"You say Vicky left you? I don't get it, Will. You told me the two of you had agreed on a divorce."

"We had."

"Then why the walkout?"

"She was behaving strangely, Sam." Will told of the night before Vicky's disappearance—the night she had come to his doorway and stood there staring in at him. And of other times when, in talking to him about even commonplace things or events, she had seemed to be out of tune with reality.

"Sister Merle," Sam said.

"I think so. Yes."

Sam shook his head and let a moment of silence go by as the car sped south through miles of citrus groves. The scent of orange blossoms was at times almost overpowering. "I don't have any doubt, Will, that when Merle got her hands on someone as susceptible as Vicky, she made the most of it."

"There's something you don't know, Sam." He went on to tell Sam about the opal Vicky had bought from the Indian woman in Mexico, and how Sister Merle had borrowed the ring and he himself had removed it from her finger when Vicky wanted it back. Sam knew, of course, who was responsible for the obeah woman's death.

After a brief silence, Sam said, "This thing that comes out of the lake. You think it's after you?"

"I do now. I didn't at first."

"And Vicky is somehow responsible for it? Created it, maybe? Why?"

"Because I told her I wanted a divorce. I suppose."

"But she's never been a wife to you. You've told me that more than once."

"That doesn't mean she wanted to be put aside, Sam. I've been just the kind of man she could live with without too much effort—successful, a good income, and too wrapped up in my work to be sexually demanding. In other words, nice to have around and still easy to handle."

"All right. She had a reason to create this thing—she wanted revenge—and she learned how from Sister Merle with maybe some help from the ring you've just told me about. Now how do we protect you?"

"That," Will said, "is why I asked you to come down here. It was you, not I, who fought Margal and beat him."

They continued the talk that evening in Will's apartment. Then after a phone call to the apartment below, Will took Sam down to meet Lynne Kimball. "She knows Jamaica," he said as they walked down the stairs. "Her husband worked for the bauxite people in Mandeville. Died there."

"That should make her easy for me to talk to."

But the Jamaican link was not necessary, Will happily

noted at once. Sam took to Lynne as quickly and completely as he had, and in only a few minutes they were talking like longtime friends. He always knew when Lynne liked someone or something. Her eyes sparkled. Her whole face glowed with inner pleasure.

They talked in Lynne's living room for hours, Lynne and he taking turns at filling in the details of what had been happening at Heron Lake. Now and then Sam interrupted with questions.

"Let me be sure I have this straight, Will. Vicky walked out on you a week after the two of you returned from Jamaica?"

"We got back here March twentieth. It was the morning of the twenty-ninth I found her gone."

"And those two people on the third floor—the Ellstroms—first saw the lake thing when?"

"April tenth," Lynne said. "Tuesday, April tenth, at night. At the Wednesday cocktail party the next day they made a point of trying to find someone else who'd seen it, and came up with Haydn Clay."

"So," Sam said, frowning as he did his mental arithmetic, "there was a gap of—let's see—eleven days between Vicky's departure and the thing's first appearance."

Will nodded.

"Then how long before the woman was found dead in the road?"

"She was killed Friday the thirteenth," Will said without hesitation. "More than a few people saw some significance in that."

"So between the first appearance of the thing—the night the dogs died, that is—and the death of the Abbott woman, we have a gap of only three days?"

"Right."

"Then what? You two saw it come out of the lake and go up to your apartment?"

"No," Lynne said. "It killed Tom Broderick first."

"When was that?"

"Sunday. The twenty-second? Yes, that's right."

"The thirteenth to the twenty-second," Sam said, frowning again. "A nine day gap. There's no pattern, is there?"

Will said, "There doesn't seem to be."

"Then—finally—you two saw the thing and discovered the footprints in Will's apartment. That was two days ago. A gap of ten days this time. No, there's no pattern. We could wait for days, or it could reappear tonight."

Lynne looked at her watch. "Do you know how long we've been talking, you two? It's half past one."

"We had a lot to talk about," Sam said.

"You must be tired after your flight." She looked toward the veranda, where the sliding glass door was open. "Have you seen our lake at night, Sam? Really looked at it? It's beautiful, even if it does seem to harbor something awful." She walked out onto the veranda. "Oh-oh. Someone's taking a boat out."

Will and Sam joined her and looked down through the screen. There was little light down there on the white sand beach; though the moon was in its first quarter, clouds scudding under it left most of the lake in near darkness.

Down on the shore two men were pushing one of the condo's rowboats into the water. When it was clear of the sand, the one at the bow stepped in and Will recognized Haydn Clay. His pant legs were rolled up, his feet bare; his silver hair matched the beach.

The other man was bigger, much taller, and also barefoot, with a mop of hair that he flung back with a toss of his head as he stepped in over the stern and kicked the craft into deeper water. Big Ed Lawson, the condo's manager. And, of course, it was nothing new, their going out together to do whatever they did on the lake.

"What are they up to at this hour?" Sam Norman asked.

"They do this pretty often, Sam. Claim they're looking for a 'gator they saw some time ago."

"An alligator? In this lake?"

"They're fairly common in this part of Florida."

"But why at night?"

"They go out in the daytime, too. It's a little weird, but they seem to be normal enough in other ways. Lawson does, at least. The big fellow. I don't know the other one, Clay, that well."

27

The Watcher

Someone else watched the building's manager and silver-haired Haydn Clay take out the rowboat that night.

Unable to sleep, Carl Helpin in 202 had been sitting in front of his television set, a drink in hand, watching a late movie. His veranda door was open. Bored with the movie, paying almost no attention to it, he heard voices from the beach only just outside and below his apartment.

Curious, he turned off the tv and walked out onto the veranda. Standing there with his nose pressed against the screen, his thumbs hooked in his belt, Helpin allowed an expression of triumph to twist his face. There was no one present to see it, however; his wife, Nicola, was asleep in her bedroom. Still, his mouth curled as he sought to see better what was happening there on the strip of white sand in the glimmer of moonlight, and suddenly he stepped back, wheeled, and hurried to a lamp table in the living room.

From its drawer he snatched a pair of binoculars with a black leather strap which he looped about his neck. Thus draped, he hurried from the apartment, deliberately slamming the hall door behind him because to his way of thinking if he had to be up at this hour checking on Lawson, his wife had no right to be peacefully sleeping. Let her wonder what he was up to.

On the ground floor he hastened along the hall to the condo storeroom where, along with lawn tools, paint, and other such items, were oars for the rowboats and paddles for the condo's canoe. The night was cool, he suddenly realized. For what might turn out to be a long session on the lake, he ought to be wearing something more substantial than the whisper-thin sport shirt he had on.

Should he go back for something? No, there wasn't time. Opening the storeroom door, he switched on the light and was delighted to see that the maintenance man had left a nylon jacket, white with red stripes on its sleeves.

He put the jacket on. Its arms were too long, but it would keep the lake breeze at bay. Lifting a paddle from the wall, he hurried from the building.

But not toward the beach. The condo's canoe was not on the beach tonight; it was where he had hidden it earlier in the evening in case he might need it. There hadn't been much likelihood that anyone else would want it at night, of course—certainly not with so many of the building's residents now staying at the motel—but he prided himself on thinking of everything and taking no chances.

Careful to keep out of sight of the two men on the beach, he trotted across fifty yards of lawn, behind hedges where possible, to a small concrete building on a canal fed by the lake. The structure housed pumps by means of which the condo obtained water from the lake for its lawns and shrubbery.

The canoe was there behind it, waiting for him. He slid it into the canal. Certain he had not been seen, he seated himself in the stern and silently dipped his paddle into the dark water.

* * *

On the veranda of 504 Lynne Kimball said suddenly, "Look! Down there by the pumphouse!"

Will Platt and Sam Norman looked where she was pointing and saw a canoe with a solitary paddler in its stern glide from the canal into the lake. There was just enough light from the cloud-veiled quarter moon for Will to be reasonably sure of himself when he said, "It's Helpin."

Sam said, "Who's he?"

"Fellow from California. No one likes him much."

They watched the canoe glide along the shore, a dim white shape that became whiter whenever the clouds let the light of the moon through to shine on it. After a while Lynne said, "He seems to be following the rowboat."

Sam said, "You know, this could mean something. Why don't we check it out, Will, in one of those other boats down there?"

"Should you?" Lynne asked fearfully. "Suppose that thing—" She looked at Will's face and was silent. Then: "All right. I know you have to do something. Just be careful? Please?"

Will drew her into his arms and touched his face to hers. "Don't worry. I've a lot to be careful for now."

They took the elevator to the ground floor, and he led Sam to the storeroom where the oars for the boats were kept. He had been in the room earlier that day to leave a jacket for the maintenance man, who had been complaining that the lake breeze chilled him when he had to rake the beach. The jacket was not on the workbench now, Will noticed as he lifted a pair of oars from their wall brackets.

The moon was lost behind clouds when Sam and he reached the shore. Shedding shoes and socks, they walked a boat into the water, and Sam said, "You know the lake. Suppose I row and you tell me the headings."

"Right. Be as quiet as you can. Sound carries here."

Will sat in the stern, leaning forward, trying to locate the canoe and the other boat in the darkness. He could see neither, nor could he hear any sound from them. There were other sounds, however. Frog voices ranged from deep bass grunts to a shrill piping. An unseen water bird, perhaps annoyed by so much intrusion at an hour when it expected none, began what sounded like a practice session on a faulty trumpet. One of Sam's oars struck a floating slab of wood that turned into a large turtle and submerged with a sound like that of water gurgling down a drain.

Then the moon fought its way free of the clouds again and Will saw the canoe some thirty yards away, near the middle of that part of the lake known as the marsh.

He saw something else, too. The man in the canoe was wearing a white jacket with stripes on its sleeves—either the same jacket he had left in the storeroom or one a lot like it.

"That way, Sam," he whispered, making a direction signal of his hand. "Go slow. He seems to have stopped."

Carl Helpin had indeed stopped, because the rowboat he was following—the one with Lawson and Clay in it—was moving along the edge of the marsh only fifty or sixty yards ahead of him, and he feared the white canoe would be spotted if he went any closer.

Leaning forward, he laid his paddle silently at his feet. Then, straightening, he took hold of the binoculars that had been slapping the front of his borrowed jacket, and lifted them to his eyes.

The two men in the boat seemed to leap at him as he focused on them. He could see their faces clearly, and the sight brought the word "Bastards!" hissing from his lips—not loudly enough to silence a frog grunting on a nearby lily pad, but still loud enough to give him some satisfaction. Then he sat there motionless, watching his quarry.

They were talking to each other but not with any great animation and not loudly, or he would be able to hear them. Anyone who didn't know better might even believe they were just a couple of guys who liked to go fishing at night. Only, of course, they had no fishing rods.

What they did have—or what Clay had, at any rate—was a leather camera bag beside him on the seat, and a camera with a scope on it dangling from his neck. Pictures? In the dark, with infrared film and an image-intensifying scope?

You could take such pictures, of course, if you knew what you were doing. No need for a light, especially here in central Florida where the air was so clean that even without a moon your eyes quickly adjusted to nighttime conditions. But what was a real-estate man up to out here with a camera at two in the morning, for God's sake?

Unless—it was a thought—he knew more about what was in the lake than others did, and wanted pictures of it in action.

The frog on the lily pad suddenly stopped grunting.

Helpin lowered the binoculars from his eyes and turned, frowning, to look toward the source of the sudden silence. Silence could be disturbing at a time like this. To make it worse, the moonlight went out again as abruptly as though someone had thrown a switch.

Something nudged the canoe, causing it to move sideways in the water. The paddle at his feet wobbled back and forth with a faint drumming noise.

The silence returned.

All at once the stern of the canoe rose three feet into the cool darkness and tipped sideways. Then with a loud grating sound it slid back into the water as though down a slope of sandpaper.

Helpin lost his balance and grabbed wildly at the thwarts, just as something swirled in the water directly beneath his eyes. The lake erupted as though a geyser had burst up from its muddy bottom.

The moon flicked on again. Helpin found himself leaning out in space, looking down on a pair of long, gaping jaws filled with teeth.

With a cry of terror he dived from the canoe just as the jaws snapped shut on it. Hitting the water horizontally with an eruption of his own, he began swimming frantically toward the rowboat and yelling for help at the same time.

28

The Taking

Will Platt and Sam Norman saw or heard it happen—a little of both—and were instantly alert. Both had lived in islands where caimans haunt the mouths of rivers and sometimes prey upon children bathing or women doing the family wash.

"The 'gator's turned him over!" Will said.

Sam Norman leaned into the oars and sent the rowboat skimming through reeds and water grass like an air boat, the marsh vegetation responding with a clawing, scratching noise as the craft bored through it. A heron rose from nowhere with huge white wings flapping and long legs dangling almost in Will's face. He leaned sideways to avoid it. When he straightened, the canoe was close enough for him to see details.

It had been overturned. More than that, it had been all but bitten in half, the bow a half-sunken white blur at a two-o'clock angle.

Carl Helpin had flung himself clear and was churning the water into froth as he stroked through a carpet of lily pads toward the other rowboat.

The two men in that other boat were trying to reach him, Ed Lawson massive at the oars, the other leaning forward from the stern as Will was, struggling to see and direct him.

237

"Damn," Will said.

A cloud had slipped under the moon again, blocking out its glow.

But near the overturned canoe something was happening that needed no light to reveal it. Out of the dark water rose a spiral of mist or fog, pale gray in the night. Up it came as though escaping under pressure from the mouth of a submerged bottle, and on reaching a point four or five feet above the surface of the marsh, it began to expand.

The spiral stopped twisting and filled out. It swelled into a shape that could have been human. It flowed over the marsh in pursuit of the man swimming through the lily pads in his bid to escape the alligator.

Sam Norman caught sight of it as he turned his head to get his bearings. The oars froze in mid-stroke. "My God," he said in a low voice. "Will, what *is* that?"

Hands gripping his knees, Will Platt could only lean forward and watch while a chill of premonition coursed through his body and made him tremble. There was light from somewhere now, at least a glow, if not from the moon then from the thing that had risen from the lake. It showed him again that the man from the canoe wore a white jacket with striped sleeves.

Mine, he thought.

And the thing from the lake was now human, or at least as human as any creature of mist or ectoplasm could be. Seemingly without effort it closed the gap between itself and the man who was roiling the surface.

The other men had seen the lake thing too, and Ed Lawson had stopped rowing. Haydn Clay was holding a camera to his eyes, and there was just enough light from the lake creature for Will to see the man's finger repeatedly working the shutter release.

All at once the misty, glowing thing attained a position directly above its victim and descended upon him. Descended *into* him, it seemed to Will. The man stopped swimming—not all at once but slowly, as though the creature were feeding on him and sapping his strength so that he could no longer make his arms obey his will.

The glow revealing his plight became dimmer as the thing flowed into him. Just before it vanished altogether, Will saw the man make a feeble effort to move his arms again. Like the last struggle of a spent fish, it barely disturbed the water

Fleeing from the alligator, hoping to God it did not really want him but was merely annoyed by his intrusion into its lair, Carl Helpin was unaware of the pursuer above him until its glow lit up the water.

Then, looking up, he saw what appeared to be a woman made of mist hovering over him, and for the first time in his life knew the meaning of terror.

He was a man who more than a few times had inspired terror in others—certainly in his wife—but had always thought himself able to outsmart or outhate anything that might threaten his own security. Now the taste in his mouth was that of hot vomit while the blood in his thrashing body turned to ice water. Not enough blood reached his heart to keep it beating properly. He could not breathe.

The misty thing in the night air hung over him for only a few seconds, as if to be sure it was properly positioned. Then it flowed down upon him and into him, and the cold in his body intensified, the little strength that was left in his limbs was sucked out of them, leaving him limp, and with all his gasping he could find no air for his tortured lungs.

He was being destroyed. He knew it. This thing he had for so long been stalking—this thing he had been so certain was a creation of that crooked California realtor, Haydn Clay—was no fake. It was real. It was killing him.

Parts of his life flashed through Helpin's mind at that

moment, while his arms and legs weakly struggled to keep him swimming despite the certain knowledge that his insides were being sucked dry. In vivid detail he relived the afternoon in Hollywood when, accused of causing the failure of an expensive film with his poor special effects, he had been told to get the hell out and stay out.

Then he saw himself asking Nicola to marry him while she thought he was still in great demand and she merely a struggling young actress.

Strange, how much of a man's lifetime could rush past him when he expected to die in a few moments.

But then something happened. The thing that had overtaken him and was sucking his life away suddenly seemed to lose interest in destroying him. He felt as though a giant octopus had let him out of its embrace. He could breathe again! His heart was again beating! He tried his arms and they worked.

The thing didn't want him, after all!

Had he been strong enough, he would have cried out in triumph—something typical of him, something obscene.

But suddenly he felt a movement behind and beneath him in the dark water. Panic caught him again. He half-turned to look behind him. And as he did so, a pair of long, gaping jaws closed on his legs.

Even as he screamed, he felt the 'gator's teeth bite through flesh and reduce bones to splinters as the monster pulled him down.

Will Platt saw it happen and heard the scream. The explosion in the water must have been caused by the reptile's tail. Even if strong enough still to have struggled, the man could never have created such a commotion.

It endured for moments as the creature thrashed about, churning the lake to froth. Now and again the great snout was thrust above the surface, and those in the two rowboats saw the mangled thing in its jaws.

Again Will was able to identify the white jacket, now in bloody shreds, as the one he himself had owned until that morning.

Then the frenzy subsided and the lake became quiet. And after a period of fear and speculation, the four men in the two boats brought their craft together to discuss what to do.

"There's no point in trying to find him," Ed Lawson said. "You think so, Haydn?"

Fussing with his camera, Haydn Clay shook his head. "No point at all, Ed."

"You were taking pictures," Will Platt said. "Did you get any of that thing?"

"The 'gator? No. I wasn't quick enough."

"Not the 'gator. The other."

"Yes, if it shows up on infrared. But what was it? Do *you* know what it was?"

Silence.

"What brought you two out here?" Lawson asked. The boats were close together now, gunnels touching; he didn't have to speak loudly. Obviously he didn't want to, either, so close to where the alligator had seized its prey just a few minutes before.

"We were following Helpin to see what he was up to," Will said. "What were you doing out here?"

"Looking for the 'gator, among other things," Lawson said.

"Other things?"

"Haydn's work. Look—hadn't we better get back and call the cops about this? A man's been killed."

Will Platt drew a deep breath. Now he would have to call Jurzak, that seemingly ordinary fat man with the watery gray eyes and computer mind. There was no way to avoid it.

The prospect filled him with dread. Because the investigator would almost certainly insist on a conference now, right now, while he, Will Platt, was overtired and likely to blunder.

For Will Platt the result could easily be calamitous.

29

A Resemblance

"Why don't we all just sit here and talk for a while?"
At 3:35 A.M. Homicide Investigator Jurzak looked
sleepy and unhappy—even more unhappy than the men
he had sent out in the condo's boats to seek the victim
of Heron Lake's alligator. "By the way," he continued,
"my name's Karl. Same as Helpin's but spelled with a
K. Might be easier for you folks than Jurzak."

He picked the most comfortable chair in Will Platt's
living room and slouched into it, thrusting his legs out
and letting his gaze linger on the ceiling while the others seated themselves.

His melon-shaped face was putty hued, Will noticed.
For some reason he looked as though he had been up
longer than anyone else in the room, though the others
had not been to bed at all. And he kept one hand pressed
hard against his bulging abdomen, as though in pain.

"You know, I'm a little weary of this business,"
Jurzak complained. "Aren't you people a little weary of
it?"

No one answered him.

He swept them slowly with his gaze: Will on his left,
Lynne Kimball next, Sam Norman beside her, then the
two men from the other boat, big Ed Lawson and

Haydn Clay. "All right. Now who wants to tell me exactly what happened? From the beginning. Which of you went out on the lake first?"

"Clay and I did," Lawson said.

"Clay and you, hey?" The watery eyes focused on Haydn Clay. "This fellow whose death we're discussing —this Carl Helpin—told me not long ago you're from Los Angeles, Mr. Clay. That right?"

"Yes."

"He said you were in real estate out there."

"No, that's incorrect."

"Pardon?"

"There *was* a Hayden Clay in real estate out there. He's doing time for some sort of swindle, I believe—you could look it up. But his name is spelled with an 'e'—*H-a-y-d-e-n*—while I was named for the composer." Clay shrugged. "We got each other's phone calls sometimes. A real nuisance. I was never in real estate. I'm a photographer."

"In motion pictures?"

"No, just a photographer. Wildlife, mostly."

"Mmm." The gray eyes hadn't blinked even once. "So what were you and Mr. Lawson doing on the lake tonight?"

"Looking for wildlife. And for the 'gator, of course."

"To take its picture?"

"If we found him. I've been taking other pictures of the lake right along. I've a contract from my publisher to do a book of Florida wildlife photos."

Jurzak's face resembled a gray balloon on which a frown had been drawn. "This thing you all saw come up out of the water—this misty thing that seemed to float out over Helpin while he was trying to escape from the 'gator—did you get a picture of that, Mr. Clay?"

"I took some. I won't know if I got anything until the film is processed."

"Maybe you ought to let me have that film, Mr. Clay.

I'll have our lab look after it."

It was Clay's turn to frown. "This isn't ordinary film, Inspector. It's infrared, and has to be—"

"I thought you said you were looking for the 'gator," Jurzak interrupted softly.

"We were."

"And trying to photograph it on infrared? I was under the impression that such film is sensitive only to objects that give off some degree of heat." He scratched his nose. "Does a cold-blooded reptile give off any heat, Mr. Clay? I'm only asking, you understand. I'm not up on sophisticated photography."

"For the 'gator, if we were lucky enough to find him, I had another camera in my bag, with color film and flash," Clay said.

"Why didn't you use it, then, when the animal attacked Mr. Helpin?"

"There wasn't time when it overturned the canoe. Everything happened too fast. Then when it attacked him the second time and pulled him under, I was busy with the infrared, trying to get some shots of the misty thing. And—well, frankly, with the 'gator that close to us, I was too scared even to reach for the flash camera." The recollection caused Clay to begin shaking, and he paused to get control of himself. "My God, if you had seen the size of that alligator, Inspector—"

"Investigator. That's my title: homicide investigator. But call me Karl, eh? With a K. Our people know a good deal about film, Mr. Clay. If this is too tricky for them to handle, they'll be sure someone reliable takes care of it. We want to see what's on it too, you know."

Haydn Clay hesitated for a few seconds, then expelled a noisy sigh and reached into his pocket. Jurzak took the film with his outthrust hand and peered at it, then dropped it into his own pocket and said, "Thank you." Then he looked at Ed Lawson.

"Mr. Lawson, there's a thing that's been puzzling me

for some time now. Want to clear it up, do you?''

Big Ed had chosen a straightbacked chair and was sitting on it in reverse, with his chin on his arms. He lifted his head now and sat straight. "Clear what up?"

"This thing about you and Helpin. I've heard from quite a few people in the building here that Helpin was trying to get you fired as manager. That so, is it?"

Lawson slowly nodded. "That's so."

"Why?"

"He thought the building could do better, I suppose."

"Please, Mr. Lawson." Jurzak's look of pain perhaps had nothing to do with his apparent illness.

"Well, hell, I don't know what he had against me. He disliked a lot of people. I guess it was mutual."

"You seem to have been a special target. Something exceptional must have happened between you."

Finding the unblinking stare of the gray eyes more than he could endure, Lawson looked down at the carpet.

Jurzak waited. Then he said gently, "Mr. Lawson?"

"Leave it alone, for God's sake. He's dead now. It has nothing to do with what killed him!"

"Being the judge of that kind of thing is what they pay me for," Jurzak said. "Why did Helpin hate you so bitterly, Mr. Lawson?"

"Oh, hell." Lawson jerked his head up and sat straight again. After looking helplessly at the others in the room, he returned his gaze to the investigator's implacable face. "He propositioned me and I told him to shove it."

"He propositioned you how, please?"

"In the pool one evening. The two of us were there alone. He got chummy, swimming up close to me and pawing me. Then he told me I was just the kind of man he'd been waiting for, and he was well off and could do me a lot of favors."

"And you rejected him."

"I told him to go peddle himself somewhere else."
Lawson's voice dropped almost to a whisper. "Then the
bastard starting *really* pawing me, begging me to change
my mind, and I got mad. I shoved his head under water
and damned near drowned him, I was so mad. From
that day on, all he wanted was to get even."

Putting an end to the long silence that followed,
Jurzak said quietly, "Well, thank you. We seem to be
solving a few of the puzzles, at least, don't we?"

Will Platt had been listening intently to every word
that came from the investigator's lips. Now with grudg-
ing admiration he said, more to break the tension than
anything else, "Karl, have you ever read Victor Hugo?"

"Victor Hugo? Why, yes, I believe I have. Some of his
books, at least."

"Les Misérables?"

"Ah, yes. One of my favorites."

"I thought it might be," Will said dryly. "May I answer your earlier question now?"

"Please do."

"Exactly what happened, you said. Very well. Mr.
Norman, Mrs. Kimball and I were talking in her apartment. It was about one o'clock—"

"Talking about what, Mr. Platt?"

"The killings. Sam Norman is an old friend of mine,
visiting from New England. Mrs. Kimball and I were
telling him what's been going on here."

"I see." Jurzak helped himself to a good look at Sam.
Perhaps not the first.

"We went onto the veranda and saw Ed and Mr. Clay
taking out a boat," Will went on. "Then we saw Helpin,
in the canoe, come from the pumphouse canal and follow them. Sam and I decided to follow Helpin and find
out, if we could, what he was up to." He finished the
story, describing the 'gator's attack on the canoe, the
appearance of the lake thing, and Helpin's death. "Have
I left anything out?" he then asked the others.

"That's about it," Sam said. "Except, of course, we don't know what the thing *is* that came out of the lake."

"Or its connection with the 'gator. We don't know that, either, do we?" Jurzak said.

The room filled with silence.

"Have you heard anything more about your wife, Mr. Platt?" Jurzak asked.

Will shook his head.

"Nothing at all?"

"Not a word."

"Perhaps you should employ a different detective agency."

"Perhaps I should. I thought this one was supposed to be competent. They charge enough."

Again silence.

"Mrs. Kimball," Jurzak said, "you haven't said anything about all this."

Lynne Kimball shrugged. "I didn't see much of it, being on my veranda the whole time. I heard someone yelling or screaming, that was all."

Jurzak gazed at her without expression, but there was something probing in his very lack of it. "Mrs. Kimball, forgive me, please, if I seem a bit rude, but certain people in this building, and in the motel now, are taking about your friendship with Mr. Platt."

"I know."

"No comment?"

"Why bother?"

"No comment from you, either, Mr. Platt?"

"Just one," Will said. "The three favorite diversions here are golf, bridge, and gossip. The greatest of these is gossip."

"Well," Jurzak said, removing his hand from his abdomen and wincing with apparent pain as he pushed himself erect, "that seems to be about it, doesn't it? For now, at least. I believe I'll just go see if my men have found anything."

* * *

It was daylight when the investigator returned. By that time Will and Sam were alone, drinking coffee to restore some energy after the total loss of a night's sleep. Lawson, Clay, and Lynne Kimball had gone to their apartments.

Responding to the knock on the door, Will rose and opened it. Jurzak stood there with a black plastic bag in one hand, peering at him out of those deceptively watery eyes.

"May I come in, please? I have something here that may interest you."

Entering, he lowered himself into the chair he had occupied before, and placed the plastic bag at his feet. Gazing at both Will and Sam, he sadly shook his head. "I had no idea alligators made such a mess of things," he said. "This must have been a big one."

"It was," Will said.

"My men found bits and pieces of Mr. Helpin, nothing more. Do 'gators have some special antipathy toward such men, do you suppose?" He smiled weakly and on getting no answer, stopped smiling and reached into the bag between his feet. "We also found this, Mr. Platt."

Out of the black plastic he lifted a ragged piece of white nylon with part of a sleeve attached. There was a red stripe, or what remained of one, running down the sleeve fragment.

"Look here, Mr. Platt," Jurzak said, turning the scrap of cloth as he handed it to Will.

Will found himself looking at the inside of the collar, where a sewn-on label bore the name Willard Platt in black script. Vicky had sewn it on months ago, he recalled, after ordering labels of both their names from a mail order house.

"He was wearing your jacket, Mr. Platt?" Jurzak said.

"It seems he was."

"I wasn't aware you were that friendly with him."

With a chill settling deep inside him, Will had trouble keeping his voice steady as he explained how Carl Helpin had been wearing the jacket. It sounded, he thought, too pat.

Murmuring "Thank you, Mr. Platt" but offering no comment, the homicide investigator quietly returned the torn piece of apparel to the bag and departed.

But at ten o'clock the following morning he was back, this time with a large brown envelope from which he silently withdrew a number of 11 x 14 black and white photographs. Laying them out on the diningroom table, face up, he stepped back and motioned Will to look at them.

Will did so. Sam Norman was at the pool.

The photos were in sequence. They showed a misty spiral rising from the lake's dark water. They showed the spiral swelling into an almost human shape and moving over the water to zero in on a swimming form below. They showed the shape descending into the swimmer's turbulence and becoming a part of it.

"Does that thing look like a woman to you, Mr. Platt?" Jurzak asked in his exasperatingly neutral voice.

Will hesitated. "In a way, yes."

"It does to me, too. So the question now is—wouldn't you say?—what woman? Does it remind you of anyone you know?"

Damn you, Will thought. "No, I don't think so."

"Do you have a full length picture of your wife, Mr. Platt?"

"I—think so. Yes."

"Shall we look at it?"

Will went into the bedroom Vicky had used and took from atop the chest of drawers there a framed photograph he was fairly sure Jurzak had already seen. He carried it back to the dining room and placed it on the table with the pictures the investigator had brought.

Jurzak picked it up and studied it.

"Am I too eager, Mr. Platt, or do I see a resemblance?"

"What the devil are you driving at, Jurzak?"

"A resemblance. Yes, definitely. What am I driving at? Who knows, Mr. Platt? But have you considered the possibility that your wife may not have run away, as you say she did? That she may have—ah—drowned herself in the lake here?"

"Why in God's name would she do that?"

"Mr. Platt," Jurzak said mildly, "I'm sure I don't know. I was just hoping you might be able to tell me. Because I keep thinking of what the man next door to you here kept saying to his wife when he was dying. You remember what he said, Mr. Platt? According to her statement he uttered just one word, the word 'bat,' over and over again in trying to tell her what, or who, had attacked him."

Jurzak's watery eyes never blinked, though he suddenly pressed a hand to his abdomen and grimaced with pain. "Has it occurred to you that he might have been saying *Platt* in an effort to tell her it was your wife?"

Will returned the man's owlish stare in silence, wondering whether the freeze he felt forming inside him was showing on his face.

"Anyway, Mr. Platt," Jurzak said then, "I trust you're not thinking of going anywhere in the near future."

"Going anywhere?"

"Leaving here."

"No, I'm not."

"I'm glad to hear that. Because I'm not very well just now and don't really want the job of going after you. Good day, Mr. Platt. I'll be keeping in touch. Meanwhile, if you find you have something you want to tell me, just give me a ring, will you?"

At the door he paused and looked back, frowning.

"You know, I'm really curious about these pictures, Mr. Platt. Do you suppose a spectral image would show up on infrared film? There have been some interesting books written by researchers—English, mostly—who photographed ghosts. I must find the time to look at them again."

30

A Truth to Tell

After Jurzak's departure Will remained deep in thought for a few minutes, then looked at his watch. It would be a while before Sam returned from the pool. Lynne Kimball was shopping and would probably be back about the same time. It was now quarter past ten.

He went into his study and sat at his typewriter. What he had to write could be done in an hour, he estimated; it didn't have to be polished for an editor's eyes. For a moment he pondered how and where to begin it, then decided on a simple letter.

Dear Lynne and Sam,
   Our friend Jurzak has just been here with the photos Haydn Clay took of the lake thing. The creature resembles my wife, he pointed out. He had seen a photo of her, and his memory appears to be as sharp as his mind. He asked me certain questions that force me to believe he suspects me of lying about her. He even suggested she might have committed suicide by drowning herself in the lake.
   There are other things friend Jurzak may come up with as he digs deeper, which he certainly in-

253

tends to do. But never mind. The point of this letter is that I have *not* told the whole truth yet—not to anyone—and want you to be the first to know it. And I would rather write it than talk about it, at least just now.

At the time of my return from Jamaica Vicky and I had agreed to a divorce, as you know. I've told you she was behaving strangely. Sam, you can vouch for the truth of that because the strange behavior began in Jamaica and you observed some of it.

I've told you both how Vicky appeared one night in my bedroom doorway here and stood staring in at me in a way that made my hair rise on end. The peculiar glow in her eyes was not natural. I think I've told you how she did the same thing just before we left Jamaica, when she was seeing Sister Merle every day.

All right. Now I have to tell you what you *don't* know.

The night after Vicky stood in my doorway I couldn't sleep. I lay awake for hours, asking myself what was happening to her, and how much of it was a result of her visits to the obeah woman. About two A.M., when I was still wide awake, she appeared in my doorway again, but with a difference.

This time, though again in her nightgown, she held a knife in her right hand. The same kind of knife, Sam—a common kitchen paring knife—that Sister Merle was killed with.

This time she stopped in the doorway only long enough to make sure I was on the bed. Then she came straight at me with her arm in the air, and if I hadn't almost instinctively reached up and caught her wrist, she would have buried the blade in my chest.

I reared up and struggled with her but, my God, she was strong. This wasn't the woman I'd been married to for so many years; it was someone I'd never known before. I managed to get up off the bed and onto my feet, and we crashed all around the room, she trying to stab me and I battling her to prevent it. I got both hands on her wrist and twisted it so she dropped the weapon, but even that didn't stop her. She shifted both of her hands to my throat and proceeded to strangle me.

To stop that I did the same to her, and there we were, the two of us, stumbling around the room trying to choke each other. I don't know how long it lasted. As I've said, she was abnormally strong —stronger than I, I'm sure—as though she were possessed in some way. And the wild look in her eyes seemed to bear that out.

You know what I mean, Sam. You've seen people possessed at voodoo services and know what they can do. Anyway, two or three times I thought I wouldn't be able to hold her off any longer. Then all at once she went limp and slid out of my grasp to the floor.

I don't know what happened, I swear. I wasn't trying to kill her, just desperately struggling to keep from being killed. My hands were at her throat but I don't recall feeling anything snap or hearing any sound of that sort. I must have done something, of course. I just don't know what.

I went to my knees beside her and she was not breathing, she had no pulse, that queer glow had left her eyes. No doubt about it, she was dead, but I even held a mirror to her mouth for several minutes to make sure. Then—what was I to do with her?

Leaving her there on the bedroom floor, I went into the kitchen and poured a drink to clear my mind, but didn't drink it. It went down the sink when I realized I'd better stay cold sober at this point.

I asked myself whether Vicky had gone mad. What had she planned to do if she succeeded in murdering me? I went into her bedroom to look for evidence that she had planned to run away—a packed suitcase, an extra large supply of money in her handbag, that sort of thing. There was nothing. Apparently in her madness she hadn't thought beyond the act of walking into my room and stabbing me.

But this train of thought gave me an idea for what *I* might do then. I had to dispose of her body, of course. Nobody was going to believe she tried to kill me and I accidentally killed her while trying to defend myself. I would put her body in the lake. Then I would tell the police she had left me. I would say she had been acting queerly—which, God knows, was true—and perhaps I could even go so far as to hire a private detective agency to find her. As for Vicky herself, if I disposed of her in the lake (forgive the seemingly callous use of that word, but I can't think of another just now), she literally would disappear, wouldn't she?

So, to keep this short, I went down to the beach, looked up to make sure there were no lights on in any of the apartments, then returned to my apartment and carried Vicky down to one of the condo's boats.

It was about three in the morning then. At this point I really needed a drink and would have finished half a bottle, I'm sure, had I brought any along. I felt like a character in a crime story, certain I was making mistakes that would trip me up, but unable to think of what they might be. That's what I meant at the beginning of this letter when I said there were things Jurzak might come up with as he digs deeper.

He won't, however, come up with the body. Of that I'm convinced. I hate to say this—it makes me even more sorry for what I did—but I believe the alligator must have taken care of Vicky, or the people dragging the lake would have found her by now.

So now you know, you two, and I can only leave the judgment to you. I didn't mean to kill her. It was an accident that happened while she was trying to kill me. What I did with her afterward was stupid but seemed at the moment to be the best way out. As for the thing that keeps coming out of the lake to attack people, I don't know what it is, but I suspect. Vicky learned something from all those long talks with Sister Merle, no doubt of it. She may have learned things from Margal, in Haiti, too, where her interest in the occult was equally strong.

Did she learn about life after death? How not to die as we know dying? How to return as demon, friend, incubus, spirit, shade, spectre, phantom, materialization—whatever one may call it? For revenge on the man who killed her? Because I killed her, no doubt of that, and the other night when she attacked Carl Helpin she thought he was Will Platt. That jacket—she herself sewed my name in it. She knew it well. And when she discovered her mistake, *she let him go*.

Which leads me to one more speculation before I close this letter. The phantom first killed two dogs. A basic, primitive killing, it seems to me. It then killed a woman, Connie Abbott. Still fairly basic but at least Connie was human. Then it destroyed Tom Broderick, a man. And now, this last time, it attacked a man wearing my jacket but let him go on discovering the man was not Will Platt. Is it becoming more selective? Getting closer?

I hope we can talk about this now that I've briefed you. The alternative, of course, is for you to hand a copy of this letter to Karl Jurzak.

31

Voodoo Woman

"I think we need Ima Williams," Sam Norman said.

They were seated, the three of them, in Will's living room, where Lynne and Sam had just finished reading Will's letter.

"Yes," Sam said, twisting his face into a frown, "I think we'd better try to get Ima up here. We can't do this alone, Will. We just don't know enough about this kind of thing."

Will said, "Why Ima? Because she was able to destroy Sister Merle?"

"And because she's kanzo."

Will nodded.

"I had some long talks with her after you and Vicky left and she was taking care of me," Sam said. "I asked her how she was able to get close enough to Merle to do what she did, and she said the loa helped her. Let's hope they'll help her again."

Will shook his head. "We can't bring her here. Have you any idea how long it would take her to get a visa, even if she already has a passport?"

"She has a Haitian passport," Sam said. "Showed it to me one day when I asked about her family in that country. And you're forgetting the U.N. owes me a large

favor for going down there to help their Juan Cerrado."
He shrugged. "All they'd have to do is pick up a telephone, and I'd be in and out of our embassy in Kingston
in half an hour."

"And if they won't?"

Sam frowned. "If they won't, there are other ways to
cut the red tape, if you're willing to pay for it. I know a
fellow right here in central Florida who's been flying to
Jamaica for pot. For a price he'd fly me down there and
bring the two of us back."

"You're kidding."

Sam smiled. "Am I? There's a spray-plane field just
outside Christiana. You didn't hear the planes over the
banana fields when you were there? Or notice the goo on
the Land Rover after they'd been working?"

"But—"

"Wait," Lynne interrupted. "Why do we have to *confront* this thing in the lake?" Why can't we just get out
of here?"

"Run away, you mean?" Will said.

She reached out to touch his hand. "Believe me, darling, I'm not proud. I want to keep you, not lose you to
a dead woman."

"We can't run, Lynne."

"Why?"

"In his own sweet way Jurzak warned me not to. Said
he didn't want the job of going after me. Besides, what's
to keep Vicky from following us? I can't believe she's
confined to any one place."

A shudder briefly touched Lynne's slender body.
"The way you and Sam speak of her as though she were
still alive . . . I feel I'm trapped in a nightmare."

"It's safer for us to think of her that way," Sam
pointed out. "She isn't alive the way we are, of course.
But she had those long sessions with Sister Merle—
learned from her, we have to assume—and both obeah
and voodoo provide for a life after death. Especially
when there's unfinished business to be attended to."

He paused, then added quietly, "Yes, we'd better think of her as being alive, Lynne, if *we* want to go on living. And Will is right. If you two left here, she'd probably follow."

"And if she didn't," Will said in a tone of finality, "she'd continue looking for us here, is my guess. As she's been doing right along. We could be responsible for more terror, maybe more deaths. That is, *I* could be. But you needn't stay, love. In fact, I wish—"

"Uh-uh." Emphatically Lynne shook her head. "If you stay, so do I." And when he would have protested, she held up a hand to silence him.

"All right," Sam said, rising. "The only problem I can see is Ima. Does she like you enough to do this for you, Will? I think she does—and she owes you for not reporting Merle's death to the police. But, of course, we don't know." He looked at his watch again. "Shall I give my U.N. buddy a ring?"

Will nodded. Sam went to the telephone and dialed a number. They watched him in silence while he toiled through the layers of explaining and at last had his man.

Lynne Kimball suddenly said then, "Will, if he can get a visa for Ima, I'm going with him."

"You what?"

"I'm going with him." Her voice was low but firm. "I'm a woman, I've lived in Jamaica—"

"She's Haitian, Lynne. Not Jamaican."

"There can't be that much difference in what I'm talking about. If I go along and tell her I'm there because I love you and don't want to lose you—" Suddenly silent, she looked the length of the room at Sam Norman.

Still talking on the phone, Sam had raised a hand to signal them, with two fingers upthrust in a V for victory.

The following morning, before daybreak, Sam Norman and Lynne Kimball left for Miami in Lynne's car, and Will was alone.

32

A Visitor from the Marsh

What, Will wondered, would he do with himself until they returned—with or without Ima Williams?

He tried working, but an hour at the typewriter produced nothing worth while, and he gave up. He tried to read and found he could not concentrate because his thoughts were with Lynne and Sam on their mission.

Would they be able to persuade Ima to leave Jamaica? Would they even be able to locate her? She had said she would be going to another housekeeping job as soon as Sam departed. That other job might be anywhere in the island, and they could be days trying to track her down.

About eleven he could stand the tension no longer and went out to work some of it off by waxing his car. He was doing that when a car with the county sheriff's seal on its doors rolled in and Karl Jurzak stepped out of it. The homicide investigator flapped a hand in salute but did not approach. Leaning against his car, he appeared to be waiting for something.

He did not have long to wait. Almost at once a pickup truck arrived, towing a trailer with a boat on it. Jurzak walked along with the men as they rolled the boat to the lake and launched it. Then one of the newcomers returned to the truck for what looked like a high-powered rifle.

After a few minutes the quiet of the morning was disturbed by the purr of the boat's powerful outboard as the craft moved out toward the marsh.

Jurzak had not gone with it. Returning to the parking lot, he veered toward Will and now leaned against Will's car, as though the effort of helping to launch the boat had wearied him.

"Has anything happened since I talked to you, Mr. Platt?"

"No, Karl."

"That's something to be thankful for, at least."

"Why the rifle?" Will said. "I thought when a 'gator invaded a place like this, you tried to capture it and take it to the Glades."

"This one killed a man, Mr. Platt. If we find him, we'll shoot him. Only safe thing to do. Besides, the restrictions on hunting them have been eased. For quite a while we've had a surplus." He smiled. "From what I hear, you can even order 'gator steak in some restaurants."

Will made a face. "You, maybe. Not me. Not after what happened to Helpin."

"I should tell you there will be other boats here before the day is over. Maybe for several days."

"Professional hunters?" The state, Will knew, sometimes hired such men to remove 'gators from places they were not supposed to inhabit.

The fat man nodded. "And we're going to drag the lake again. More thoroughly this time."

"A good idea."

"You think so? Suppose they find your wife."

Will hoped his shrug was convincing. "They won't. Ever since you suggested she might have drowned herself, I've been thinking. I don't buy it, Karl. It won't stand up."

"You told me she was acting strangely even before the two of you returned from Jamaica."

"Not that strangely. In any case, if she had wanted to kill herself, she wouldn't have done it that way."

"Why not?"

"She never swam in the lake. Some of our people do at times, but she couldn't persuade herself to try it, not even once. The thought of being caught up in weeds and lily pads like a fly in a spiderweb gave her the shivers. She used the pool."

The watery eyes seemed to appraise Will's face intently for a few seconds, then Jurzak shrugged. "You may be right. I think if I were you, though, I might be somewhat relieved if we did find her in the lake. The uncertainty must be getting to you."

Limply flapping a hand in farewell, he walked away.

There were four of Jurzak's boats on the lake before the day ended. Each was manned by two or three men, and no two of them were alike. At times Will could not resist walking out onto his sixty-floor veranda to watch them.

In a marshy body of water three miles long, it might take weeks to home in on an alligator, even one as large as this. Still, experts familiar with the reptiles' habits would not have to search the entire lake, would they?

What else would they find? Will wondered. They had already found pieces of Helpin's body and might drag up more. But after all this time would there be anything left of Vicky to be found?

He doubted it. She had been wearing nothing but a nightgown when he committed her body to the lake's dark water. Not even slippers. If the 'gator had taken her—and it must have—there would not be enough left of the nightgown for it to be identifiable. Even the jacket worn by Helpin, recovered almost immediately after his death, had been in shreds.

Relax, he told himself. They won't find anything.

When darkness came and the boats returned to the

condo's beach for the night, he found himself pacing the apartment. He realized suddenly that he had to get out of the apartment for a while. Waiting for the phone to ring was not the answer; he was too tense—something would snap. Besides, what assurance did he have that the phones in Christiana were working or that Sam or Lynne would call so soon.

He slammed the door behind him and went down to his car. Got into it and slammed the car door too. On Highway 27 he headed north with no destination, just to breathe a different air and see something other than the apartment walls and the lake. After he'd been out for a couple of hours—he'd stopped at a diner for a sandwich —he felt relaxed enough to head for home.

It was after eleven when he got out of his car in the condo parking lot and walked into the building. Riding up to the sixth floor, he fished his key from his pocket and opened his door.

An odor assailed his nostrils. A smell of the marsh, of stagnant water, of swamp muck. It gagged him, it was so strong. He reached out blindly for the light switch on the wall and fumbled it on. Took in a deep breath and felt himself become cold and brittle.

The carpet was wet with footprints again. Footprints all over the living room. Footprints leading to the bedrooms and the study. Their maker must have prowled the whole apartment, looking for him.

He quickly put the light out and stepped back into the hall, but stood there with the door still open, peering into the now dark apartment. The thing could be seen clearly in the dark now, couldn't it? He had distinctly seen it attack Helpin in the marsh. A human shape, Vicky's shape, made of mist—or ectoplasm—internally glowing. If it were still here, he should see it now. Or the glow from it.

Nothing. It must have departed.

Snapping the light back on, he hurried through the

living room to the veranda and saw where the thing had come through the screen, wetting the plastic. Shaken, he peered into the bedrooms and his study, even into the bathrooms and the kitchen.

Footprints everywhere. And that sickening smell of the swamp. But nothing else.

It knew where he lived now, for certain. It was homing in on him, becoming smarter all the time. There would probably be no more Connie Abbotts or Tom Brodericks or Carl Helpins. But it hadn't killed Helpin, had it? Only rendered him helpless long enough for the 'gator to get him. My jacket, Will thought. Platt, for God's sake get out of here before it returns!

He hurried back to the hall door, putting lights out as he went. Turned there for one last look into the dark apartment, one last shudder of apprehension that racked him from head to foot.

Pulling the door shut after him, he went along the hall to the stairwell, where the thump of his shoes on the uncarpeted concrete stairs was not much louder than the thudding of his heart as he descended to the floor below. His hand shook as he fumbled Lynne's key from his pocket and opened her door.

This time he sniffed the air before lifting his hand to the light switch. There was no swamp smell here. The thing was after him, then, not Lynne, and wasn't aware yet that he spent much of his time in this apartment. He might be safe for a while.

He switched the light on. There were no footprints. He shut the door behind him, walked to the livingroom sofa, and sank onto it with a noisy exhalation of relief.

Almost at once, though, he got up to put the light out and draw the drapes at the windows and across the veranda door facing the lake. Then with only one lamp on, he sat to wait, ready at the first sign of danger to leap to his feet and race to the hall door.

An hour passed. Two. Nothing happened.

He fell asleep at last on the sofa, sitting up, and dreamed of Lynne and Sam in Jamaica. In the dream they were with bearded, loyal Ken Daniels in Ken's battered old taxi, driving through the night in search of Ima Williams. When he awoke they were still searching, and it was daylight in both Jamaica and Florida, and the telephone was ringing.

He answered it with sleep and bewilderment in his voice. Who would be calling Lynne at this hour?

"Morning, Will." It was Sam Norman. "We thought we might find you there when you didn't answer your phone. Any reason, other than the obvious one?"

Will hesitated. Should he tell them? They would worry if he did. On the other hand, they might not realize the special urgency of their mission if he didn't. "My own place is full of footprints again, Sam."

"No."

"I went up the road last night for a bite to eat. Found them there when I got back. What luck with Ima?"

He heard Sam telling someone else—Lynne, no doubt —about the footprints. Then Lynne took the phone.

"Darling, we've found Ima and she's coming. We're waiting right now for Ken Daniels to drive us to Kingston."

"Where are you?"

"At the Villa Bella." It was a guest house just outside Christiana, on the road to Spaldings. "Ima is with us. She shared my room last night. She was working in Mandeville." A pause. "Will, use my apartment until we get there. Don't go back to your own!"

"Thanks. I'll be glad to take you up on that."

"Sam wants to talk to you again. Will, I love you. Be careful."

Sam took the phone and said, "If we're lucky at the embassy, old boy, we may be able to catch a plane for Miami this afternoon. At worst we'll be on the first one out tomorrow."

"I'll keep my fingers crossed."

"Ima wants a word."

The phone changed hands again. Ima Williams's warm voice said, "Mr. Will? This is Ima. I just want to say that I hope I can help you. I will do my best."

"Thank you, Ima. I know you will."

"I have been back to Haiti since I saw you last. Not for long—just a visit—but I stayed with Manman Lespri, my mambo, and received instructions that will make me more knowledgeable, I am sure."

"Good."

"Your Miss Lynne is nice. I like her."

"Thank you, Ima."

He heard a tangle of voices then, after which Lynne took over the phone. "Will, Ken Daniels is here and we're leaving. Take care of yourself, darling. Bye for now."

"Goodbye, love," he said. But she had hung up.

That day was better than the one before. Knowing they would soon be arriving with Ima, and telling himself she would know how to help him, he was not so tense. The boats on the lake were not such a lodestone for his attention, either. He could accept their presence now without constantly imagining they might drag up something to bring Karl Jurzak to his door again.

Would Sam succeed in getting a visa for Ima Williams in time to catch a plane today at the Palisadoes airport? Will climbed the stairs to his apartment and looked for a Jamaica-Miami timetable but failed to find one; must have thrown away the one he had. Platt, you're a writer; you should keep things like that, damn it! He remembered the departure times from Montego Bay, but Kingston's were different.

Anyway, it was highly unlikely the embassy would be that cooperative, even with the urging of Sam's United Nations friends.

Tomorrow, then. They would be turning up tomorrow.

If no hitch developed.

33

"He Wants to Find Her Again"

Will watched the boats while eating lunch on Lynne's veranda. There were six today. He had never witnessed a dragging operation before and could discover no apparent pattern in this one.

When tired of watching, he washed and dried the lunch dishes, put them away, and went up to his own apartment to change into swim togs. When he got to the pool, he was happy to find it deserted.

His mood changed as he swam. Forgetting his problems, he found himself thinking of the day he had met Lynne Kimball here. Absolutely an arranged-in-Heaven encounter, not a mere accident, he told himself again.

What a woman she was! And what a miracle he had at last found her, after writing her into book after book while convinced there really was no such woman in the world.

Thinking about her, he swam contentedly back and forth until he was too tired to continue. Then he returned to Lynne's apartment and, after drying himself, lay naked on her bed and slept for an hour. The sleep refreshed him, and he was able to get through the remainder of the afternoon without pacing the floor.

It was still daylight—the boats were still plying the

270

lake—when he began to wonder just how Ima Williams would try to help him, and what her chance of success might be.

As a hounsi kanzo she would know most of the voodoo ceremonies, of course. Her own hounfor's version of them, at any rate, for the rituals varied widely in different parts of Haiti. The awesome rite by which a person *became* kanzo was one he himself would never forget: the servitors all in white, the seven black iron pots turning red over individual pine-stick fires, the houngan filling them with oil, the peristyle reeking with the smell of it as the oil began to boil and smoke.

He could picture Ima at the time of her initiation, being led from the secret djévo, that room in the adjoining hounfor where for the past seven days she had been left alone to meditate in silence on the commitment she was about to make. The houngan would have taken her by the hand and walked her into the peristyle, where the three drums were almost silent now, just barely whispering, and the crowd of onlookers all but held their breath while watching.

By the hand he would have led her to the first of the zins, those now glowing iron pots in which the boiling oil bubbled. He would have shifted his grip to her right wrist and slowly dipped her hand into the oil and held it there for ten seconds or so. Then he would have walked her to each of the other six pots and repeated the dipping.

After that, Ima would have been returned to the hounfor for a further three days of meditation from which she would emerge kanzo, with knowledge and powers she had not possessed before.

That knowledge and those powers, Will reflected, had not been enough to enable her to match wills with Sister Merle in Jamaica. But perhaps her recent stay with her mambo in Haiti had sharpened them.

As for a ceremony by which she might undertake to

protect him from the dead, he could think of only one such that he had ever attended, but there were several. Voodoo involved scores of ceremonies. There were the gardes to protect one against evil magic. The more powerful arrêts to safeguard whole families from the loup-garou and evil spirits. The mysterious and legendary gros arrêts used in the old days to secure the safety of whole villages when the people-devouring baka were on the prowl.

Ima would know about those.

She knew, too, about the unusual powers of the cocomacaque, of course. He well remembered the night in Jamaica when he had inched her door open to see what she was up to, and discovered her brandishing a monkey-palm stick while calling on the loa for help in finding Sam. He had such a stick in his closet at this moment, if she wanted to use one here.

There had not been another phone call from either Kingston or Miami. Sam had not made the hoped-for connection, then. As the day faded, Will went out onto the veranda for a final look at the boats, and found them returning to the condo beach.

If Lynne and Sam would not be returning tonight, he might as well go out for something to eat. The motel, maybe. The food there was seldom better than awful, but he felt no need to drive as far as he had driven yesterday. Locking Lynne's door behind him, he went down to his car.

He found some of the condo's people in the motel restaurant, and one of them beckoned to him. Pearl Gautier was eating alone, or rather waiting alone to be served, and he accepted her invitation.

"Have the boats found anything, Will?"

"Not yet, so far as I know."

"God, I'm so frightened," she said. "Do you know I haven't slept, not really, since Connie was killed?"

She leaned toward him just as a waitress stopped to take his order. There was a moment of confusion, the waitress not knowing whether to retreat or not. Pearl sat back to wait for privacy. Will said, "I'll just have the special, whatever it is."

"Yes, sir, it's fried clams." The waitress went away.

"Someday I'll learn to take the special in this place, even when I don't want it," Pearl said. "You can wait forever if you shake the kitchen up." She went on at some length about the service, the food, and other motel trivia. Then for a time both of them were silent. Then she said, frowning at him, "Tell me something. Has Karl Jurzak been to see you?"

"More than once."

"What do you think of him?"

"I wish I had his mind. I might write better books."

"I knew him before any of this happened," she said. "Shall I tell you about him, so you'll know what to expect?"

The waitress came with Will's food, but curiosity kept him from touching it, and he nodded. The nurse still had nothing in front of her but a glass of water.

"He came here from New York when his wife was killed in a car accident," Pearl said, speaking so quietly now that other sounds in the restaurant intruded enough to be annoying. "He was in love with her. Really in love, I mean. He told me once it was a very special thing, spiritual more than physical, as if—well, this may sound awfully corny, but it's what he said—he said he was convinced they'd been *selected.*"

She paused to stare at him. "You know what I mean? They found each other late in life for both of them, after each had made mistakes and been divorced, and it was special. Then she died, and he felt he was only hanging around—that's how he put it—until his time came to be with her again. It won't be too long. He has terminal cancer."

"What?"

"Haven't you noticed how he hangs onto his stomach all the time? He's always in pain. About six months, that's all he can hope for at the most. I've nursed him through some bad times. I know."

"Lord," Will said.

"He isn't bitter," she said. "He wants to find her again." The waitress came at last with her food and she stopped talking until it was arranged in front of her. Then she said, frowning at Will's untouched plate, "I'll bet I've spoiled your appetite. I'm sorry."

He shook his head as he picked up his fork. "I kept thinking of *Les Misérables*," he said, and looked at her to see whether she understood.

She nodded. "The policeman. So relentless and efficient."

"But there was something more. This man had compassion. Now I know why."

The rest of his conversation with Pearl Gautier was ordinary. Will said he hoped those residents of the condo who were spending their nights at the motel would soon be able to return to their apartments. She hoped Jurzak's people would catch the alligator before it killed someone else. Then, leaving her, he returned to Lynne's apartment intending to switch on the tv and idly amuse himself until bedtime.

And, on opening her door, he felt the swamp smell explode in his lungs, and slammed the door shut again.

After trembling outside for a moment he opened it a second time and reached for the light-switch. Footprints? Yes, they were there, leading in wet trails from the veranda to all parts of the apartment. Last night repeated.

He shut the door and walked to the elevator. Pushed the button. Stood there looking back at the apartment door while fearfully waiting for the car to come up to him. It seemed to take forever. The doors opened when they were good and ready, as though deliberately taunting him. He quickly stepped in and sent the car down to floor one.

At his rapping on the manager's door, big Ed Lawson

appeared—the first time Will had faced him since the night on the lake. In his usual deep voice he said, "Well, hello, Will. Come on in."

Will walked in and sat down, still cold, still shaking. "Ed, I need a favor."

"You look as though you need a stiff drink. What's happened?"

"The thing that attacked Helpin before the 'gator got him—you remember?"

The manager nodded.

"It's after me now." Will described the footprints he had found in his own and Lynne's apartments. But be careful, he warned himself. This is a man with a no-nonsense mind. A man who damned near drowned Carl Helpin in the pool when Helpin stupidly propositioned him. He isn't going to believe too much.

Big Ed listened. His shrug was accompanied by a frown of genuine bewilderment. "So what do you want me to do?"

"You have apartments for rent in this building, don't you?"

"A few."

"Rent me one for tonight."

"Will, we don't rent by the night. The by-laws don't permit it. A month. Nothing less." Lawson rose from his chair and went to another part of the apartment. Returning with a key, he dropped it into Will's hand. "Be careful," he said. "All I've got that's ready to sleep in is 102, next door to me here."

Where you can keep an eye and ear open, Will thought. To protect me or to check on me?

"Just remember," Ed said, offering his hand and exerting pressure that made Will wince, "that damned thing won't have to climb the building if it wants you tonight. You see or hear anything, you holler real loud."

34

Hidden Fire

He spent most of the night watching the lake, but nothing happened. Something must have come *out* of the lake when he was not on sentry duty, however, for when he left the first-floor apartment at daybreak and went up to Lynne's, he found more of the wet footprints. There were fresh ones in his own place, as well.

At quarter to eleven he walked out onto his veranda to watch Jurzak's boats through binoculars. Some were equipped with outboard motors this morning, some powered by oars. One of those being rowed was alone in a patch of marsh about half a mile from the condominium.

It held two men. One stood in the stern, peering at the marsh as the craft moved slowly through it. Suddenly he bent down and came up with a rifle, took aim, and fired.

The sound of the shot was a single sharp crack, as though a bullwhip had been snapped over the lake's quiet waters. Ten yards from the boat's bow something in the reeds erupted in a furious splashing.

The rifle cracked again. It cracked a third time. The eruption subsided.

The man with the gun waved his weapon over his head in a gesture of triumph, and appeared to be yelling.

At once the other craft of Jurzak's fleet made for the marsh, those with outboards filling the morning stillness with a rumble of motor noise and trailing wakes full of foam and disturbed vegetation.

In the marsh something long and pale came up alongside the killer boat—a 'gator, belly up—and the man who had slain it exchanged his rifle for a pole. He poked at it a time or two, then put the pole down. Kneeling, he leaned over the boat's side with a loop of rope in his outthrust hands.

Other boats arrived then, and Will could not make out what individual men were doing or trying to do; it appeared to be a group effort accompanied by some confusion. It lasted all of five minutes, with the boats milling about and bumping one another. Then with all six craft present and the 'gator apparently secured, the fleet moved toward a strip of shore where a smooth patch of meadow dipped gently to the water's edge.

Will watched them beach the boats and haul the creature up onto the grass. There were some big 'gators in Florida these days, due no doubt to the length of time they had been protected as endangered wildlife. This one looked huge. At that distance, with so many men standing around it, he could not be certain *how* huge, but it was surely sixteen to eighteen feet long.

Would they open it up right there on the grass, to find out what its stomach contained? He watched until he was tired of watching. When he gave up and went inside, some of Jurzak's men were on their knees, others standing around looking on.

Presently his phone rang, and it was Sam Norman at the airport in Miami.

"Sorry we couldn't make it yesterday, old boy," Sam said cheerfully. "But we did get out first crack this morning. Are you okay?"

"I'm okay, Sam. Lynne's with you? And Ima?"

"Both here. We're headed for the parking garage

where I left the car. Be seeing you."

With a deep sense of relief Will hung up and went to
the veranda again. Someone had driven a pickup truck
in from the highway, and men were lifting the 'gator into
it. Karl Jurzak's car was· parked beside it and the investigator himself was directing the operation. As Will
watched the fat man squeeze into the car and drive out
through the meadow with the truck following, he
thought of what Pearl Gautier had told him in the motel
restaurant.

Fifteen minutes later, when his doorbell rang and he
drew the door open, Jurzak was standing there.

"May I come in, Mr. Platt?" The voice was almost
too gentle.

"Of course."

The man with terminal cancer entered and, seemingly
weary from his morning's work, lowered himself gingerly into an easy chair. After waiting for Will to sit, he
said, "You saw us catch the 'gator, Mr. Platt?"

"Yes."

"Relieved, are you?"

"I suppose so, after what happened to Helpin."

"And to your wife."

"Oh, my God. You don't mean—"

Jurzak slowly nodded. "We didn't find anything—ah
—conclusive, mind you. I mean to say, there was nothing of hers in the animal's stomach where we found
some fragments of Mr. Helpin along with his belt and
one of his shoes. We did find this, however."

Reaching into his shirt pocket, he held something out
for Will to accept. "And, of course, it may not have
belonged to your wife at all. Mrs. Helpin says it did,
though. I took the liberty of showing it to her when I
went to tell her about the shoe and the belt."

His flabby shoulders moved very slightly. "I thought
I wouldn't bother you unless I had to, Mr. Platt. Was it
your wife's?"

Staring down at the opal ring in his palm, Will slowly nodded.

"I am sorry," Jurzak said. "It was wedged in one of the creature's tooth-pits. Are you quite certain it was hers?"

"Yes."

"It's rather an odd stone. I mean, I know a little something about such things. So dark and—ah—murky, for an opal. I believe it was Orpheus, the poet of Greek legend, who said they filled the hearts of the gods with delight." He paused and frowned. "But this isn't that kind of opal, is it? It awes one a little. Do you recall where your wife obtained it?"

Tonelessly Will said, "We bought it for three hundred dollars from an old Indian woman in Mexico who said it had certain powers. And I believe it has."

"Some do, it's said." Jurzak pursed his lips and moved his head up and down as he leaned from his chair for another close look at the stone in Will's palm. "In ancient Greece opals were thought to give their wearers the power of foresight and prophecy. Did you know that?"

"Well, yes. I've read it, at least."

"Eastern peoples still believe they are sacred stones endowed with a power to command the truth." The word "truth" hung in the air between them as the investigator gazed solemnly at Will's face.

Will said uneasily, "Karl, tell me something. Do you believe my wife drowned herself?"

"Should I?"

"Answer me, please."

Jurzak gazed into space, then shrugged. "She was acting strangely when you returned from Jamaica, you said. You awoke in the morning and found her gone. You thought she had left you. But if she had planned merely to leave you, why did she not take her car? It isn't easy to get from here to an airport. Not easy at all in the middle of the night. And if she meant to remove herself from your presence and live apart from you, why didn't she withdraw a sizeable sum of money from her account at the bank? She didn't, you know. After your return from Jamaica all she withdrew was a little pocket money, a hundred dollars. I've checked."

"So?"

"So in answer to your question I would have to say yes, she deliberately drowned herself. Then the 'gator found her body." Jurzak paused. "Now about the ring. You say you believe it has powers."

"I believe it's responsible—partly, at least—for what has been happening here. I don't mean the 'gator. I mean the thing Haydn Clay got the pictures of when Helpin was killed."

"Our ghost."

"That's as good a word as any, since we don't know what it is. In Haiti, Karl, my wife became much too friendly with a man named Margal, one of the most feared bocors—sorcerers, if you prefer—in a country where sorcery is a fine art. In Jamaica she was taking lessons from an obeah woman. Do you know about bocorism and obeah?"

"Only from reading about them."

"Vicky was deeply interested in occult studies of that sort. Attuned, you might say. She went to see this obeah woman daily in spite of my objections. One day the woman asked her about this ring, and when Vicky told her its history and what the Indian woman had said about it, she asked if she might wear it for a time. I happen to think, Karl—smile if you want to—that the ring absorbed something from her, and Vicky came into possession of that something on taking it back and wearing it again."

Jurzak reached for the ring and gazed at it in silence. "A smothered mass of hidden fire," he said at last.

"What?"

"Some writer said that once about black opals. I forget who. A famous stone called the Flame Queen, from Australia, is black with a flame-red center."

He looked up at Will with such an innocent stare that he might have been a small boy enthralled by what they were discussing. "It seems they sometimes arouse passions, these strange stones. Did you know that Antony once wanted one that was owned by a Roman senator—wanted it for Cleopatra, one supposes—and when the man refused to part with it, Antony became furious and sent him into exile? This *is* a black opal, of course," the investigator went on calmly. "Strange that you found it in Mexico. I thought the best from there were fire opals. But, of course, it may not have originated there. Perhaps it's old, even very old. Three hundred dollars, you say? Why do I have a hunch that the old woman who sold it to you may have been desperately in need of money?"

He dropped the ring into his shirt pocket.

"Are you going to keep it, Karl?"

"I believe I'd better, Mr. Platt. At least for the time being. It's the only evidence we have, isn't it, that your wife may be dead? And even so, it's pretty flimsy proof . . . wouldn't you say?"

35

The Cocomacaque Again

The three from Jamaica arrived in mid-afternoon,
tired and hot after the long ride from Miami. Will was
waiting in Lynne Kimball's apartment, where the Haitian woman would be staying. Clasping Ima's long-fingered hands, he said fervently, "Bless you for coming."

She looked the same as when he had last seen her: tall,
handsome, proud. Seeing America for the first time had
obviously not fazed her, though like most of the Jamaican farm workers who came to toil in Florida's sugarcane fields, she probably thought all America was flat
and therefore not nearly so attractive as her adopted little Caribbean island with its verdant mountains.

"Did you stop for lunch?" he asked them.

Lynne said they hadn't. "We didn't want to take the
time."

"I thought you wouldn't. Sit down. Everything's
ready and waiting."

He produced a meal of chicken and vegetables he had
prepared between the time of Karl Jurzak's departure
and their arrival, and was delighted when Ima Williams,
who so often had served him, accepted both the food
and the service with complete composure.

Will told them of the footprints in both his apartment

and this one. Of his sleeping, if it could be called sleeping, in the apartment the manager had let him use last night. Of the killing of the 'gator, and Jurzak's visit with the ring.

"We don't have much time, do we?" Sam said. "Not if that thing is watching both apartments."

"I'm sure we don't."

"We'd better do some fast thinking, then. Plan something before dark. What do you say to that, Ima?"

Her fine face fixed in a frown of deep thought, the Haitian woman slowly nodded. Then she said, "What is this ring you speak of, Mr. Will? The same one your wife wore in Jamaica?"

"Yes. Sister Merle asked if she might wear it, and my wife lent it to her. It was on Merle's finger when she was dying and caught hold of Vicky's hands. I took it from her after she died and gave it back to Vicky."

Ima said, "I wish I could see it. If it has powers—"

"I'm afraid that's impossible."

"The ring could be very important to us if something of Sister Merle passed through it into your wife," Ima persisted. "Some knowledge or power, I mean. Certain objects are used in that way, you know. In voodoo the cocomacaque conveys power. Through this ring your wife . . ." Shaking her head, she was silent.

"Well," Will said reluctantly, "I suppose I could phone Jurzak and ask him. I'll have to tell him what you want it for, though. How will you use it?"

Ima looked across the table at Lynne. "I can look around, please?" When Lynne nodded, she rose, though her meal was but half finished, and walked through the apartment.

The familiarization tour took several minutes, during which time those left at the table waited in silence. Returning, the hounsi seated herself and said, "It comes from the lake?"

"Yes." Will nodded. "It comes from the lake."

"And will come here?"

"Or to my place, directly above this one. Wherever we are. Wherever we have lights on."

"We should all be in one place, then, I think," Ima said. "Miss Lynne, do you have candles? White ones?"

"How many?"

"Perhaps ten, twelve? The more the better."

"I don't have that many, I'm sure. But we can get some. Can't we, Will?"

He nodded. "Just a trip to a store. Am I right in thinking you'll try a gros arrêt, Ima?"

"Yes, Mr. Will. I brought some things with me. Mostly it is not *things* we need, though, but to believe. To have faith in the candles and the gros arrêt and—well, I wish we had a cocomacaque. And, of course, the ring Sister Merle wore when she was dying and held onto your wife's hands."

Will got up and went into his study. His cocomacaque leaned in a corner of a closet there. Taking it out he looked at it, recalling the day he had found it growing near the top of Haiti's highest mountain.

He had earned a good deal of respect in Haiti by carrying this with him on some of his forays. Here in Florida he occasionally used it as a walking stick, simply because he liked the feel of it. It weighed only a few ounces —ten and a half, to be exact—but was tough as steel. More than once, on handing it to friends for their examination, he had said lightly, "Break it if you can. Put your knee to it."

No one had snapped it yet.

Carrying it back to the dining table, he offered it to Ima Williams. Her eyes nearly doubled in size as she accepted it and held it horizontally against her breast, grasping it so tightly he could see her knuckles change color.

Her eyes closed. Her lips moved but made no sound;

the words they formed were for herself alone. The others watched her in silence.

She opened her eyes. "Where did you get this?" she whispered.

"On Morne La Selle."

"*You* found it? Yourself?"

He nodded. "There was a Haitian friend with me, but we were not together at the time."

"You yourself *cut* it?"

"With a jackknife." They were not really difficult to cut. The steely hardness came later, when they dried.

"Wonderful," she said. "But I would like to bless it, too, before we use it, the way we do the drums. You would permit that?"

"Ima, you're to do whatever you think best. No one here is qualified to instruct you."

Solemnly she said, "It has power now. I can feel it. But there can be no harm in asking the loa to help us." Still holding the cocomacaque in both hands, she looked up at him. "And will you get the ring for me, Mr. Will?"

"Finish your dinner while I make a phone call."

Karl Jurzak had long ago written his number on a bit of paper and left it on the telephone table. Will dialed it and found himself talking to a woman in the county sheriff's office.

"Karl Jurzak, please. This is Will Platt at Lakeside Manor."

"Just a minute, Mr. Platt. I don't think he is in right now." She checked, and the homicide investigator was not. "Would you want him to call you when he returns?"

"It's urgent. Can you tell me where he is?"

He had to wait while she tried to find out. Then she said, "I can't be sure, but I believe he has gone home. He told someone he wasn't feeling well."

"Oh Lord. Have you his home address and phone number?"

She provided the needed information, and he dialed Jurzak's home. There was no answer. "Damn," he said aloud with a helpless look toward the three at the table, who were watching him. Then he thought: terminal cancer. Not feeling well. He could be there but not answering his phone.

He glanced at his watch. There was plenty of time. Give the man half an hour, then call again.

The others finished their lunch and Ima said, "I will do the dishes," but Lynne would not let her.

"You have to get ready for tonight," Lynne said. "Let me show you your room. Then you can be alone to do as you wish."

Ima took the monkey-palm stick with her, and when shown her room, stayed in it. The kitchen chores finished, the others sat in the living room and talked.

Lynne and Sam told how they had found Ima in Jamaica by first finding the taximan, Ken Daniels, and asking him where she was working. At the embassy in Kingston they had run into unexpected delays when the man they sought was absent and they had to deal with an officious substitute. Then they had just barely beaten a threatened airline strike in getting off the island this morning.

With frequent glances at his watch, Will told them of his talk with Pearl Gautier in the motel restaurant. Then he tried again to reach Karl Jurzak by phone, and again got no answer.

Was the man at home? Or could he have gone to a doctor, perhaps?

He called the sheriff's office and talked with the woman again. Had she heard from Karl? No. "Tell me, please—do you think it possible he may have gone to his doctor?"

She thought it possible. She gave him the name and

phone number of Jurzak's physician. He called.

The man had not been there.

On hanging up, he became aware of sounds from Ima's bedroom and looked at the others. She had closed her door; the sounds were muffled. Still, they were clearly audible, and he caught himself thinking that this was surely the first time any such chanting had been heard in Lakeside Manor.

He recognized a voodoo chant to Legba, guardian of the gate between the world of the loa and that of mortals. *"Papa Legba, ouvri bayé! Papa Legba, ouvri bayé pou mwê!"* Until the keeper of the gate complied, she could summon no other deity to help her.

The chanting continued. In the hounfor it would have been accompanied by drumming. To the rhythmic throbbing of the three ritual drums, servitors dressed in white would be moving unhurriedly through the sinuous, shoulder-swaying steps of a yanvalou. There would be a pouring of water on the ground by other participants in the just-beginning ceremony, and repeated cries of *"Abobo!"*—amen, or so be it—as the service continued. Here in a Florida condominium at five in the afternoon, the chanting was profound in itself.

It went on and on, changing at times into nonmusical prayers intoned in the Creole of the Haitian peasant, then gently lilting into melody again. He heard prayers to Agoué, Damballa Ouédo and Simbi, and was not surprised. Though the three had different functions, all dwelt in water. He heard songs or chants to obscure loa whose functions he simply did not know.

Tiring of it after a while, he looked at his watch again and realized he must do something about Karl Jurzak. The afternoon was nearly over. In a few hours darkness would come down on the lake, and the thing in its waters would be on the prowl again.

Besides, he had promised Ima to obtain some white

candles. Those in Sister Merle's house had been black, he recalled.

He dialed the fat man's number again. No answer. Once more he called the sheriff's office. Jurzak had not returned. To Sam and Lynne he said, "He may be just too sick to answer his phone. I'd better go to his place and find out."

"How far is it?" Lynne asked.

"Twenty miles. Don't worry. I'll be back long before dark."

Sam offered to accompany him but he refused, not liking the idea of leaving the two women alone in the apartment. Once out on the main highway, he turned north and ignored the speed limit. But on reaching the town in which Jurzak lived, and looking at his watch again, he stopped at a store and bought the candles before going on.

Showing the woman at the cash register the piece of paper on which he had written Jurzak's address, he asked directions and was given them. It was a street not easy to find, in a part of the town that had gone seedy. The house itself was large but old. Its porch steps looked rotten enough to crumble under him as he climbed them.

He rang the bell. No one answered. He rang it again, then tried the knob and found the door open.

Stepping inside into a dark entrance hall that smelled of mildew, he called out, "Karl? Karl Jurzak? Are you home?"

The silence mocked him.

"Jurzak! Are you here?"

Still nothing. So the man was not at home, and had left the front door unlocked through carelessness. Hardly the kind of behavior, though, to be expected from one so efficient.

The ring. Would it be here or at the sheriff's office? With a man like Jurzak you couldn't be sure. He had his

own way of doing things and probably ignored many a
regulation. Will frowned at a staircase in front of him,
dim now in the late afternoon gloom. He began climbing. Ima felt the ring was important. If it were just lying
here on Jurzak's dresser . . .

At the top of the stairs he turned toward an open door
on his right. It was a bedroom.

Karl Jurzak lay there on the bed, on his back, fully
dressed and snoring.

Will went to him and looked down at him. There
seemed to be nothing wrong; the man was simply asleep.
He said "Karl" and put a hand on a shoulder and gave
it a shake. Gave it a second shake and then a third, the
last one hard enough to rock the old-fashioned double
bed on which the man lay.

Jurzak opened his watery gray eyes and looked up.
"Mr. Platt? What's the trouble?"

"Are you sick, Karl?"

Using Will's arm to haul on, the fat man struggled to
sit up and finally managed it. "One of my bad days," he
said. "Sorry. It happens. What can I do for you?"

"I want to borrow my wife's ring for a few hours."

"What for?"

It took a desperately long time to explain the situation, but Will made himself do it. After all, the man
had not slammed the door on his request with a blunt
no.

"And you think this Haitian woman can solve the
case for us?" Jurzak said.

"If obeah created this thing," Will said, "perhaps
voodoo can destroy it."

"Which of the two is more powerful?"

"I don't know, Karl." And in any case, gentle Ima
Williams might not be more powerful than a spirit-
world demon created by that murderous woman from
the Cockpit.

The fat man squirmed off the bed and stood swaying

on his feet. "All right," he said. "I shouldn't, but I will."

"Thanks, Karl." So the ring was here in the house, and he would not have to waste time going to the sheriff's office for it. Thank God for that.

"I go with it, though. I want to see this for myself."

"But you're ill, man!"

"Do me a favor. Go downstairs to the kitchen and bring me up a drink."

"What kind of drink?"

"There's only one kind. Brandy. Bottle's in the ice box—I take it cold. Just pour me half a water glass and bring it here while I'm getting some shoes on."

Will did as asked, shuddering when he saw the filthy condition of the man's kitchen. There were dead roaches on both the floor and the counters, and dishes in the sink that must have been there for days. Jurzak was a very sick man, obviously. When handed the half glass of brandy, the investigator nodded thanks and drank it down steadily but slowly, with his eyes shut, as though it were a foul-tasting medicine.

On the way down the stairs Jurzak used one hand on the old, scarred bannister and kept the other pressed to his stomach. His mouth was tight with pain. Downstairs he shuffled to a desk in the living room, with some difficulty opened a drawer, and lifted out a small brown envelope which he thrust into his pants pocket.

"Okay, let's go."

On the twenty-mile drive back to Heron Lake he spoke but seldom, obviously being more concerned with what was going on inside his body. When he did talk, it was merely to ask a few basic questions about voodoo, which Will answered as effortlessly as he would have replied to similar questions after a lecture.

The real question, Will thought, was whether Karl Jurzak ought not to be in a hospital at this moment, getting the care he so obviously needed.

36

A Ring of Candles

Perhaps in a way it was a kind of séance. Certainly it was unlike any voodoo service Will had ever attended.

At Ima's request he had seated himself on a straight-backed chair in the center of the living room. On the sofa to his right sat the woman he loved, and on the veranda in front of him, watching the lake, stood his best friend, Sam Norman. Both had flatly refused to leave when he questioned their need to expose themselves to danger just to be with him.

To his left, in an easy chair and still clutching his stomach, sat the homicide investigator Karl Jurzak. In pain, palpably, but alert and curious.

Will had wanted to hold the affair in his own apartment upstairs, but Ima had vetoed the request. It was here, she pointed out, that she had talked to the gods and blessed the cocomacaque, the candles, and the ring. The service, therefore, should take place here.

The room was beginning to darken now as she walked about relighting candles which had been set upright earlier in gobs of their own wax on saucers from Lynne's china closet. There were thirteen of them, arranged around him in a circle. Ima had explained why the candles had to be white. "Bocors and obeah persons always use black ones."

As the Haitian woman completed her preparations, Will sat there in the ring of small flames, watching her. She wore the opal ring now. Jurzak had given it to him when they arrived, and he had handed it to Ima. She wore it on her left hand, with the gem turned inward.

Now she stepped to the wall and took up the cocomacaque leaning there. On it she had tied inch-wide strips of colored cloth—green, pink, lavender—and bits of braided white string. He recalled a visit he had once made to a sacred voodoo waterfall in the mountains of Haiti—Saut d'Eau it was called—where similar bits of cloth and string had adorned a number of dead trees leaning into the mist that filled the grotto.

The cocomacaque was now a gros arrêt, he suspected, meant to protect him and perhaps to protect her as well. She must have brought the bits of cloth and string with her from Jamaica.

Holding the monkey palm, she turned to look toward the veranda, where Sam was on sentry duty watching the lake. Sam shook his head at her. The sliding glass door being only partly open, she went to it and opened it wide, at which a light breeze entered that caused the candle flames to flicker. Will looked at the flames and supposed he ought to feel slightly foolish in such a position, a grown man sitting in a circle of candles in the living room of a Florida condominium. Yet he did not feel the least bit foolish; this was deadly serious.

"Are you afraid, Mr. Will?" Ima asked quietly, turning to look at him.

"Yes." Why lie? A prickling sensation had taken hold of his whole body, especially his hands and feet, and he could feel the blood pounding in his ears. Why shouldn't he be afraid? He was the bait in a God-awful trap, knowing the thing in the lake would come for him, and not knowing whether this quiet Haitian woman with her knowledge of the occult would be able to protect him.

His fear must have been visible to them all, for Lynne Kimball suddenly rose from the sofa and stepped through the ring of candles to his side. Sinking to one knee beside his chair, she looked into his face. "Will, I'm frightened," she whispered. "Do you have to go through with this? Can't we just run?"

"Hon, there's just nowhere to run to."

Her eyes closed. Almost inaudibly she whispered, "Dear God, if this man and I are really something special to you, as we've dared to think, please help us now."

Reaching out, he took her hand and squeezed it.

The room darkened. Ima had said she did not want the lights on, only the candles. Beyond the veranda the lake had become dark, too. Most of last night an almost full moon had been dimmed by clouds. Tonight it was hidden completely.

The light from the ring of candles would be clearly visible to anyone or anything on the lake. Or in it.

Karl Jurzak said unexpectedly, "Is it always this noisy here, Mr. Platt?"

Noisy? When you lived here you scarcely noticed it, but yes, it was noisy. Some of the lake's inhabitants seemed to find a special voice at this hour. At the moment, the loudest were two frogs talking to each other tirelessly in xylophone tones, one slightly higher on the scale than the other. To a man whose stomach was keeping his face contorted with pain, it must be annoying.

"It will quiet down, Karl," Will said.

But Jurzak wanted to talk. Perhaps it helped him to combat the pain. "Brief me again, will you? What's going to happen here?"

"I wish I knew."

"Well, then, how will the opal *affect* what happens? You must think it will play a major role or you wouldn't have chased me for it."

Will hesitated. It was the first time he had been asked

to be specific. "What we think, Karl, is that when the obeah woman wore this ring it absorbed from her some power that my wife was able to use when she took the ring back."

"Do you believe in life after death, Mr. Platt?"

"I think so. Do you?"

"I must. It is what I have left—*all* I have left—to know I'll be with my wife again. And it may be we can achieve a life after death by believing in it. That would not surprise me, Mr. Platt. Not at all."

Will was silent.

"And, of course," Jurzak said, "you believe, too. Because what you are saying is that your wife is able to use this obeah power of hers even in death."

"Am I saying that?"

"It *is* your wife you expect tonight, isn't it?"

"Of course."

"And she is dead?"

"I believe so."

"You really know so, don't you, Mr. Platt? She didn't drown herself. If she was so afraid of the lake that she never swam in it, she would not have killed herself *that* way, as you yourself pointed out to me when I first brought up the possibility of suicide."

The fat man shifted his hands on his stomach, now pressing a few inches higher up. A grimace of pain accompanied the change. "Ah, no, Mr. Platt. Never would such a person have swum out into those slithery weeds and deliberately filled her lungs with water she considered so unwholesome. Fastidious women like your wife don't destroy themselves in ways they consider ugly. They look for the nice ways."

Pausing again, Jurzak looked down at his hands as though surprised to find them exerting such pressure on his body. "You killed her, I think, Mr. Platt. Of course, I don't suppose I'll ever be able to prove it, nor will anyone else. If she was a true pupil of the obeah woman you've told me about, perhaps I don't want to."

Will continued to stare at him.

"*Is* that why you killed her, Mr. Platt? Because she had become a creature of evil?"

Will glanced down at a thing Ima Williams had hung about his neck when she led him to his chair. It was fashioned of fragments of colored cloth sewn together to form a small drawstring bag. The colors were the same as those on the cocomacaque.

What was in the bag he did not know, but it reminded him of similar pouches, containing lumps of camphor, that his mother had made him wear around his neck when he was very young. Those had been to ward off colds, she had insisted. But she had been a deeply religious woman. In her nightly recitation of the Lord's Prayer she had always borne down heavily on the words "Deliver us from evil."

He had, in fact, always suspected that the camphor bags were meant to protect him more from evil than from anything as ordinary as colds.

If I live through this night, he thought, frowning now at Jurzak but still maintaining silence, maybe I'll show him the letter I wrote to Lynne and Sam. He just might understand.

Suddenly from the veranda Sam Norman called, "I see it! It's coming!"

37

"I Hope He Finds Her"

Ima Williams at once came out of a seeming trance inspired by Jurzak's questioning of Will. Holding the cocomacaque stick horizontally in front of her at arm's length, she began a slow walk around the circle of candles.

Her shoulders dipped and swayed. Her bare feet performed a shuffling yanvalou step on the carpet—or what would have been a yanvalou had her hands been free to rest on her knees.

From her mouth came the chant Will had heard from the bedroom earlier.

"Papa Legba, ouvri bayé! Papa Legba, ouvri bayé pou mwê! Abobo!"

The song ceased. But her lips still moved, and Will guessed she was praying to certain of her gods, calling on them to help her in this moment of terrible need.

Were they hearing her? Was there anyone out there *to* hear her, really? He thought there was. He had seen too much at voodoo services to retain many of his original doubts. So many improbable acts were performed in voodoo. It was stupid to deny them because they could not be explained.

Sam Norman said from the veranda, "It's rising from the marsh out there. A misty kind of thing, white. No

296

particular shape to it." His voice droned on; leave it to Sam to be more curious than alarmed, even at such a moment. "Now it's floating above the water toward the beach. It's drifting over the lawn. It's rising."

Ima Williams continued her ritual slow dance around the candles. On the sofa Lynne Kimball leaned forward, staring at the veranda as she waited for the appearance of the thing Sam was describing.

Glued to his chair within the circle, Will felt his hands clench at his sides and his body begin to tremble as it turned cold again.

Karl Jurzak, clutching his belly, slowly got out of his chair and onto his feet. Swaying from side to side as though about to crash to the floor, he too gazed fixedly at the veranda.

Silent now, Sam Norman walked backward through the open veranda doorway into the room. As Lynne Kimball rose trembling from the sofa, her face ashen, he reached her side and took hold of her hand. Then as the thing from the lake rose into view outside the veranda screen, he said in a low voice to Will, "This is it, man. Be careful."

"Damn it, get out of here!" Will ordered loudly. "Both of you!"

They did not reply. Did not move.

"Get out!" he shouted again. "Go up to my place and wait there!" Reaching into his pocket for a key, he tossed it to Sam. "Please," he begged them. "Can't you see I've got trouble enough?"—*without having to worry about the two persons I care most for in this whole crazy world,* he silently finished. "Lynne, Sam—please. There's nothing you can do to help me here."

They looked at each other and could find no reason to deny his plea. Sam touched him on the shoulder in departing. Lynne's lips brushed his face. The door closed behind them, and suddenly Will felt enormously relieved.

Ima Williams stepped into the circle of candles and took up a position almost in front of him, facing the veranda but leaving him room enough to see the thing float through the screen and assume human shape.

Vicky, his wife. Made of mist, fog, teleplasm, ectoplasm—whatever it was—but still as tall as Vicky, as slender as Vicky, as attractive as Vicky. And the shape walked toward him the way it must have walked through this apartment and the one above when it left the footprints.

Fascinated, he watched the carpet turn wet behind her now as she created more of the footprints. And the odor, the same dreaded swamp smell—or was it really some kind of *death* smell?—clogged his nose and throat, threatening to choke him.

At the ring of candles she halted to look down at the flames and studied them for a moment, motionless. Then she looked up again, straight at him, as though mocking him the way she so often had in life.

As she stepped through the ring and continued her advance toward him, he would not have been surprised to hear her sneering at him in his helplessness. The candle flames flickered as though touched by a sudden brief gust of wind.

Aware that something like death was about to happen to him, Will froze on his chair, incapable of movement.

But the hounsi kanzo from Haiti was not so stricken. Holding the cocomacaque like a lance, she lunged forward and plunged it into the midst of the thing. From her lips burst a cry of "Abobo!" that rang like a bell through the apartment. Then she thrust her left hand, with the opal ring on it, palm forward into the creature's ill-defined face.

The thing that was Vicky stopped in the midst of its relentless advance as though impaled on the monkey-stick. Its hands, if they were hands, groped in vain at the stick, then weakly writhed up to its misty face and struggled there in a confulsive effort to push the ring away also. It swayed like a column of white smoke bent by a strong wind and then, still swaying, began to change both shape and color.

The tall, slender thing of white turned gray. Turned darker gray. Turned almost black. It began to shrink in size. While writing on the cocomacaque that had pierced it, it slowly lost its proportions and changed into a dwarf.

A new face took the place of the one that had almost been Vicky's. But this one was familiar, too, in a horrible kind of way. Will had seen it first when he went with Sam to that hell house in the Cockpit. Had seen it later when he went there with Vicky and found Sister Merle dying in a pool of blood on the bed.

"My God!" he whispered while struggling in vain to overcome his paralysis.

The obeah woman was alive again now. At least, she was alive in what Karl Jurzak had called a life after death. The transfiguration complete and Vicky done away with, she stood before him. The creature writhing on the cocomacaque, slapping furiously at the opal ring, was not Will's wife but the woman who, in Jamaica, had jabbed a finger into his face and shrieked a curse at him just before she died.

And she was much stronger than Vicky. Much more powerful in every way!

She slapped the monkey-palm stick aside with such force that it was torn from Ima's grasp and hurled halfway across the room, to clatter to the floor in front of Karl Jurzak. She must have nearly broken the Haitian woman's wrist in driving an upthrust arm against Ima's ring hand to slam it away from her face.

Ima staggered back and sank to her knees, moaning.

The spectre from Jamaica pursued her with incredible swiftness, seizing her by an arm before she could rise. One misty hand locked itself around Ima's wrist and savagely twisted, wringing a cry of agony from the hounsi's lips. The other tore the opal ring free and held it aloft in triumph.

In the lesser glow of the candles, the opal pulsed now with an incredible kind of fire, its colors seeming to mate in some unholy union of evils. Then, thrusting the ring onto the third finger of her misty left hand, the obeah woman turned and hurled her dark, twisted shape at Will as he at last came to his senses and struggled to his feet.

Her attack slammed him back onto his chair. Like a cloud of poison gas she enveloped him.

While he struggled to fight her off, his mind strained to comprehend what was happening. Was it really Merle, not Vicky, who had tried to plunge the knife into him in the apartment that night? Was it *Merle* he had disposed of in the lake?

He could not make himself believe it. At worst there might have been a merging of their psyches at that time because of the sessions at the obeah woman's house and their sharing the black opal's powers. But it was both of them he had been forced to deal with, not Merle alone.

Why, then, was Merle destroying him now?

As he struggled without hope to save himself, he recalled what Ima had told him just before his departure from Jamaica.

"Mr. Will, who knows what death is? Be on your guard. She will seek revenge!"

Ima was right. From the moment of Merle's dying, when through the ring she had poured herself into the living body of her pupil, she must have wanted only that: revenge. He remembered again her death-bed curse.

Be on his guard? God help him, he had tried to be. And now she was about to have her way with him, because Ima could not save him, after all. The chants, the prayers, the candles and the cocomacaque, the arrêts to

protect him from evil . . . all of them together were not
strong enough.

This was the end.

He wondered whether the earlier victims had felt the
way he did now. It was not pain, exactly. He almost
wished he could cease struggling and let it happen and
get it over with. Some primal instinct for self-preserva-
tion made him continue, but the struggle was barely
physical. It was more a thing of the mind, a refusal to
admit the power, even the existence, of anything so unreal.

He was in quicksand, slowly sinking to his death but
willing himself not to. He was naked in a pool of dark
water filled with leeches that had attached themselves to
all parts of his body and were slowly draining him. He
was weakly pushing with both hands at a smothering
mist through which he could see in spite of its blackness.

He saw Ima Williams, on her knees, apparently
stunned but trying to crawl to the cocomacaque which
had been knocked from her grasp.

Just behind her, Karl Jurzak swaying crazily from
side to side as he stumbled forward to try to help her.

Whatever was destroying Will slackened its grip for a
moment. An arm of darkness reached out with almost
insolent lack of haste to confront Ima as she crawled
toward the monkey-palm. A shadowy hand with the
hellfire opal glittering on its third finger fastened on the
hounsi's shoulder.

Jerking Ima back on her knees, the hand transferred
its grip to her throat as she cried out in Creole, imploring her voodoo gods to help her.

When the hand with its blazing opal was withdrawn,
the Haitian woman collapsed on the carpet, to lie there
twitching and moaning.

The stunted shadow of Sister Merle turned back to
Will then, but again he won a reprieve through no action
of his own. Karl Jurzak had reached for the cocoma-

caque and was bending to pick it up.

She whirled toward the investigator like a small, dark funnel cloud, and he tried desperately to bend more quickly. Perhaps, having seen what had happened when Ima plunged the voodoo stick into Vicky's astral form, he hoped to repeat the attack. But his groping hand was still inches above its objective, violently unsteady, when his face suddenly filled with agony.

It was an agony that had nothing to do with Sister Merle or leeches or quicksand. It was inside him, at the very core of his being, affecting his life source.

Will saw him suck in a great, chest-filling torrent of air. Saw him grab at his balloon of a belly with both hands as though to keep it from exploding.

His knees buckled. Almost at the obeah woman's feet he crashed to the floor like a felled tree.

Merle looked down at his still form. The monkey-palm was under his huge, inert body, only an inch or two of it still visible. Anyone trying to pick it up would have to roll him over first.

There was a disdainful air of triumph in the sway of the obeah woman's ghostly figure as it turned back to Will.

From some unsuspected reservoir inside him, Will summoned the strength to stagger up from his chair and face her. As she reached for him, to draw him into her deadly embrace, he concentrated with all his mind on the opal ring that blazed on her finger.

With both hands he clawed for it. She had not expected that, it seemed. She was unprepared. One of his clutching hands reached its objective and the ring slid free into his palm. But before he could even think what to do with it, the woman became a swirling cloud of blackness and swamp-smell—the same awful swamp stench that had accompanied the maker of the wet foot-prints—and he felt himself in quicksand again.

No, not in quicksand this time. In something beneath

it, some lower deep from which he could emerge only in a form like hers. His hand opened limply and the opal ring dropped to the floor.

But, behind Sister Merle, something was happening to Karl Jurzak.

The man himself had not moved. His body still lay where it had fallen, with the cocomacaque under it. But tendrils of white smoke were rising from it now as though it had begun to smolder.

Will was still conscious enough to wonder what in God's name was happening. Was it because in dying— if, indeed, the man was dead—he had clung to the cocomacaque and absorbed something of its power? Because, after all, voodoo gods summoned by Ima Williams had blessed the monkey-palm, had they not? And its awesome force had already been demonstrated in the hounsi's attack on Vicky.

The tendrils detached themselves from Jurzak's unmoving body and curled upward. They writhed and twisted above him until they began to assume a shape. A human shape. Big. Broad-shouldered. Obese. Like Jurzak himself.

It flowed over the carpet. Unaware of it, Sister Merle concentrated on finishing what she had begun with Will. Her spectral form embraced him like a fly-eating flower, absorbing and draining him.

The hands of Karl Jurzak took her from behind and slowly tore her from her intended victim.

Will felt himself released. Felt himself falling. He crashed back onto his chair and the chair tipped and he was on the floor, looking up at two straining shapes.

Good versus evil, he thought. Love against hate.

He began to crawl away from the struggle, aware that Ima Williams, on her hands and knees, was doing the same thing. Reaching the sofa, he turned to see how the conflict would end.

Both figures were fainter now, but he could still iden-

tify them. The astral form that had risen from Karl
Jursak's body stood by the overturned chair in which he,
Will Platt, had been sitting in anticipation of a horrible
death. Its arms were extended. Its hands were locked
about the throat of the other figure, which was kneeling.
In the flickering light of the candle ring the struggle
seemed unreal, like a scene in a motion picture viewed
through a curtain of gauze.

The kneeling figure slowly became transparent as it
struggled to break Jurzak's grip. Through it now Will
could see some of the candle flames and, brighter than
those, the glowing opal that had fallen from his own
hand but a few moments before.

Sister Merle seemed to make a last desperate effort to
lean from Jurzak's grip and reach out for the opal, but
in vain. Even as Will stared at her, her struggles dimin-
ished. Under her a dark, wet stain began to spread over
the carpet.

Before Will's eyes the woman from Jamaica's Cockpit
Country disappeared, leaving only the image of Jurzak.
That, too, was all but invisible now.

Will saw it look down at the wetness and turn away.
Saw it walk slowly over to the body of Karl Jurzak and
look down at that and turn away from that also. He
recalled certain passages in books he had read about life
after death: statements from people who, though believed to be dead and in some instances actually declared
dead, had recovered.

There had been a startling similarity in their accounts
of how in spirit form they had departed from their dying
bodies and looked back at them, even floated above
them in hospital operating rooms and watched the medi-
cal teams still at work.

As the fading form of Karl Jurzak turned from Karl's
body and walked out of the circle of candles, it was
almost nothing. A wraith. A shade. A thing of the imagination.

Suddenly it was no longer there.

Gone to look for his wife, Will thought. *I hope he finds her.*

Ima came to him, looking older and on the verge of exhaustion. Anxiously she peered at his face. "Are you all right, Mr. Will?"

"I think so. What about you?"

"We will both be all right now, I believe."

Taking her by the hand, he walked her through the ring of candles to the chair where he had been the bait in the trap. The opal was there where he had dropped it and, frowning, he bent to pick it up. After peering at it for a moment, he handed it to Ima and said simply, "Look."

No one would ever again say of this opal that it filled the hearts of the gods with delight. It was dark and lifeness now.

"Its fire has gone out," Ima said wonderingly, and turned to gaze at the wet stain on the floor. "Mr. Will, I don't understand."

"We may never understand what happened here to-night," Will said. "But thank you, Ima. Thank you for everything." Lifting her hand, he touched it to his lips. "Now let's put these candles out and go tell Lynne and Sam what happened. If we can find words for it."

38

Epilogue
Jamaica

The Villa Bella guest house, on a hill outside Christiana, is a pleasant place in which to wake up in the morning. Behind it runs a mountain valley that often fills with pockets of morning mist resembling small lakes.

Waking at daybreak, Will turned to the woman beside him and drew her into his arms, to find she was awake, too, and waiting—wanting—to be loved. Afterward he said, "How about a walk in the garden before breakfast?"

"I'd like that."

They had arrived on the island the day before, with Ima. Had been met at the airport by Ken Daniels in his battered taxi. After dinner that evening at the guest house, Lynne and Will had gone along for the ride when Ken drove Ima to the home in Mandeville where she was employed.

There had been an exchange of money, of course. More important, an exchange of embraces between Ima and Lynne and a promise that the Haitian woman would come again to the States one day to stay with them longer. "Everything in its time," Ima had said, smiling.

In the guest-house garden now, Will put an arm around the waist of the woman beside him and they gazed together at the lakes of mist in the valley. Able to see the house he had lived in on coming to Christiana to help Sam Norman, he pointed it out to her. Sam was back in Massachusetts now. Then he said, "What would you like to do while we're here? A week is a fairly long time, you know. We can't spend it all here at the guest house."

"Let's take turns," she said.

"Turns?"

"Telling Ken Daniels where we want to go each day, and what we want to see."

"You like him, don't you?"

"I like all your friends, Will Platt."

That was something new for him after so many years of marriage to a woman who had tried her utmost to alienate every friend he had. "Thank you," he said, kissing her. "And with Ken helping us, we'll do the island. A honeymoon."

They were not married. They might never be, with nothing and no one to prove—really prove—his wife was dead.

"What are we to do with our nights?" Will asked. "There's nothing much after dark here, you know."

"I'll think of something," Lynne told him, solemn as any of the little country churches they could see on the surrounding hills. "Trust me, darling."

More Fiction Bestsellers From Ace Books!